monsoonbooks

OPERATION BLACK ROSE

Lt. Col. JP Cross is a retired British officer who served with Gurkha units for nearly forty years. He has been a⸻ ⸻ frontier soldier, jungle fighter, policeman, military at⸻ ⸻ a recruitment officer and a linguist researcher, ⸻ ⸻ of nineteen books. He has fought in Bur⸻ ⸻ ⸻d Borneo and served in India, Paki⸻ ⸻ Nepal where he now lives. Well in⸻ ⸻ four hours daily.

Operation Black ⸻ a series of historical military novels set in Sou⸻ ⸻mprising, in chronological order, *Operation Black R*⸻ *eration Janus*, *Operation Blind Spot*, *Operation Stealth* and *Operation Four Rings*. The books, which may be read in any order, involve Gurkha military units, and the author draws on real events he witnessed and real people he fought alongside in various theatres of war in Southeast Asia and India.

'Nobody in the world is better qualified to tell this story
of the Gurkhas' deadly jungle battles against Communist
insurgency in Malaya in the 1950s. Cross spins his tale
with the eye of incomparable experience.'

John le Carré, on *Operation Janus*

'... a gripping adventure story ...
learn the ins and outs of jungle warfare from a true expert'

The Oldie, on *Operation Janus*

Also by JP Cross

FICTION
The Throne of Stone
The Restless Quest
The Crown of Renown
The Fame of the Name
The Age of Rage
Operation Black Rose
Operation Janus
Operation Stealth
Operation Four Rings

NONFICTION
English For Gurkha Soldiers
Gurkha – The Legendary Soldier
Gurkhas
Gurkha Tales: From Peace and War
In Gurkha Company
It Happens with Gurkhas
Jungle Warfare: Experiences And Encounters
Whatabouts And Whereabouts In Asia

MEMOIRS
First In, Last Out:
An Unconventional British Officer In Indo-China

The Call Of Nepal:
A Personal Nepalese Odyssey In A Different Dimension

'A Face Like A Chicken's Backside':
An Unconventional Soldier In South-East Asia, 1948-1971

ORAL HISTORY
Gurkhas at War

OPERATION BLACK ROSE

JP Cross

monsoon

monsoonbooks

First published in 2019
by Monsoon Books Ltd
www.monsoonbooks.co.uk

No.1 The Lodge, Burrough Court,
Burrough on the Hill, Leicestershire LE14 2QS, UK

ISBN (paperback): 9781912049585
ISBN (ebook): 9781912049592

Cover design by Cover Kitchen.

A Cataloguing-in-Publication data record is available from the British
Library.

Basic details about Indian Army prisoners-of-war have been taken from
*The Forgotten Army, Indian's Armed Struggle for Independence, 1941-
1945*, Peter Ward Fay, Ann Arbor (The University of Michigan Press,
1993).

Printed and bound in Great Britain by Clays Ltd, Elcograf S.p.A.
21 20 19   1 2 3 4

I dedicate this book to all those soldiers who,
in the horrifying conditions of being
Prisoners-of-War under the Japanese,
stayed true to their 'oath of salt',
especially to those of my old regiments
1st King George V's Own Gurkha Rifles (Malaun Regiment).
You all deserve to be remembered with pride.

List of Characters

Ah Fat   boyhood friend of Jason Rance, q.v.

Ah Hong   drink shop proprietor in Kuala Lumpur

Arnold, Albert (Bert)   Major General, Director of Operations, GHQ, New Delhi

Bahadur Shamsher Jang Bahadur Rana
son of Juddha Shamsher Jang Bahadur Rana, Prime Minister and Maharaja of Nepal, q.v. General, the Maharaja's first representative in Delhi

Balbahadur Rana   Rifleman, 2/2 Gurkha Rifles

Beamish, Victor   Lieutenant Colonel, First Secretary in Nepal

Bethem, Sir Geoffrey, KBE, CIE
Minister Plenipotentiary and Ambassador Extraordinary in Nepal

Boatner, Haydon L   Colonel, Chinese interpreter, United States Army

Buddhiman Dura   Jemadar, 2/1 Gurkha Rifles

Chiang Kai-shek   Generalissimo, Chinese Army and Head of Chinese National Government

Churchill, Winston   English politician

Dilbahadur Pun   Havildar, 1 Gurkha Rifles, in charge of Bren Gun training at Ramgarh

Ekai Kawagushi   Japanese monk who visited Nepal in 1905

Fujiwara Iwaichi   Major, Japanese liaison officer with Indian National Army with his Hikari Kikan

Gajendra Singh   Jemadar of troop of dismounted Gwalior Lancers

Ghandi, Mohandas 'Mahatma'   Indian politician

Gracey, D D   Major General, (later General Sir Douglas) General Officer Commanding 20 Indian Infantry Division

Gurbaksh Singh Dhillon Captain, 1/14 Punjab Regiment, later Colonel, Indian National Army

Hajime Sugiyama   General, Imperial [Japanese] Army Chief of Staff

Hakim Beg   Naik, 9/12 Frontier Force Regiment

Hata Shunruko   Field Marshal at King Emperor's durbar in Delhi, in 1911

Hideki Tojo   senior army officer and Prime Minister, Japan

Hisaichi Terauchi, Count   Field Marshal, Southern Army,

Hitler, A   German leader

Hitman Gurung   Rifleman, 1 Gurkha Rifles

Hirohito   124th emperor of Japan

Jenkins, Joseph (Jo)   Admiral, senior Royal Navy officer in General Headquarters, New Delhi

Juddha Shamsher Jang Bahadur Rana
                                    Prime Minister and Maharaja of Nepal

Khan, Abdul Hamid ⎱ cousins and members of the Tor Gul Gang
Khan, Abdul Rahim ⎰

Khan, Akbar   Pathan lawyer for Indian Association and, subversively, the Indian Independence League, in Malaya

Khan, Tor Gul   Son of Akbar Khan, q.v.

Krishna Shamsher Jang Bahadur Rana   General, Maharaja's second representative in Delhi

Ksatra Bikram Rana   Commanding Officer, Mahendra Dal

Lakshmi Swaminadhan Sahgal   Captain, Commander, Rani of Jhansi Regiment

Lalsing Dura   Naik, 2/1 Gurkha Rifles

Lambert, William (Bill) Brigadier, Director of Intelligence, General Headquarters, New Delhi

Liao Yuan-hsiang   Major General, General Officer Commanding Chinese Nationalist 22nd Division

Loo Soong   Chinese guerilla in Thailand

Longden, R ('Bobby') P Headmaster of Wellington College

Luo Shuo-ying	Cantonese-speaking General
Macauly, Lord	Historian and Whig politician, 1800-1859
Manbir Gurung	Rifleman, 2/1 Gurkha Rifles
Mangal Pande	one of the best-known figures in anti-British Indian historiography as the man who started the 1857 'sepoy rebellion'
Mason, Hector	younger son of Peter Mason, q.v.
Mason, Lance	elder son of Peter Mason, q.v.
Mason, Peter	Britain's Intelligence representative for Asia
McCabe, E R W	Colonel, United States Army at Chinese Army training camp, Ramgarh
Mohan Singh	Captain, 1/14 Punjab Regiment, Major General Indian National Army
Mountbatten, Lord Louis	Admiral, Supreme Allied Commander, South East Asia Command
Muhammad Taki Khan	Sepoy, 9/12 Frontier Force Regiment
Mussolini, B	Italian leader
Narbahadur Gurung	Subedar, 2/1 Gurkha Rifles
Nehru, Jawaharlal	Indian Congress politician
Ochterlony, Sir David	East India Company General, victor of the Anglo-Nepalese War, 1814-15 & 1816
Parsuram Thapa	Havildar, 2/1 Gurkha Rifles
Percival, A E	Lieutenant General, General Officer Commanding Malaya
Rabilal Rai	Malayan-based Gurkha
Raghavan, Nedhyam	Penang lawyer, head of the Indian Independence League in Malaya
Rahu Dura	Quartermaster Jemadar, 2/1 Gurkha Rifles
Rance, Jason	son of Philip Rance, q.v.
Rance, Philip	Britain's Intelligence representative in Malaya
Ranjit Singh	Captain and Adjutant, 9/12 Frontier Force Regiment
Rash Behari Bose	founder of the Indian Independence League
Riggs, George	Captain, ADC to the Director of Military Intelligence, q.v.

Saeki	Japanese major in north Malaya
Shafqat Sharif	soldier in the 9/12th Frontier Force Regiment
Shah Nawaz,	Captain, 1/14 Punjab Regime, Colonel, Indian National Army
Som Bahadur Dura	dead 2/1 Gurkha Rifles havildar
Stillwell, Joseph W ('Vinegar')	General, Commander, Northern Combat Area Command
Subhas Chandra Bose	scholar, anti-British politician and Commander-in-Chief of the Indian National Army: a.k.a. Neta-ji
Sugiyama Torashira	Japanese manager of Nakajima Photo Shop in Kuala Lumpur
Sun Li-jen	Major General, General Officer Commanding Chinese Nationalist 38th Division
Theopulos, John	Manager of Bhutan Estate with Gurkha workforce
Tomoyuki Yamashita	Major General, Commander, Japanese 25th Army, 'The Tiger of Malaya',
Victoria	Queen Empress of India
Wavell, Sir Archibald	General Commander-in-Chief, Indian Army and Later Field Marshal and Viceroy
Wingfield, C M H	Lieutenant Colonel, Commanding Officer, 3/1 Gurkha Rifles
Yamani	Japanese captain in north Malaya
Yonai Karechika	Japanese agent
Yoshimichi Hara	President of the Privy Council in Tokyo in 1941

Glossary

CHINESE

bo leng gei gwaan cheung
    Light Machine Gun (with 'Light' not required),
    was not used but 'cow horn weapon', *ngau kok
    cheung*, was used instead

hak   black
mui gwai   rose
doh che   thank you
samsu   sam = 3, su = burned, so 'triple-distilled' rice
    wine
song wai   captain
sook ching   purification by elimination

HINDI

Azad Hind Fauj   Free India Army a.k.a. Indian National Army
    (INA) but Jiffs, Japanese Inspired Fifth column,
    to British servicemen
badmash   rogue
bahadur   brave
boké   like a goat, a deadly insult to a Sikh
chalo Delhi   'On to Delhi!'
doolally   British slang for Deolali, a British Army camp
    100 miles northeast of Bombay, meaning 'made
    mentally unstable while waiting for a boat back
    to Britain'
djinn   (from Arabic) spirits in Muslim mythology who
    could assume human or animal form and
    influence man by supernatural powers
ghadr   revolt
gora   fair-skinned. Term for lower-class Europeans
gulab   rose
havildar   Indian Army sergeant equivalent
hazur   your

jai	long live
jai Hind	Long Live India
jawan	modern name for 'sepoy'
jemadar	lowest of three Viceroy's Commissioned Officers
ji	polite suffix
kaida	method, custom, the quintessential 'backbone' of the Indian Army
kala	black
luñgi	a lower-limb cloth covering
munshi	teacher
neta	leader
paratha	pancake-like preparation from kneaded flour and fried in ghee
raj	realm
'*rangrut*'	recruit
saitan	devil (for Hindus)
'*Sardar-ji*'	polite form of address to a Sikh
sarkar	government
saudhan, sabdhan	Attention!
zamhareer	(Urdu) the worst and coldest Muslim hell

JAPANESE

ah, so desu	yes,
bakayaro	bastard
banzai	(in full Tennō heika banzai) a wish for the Emperor to live for ten thousand years and a war-cry for kamikaze (q.v.) pilots and soldiers
bara	rose
choho	covert Intelligence
Chuo Kikan	the Imperial Japanese Navy's Intelligence Department
domo	thank you
gaijin	foreigner
gomen nasai	so sorry
gyanpuku	ceremony for wearing Samurai hat
hakko ichiu	eight corners of the world under one roof
hikari	Light from the East
iyé	no
notkami	spirit

kamikaze	'divine wind', a Japanese on a suicidal mission
kanpai!	cheers!
kikan	agency
kinjiru	forbidden
kodo	loyalty to the emperor
Ko-hyoteki	a class of Japanese mini-submarine
kuroi	black
san	polite suffix to a name
Shonan	Brilliant South, Singapore

MALAY

hitam	black
jalan	road
Mat Salleh	a legendary Malay who always thought he knew more than he actually did, used as slang for an Englishman
mawar	rose
orang	man
orang puteh	white man, 'European'
stengah	(from *sa-tengah*) half, colloquially 'a drink of half whisky and half water'
tuan	sir, master

NEPALI

ath pahariya	[the one who is] on duty for eight hours, an ADC
banchoot	a scurrilous epithet of opprobrium
bhai	younger brother. Also used to one younger than the speaker
boké	an insulting name for Sikhs, 'the one with the goat's beard'
chhatiwan	tree, *Alstonia scholaris*
daju	elder brother. Also used to one older than the speaker
dal	(Kathmandu Nepali) battalion
Desi	an Indian
Gorkha	district of that name and post-1948 the Indian Army word for a soldier of the Gorkha Brigade
Gorkhali	belonging to the district of Gorkha
Gurkha	English word for a Nepalese soldier

Gurkhali	English word for the Nepali language post-1948 for 40-odd years
kaida	the proper way of doing things
Khaskura	the lingua franca of Gurkhas pre-1948
Nepali	the language spoken by Nepalese royalty and court officials
raksi	country spirit
saitan	devil
sarkar	government
shabash	(Hindi also) well done
shikar	(Hindi also) big game

MILITARY TERMS AND ABBREVIATIONS

Acorn	Intelligence Officer of any unit
ADC	Aide de camp,. General or equivalent officer's personal staff officer
APM	Assistant Provost Marshal
BOR	British Other Ranks
Bren	a particular light machine gun
C-in-C	Commander-in-Chief
CO	Commanding Officer
CSDIC	Combined Services Detention and Interrogation Centre
Cwt	hundred weight
D Day	the day fixed for an operation to be launched, so D- and D+ are used
DMI	Director of Military Intelligence
DMO	Director of Military Operations
ETA	Estimated time of Arrival
ETD	Estimated time of Departure
KD	Khaki Drill
GHQ	General Headquarters
GR	Gurkha Rifles
havildar	Indian Army equivalent to sergeant
IAMC	Indian Army Medical Corps
INA	Indian National Army, POWs working for the Japanese, q.v. Jiffs

ID	Identification [card/document]
IMA	Indian Military Academy
IO	Intelligence Officer
IOR	Indian Other Rank
JIFC }	Japanese Inspired Indian Fifth Column, but
Jiffs }	pronounced and usually written as Jiffs
lance naik	Indian Army equivalent to lance corporal
LMG	Light machine gun
naik	Indian Army equivalent to corporal
NC(E)	Non-Combatant (Enlisted), civilians employed in menial tasks
NCO	Non Commissioned Officers
OG	Olive Green
'O' Group	'Orders Group', those to whom orders must be passed on before any operation
QMJ	Quartermaster Jemadar
POW	prisoner of war
RAP	Regimental Aid Post
recce	reconnaissance
RNLN	Royal Dutch Navy
RMO	Regimental Medical Officer
SM	Subedar Major
SMG	sub machine gun
Starlight	Medical officer of any unit
Sunray	Commanding Officer of any unit
WEC	Wireless Experimental Centre
wilco	wireless jargon for 'will comply with ...'
WTO	Weapon Training Officer
VCO	Viceroy's Commissioned Officer

NON-MILITARY

IIL	Indian Independence League

Preface

April 1938, Malaya: 'Did he say seven men would try to kill me or did I mishear him?' The 16-year-old English lad, Jason Rance, turned to his Gurkha friend, hoping he had misheard.

'No, you heard correctly.'

'I'm not very good at speaking Gurkhali – please tell me again what the old shaman actually said.'

Jason had been inveigled into meeting a Nepalese shaman who spent his time at one or other of the three rubber estates with a Gurkha labour force and occasionally went back to Darjeeling. 'He'll tell you your future if not your fortune,' Jason's Gurkha friend had said. 'Give him some unhusked rice which I'll get from home and he will tell you where to place it on a wooden board he puts on the ground in front of him.' He looked at Jason coaxingly. 'You must also give him some money. I suggest ten dollars.'

Jason, looking wide-eyed at his friend, had hesitated momentarily before saying, 'Yes, I'd like to go along with you. It'll be something entirely different for me.' *My parents would call this mumbo-jumbo but why not?*

The shaman was old, rheumy-eyed and long haired with a wispy grey beard and exuded an aura of authority. Jason was shown the board, not much bigger that a child's slate and now wiped clean from the last occurrence, and the shaman covered it with fine dust. Jason was told where to put the rice on it. He placed the ten-dollar note on the ground beside the board and was bidden to sit. The old man started by putting his liver-spotted, grave-marked hands in the rice, feeling it, lifting some and letting it fall, and gently kneading it. He asked Jason his name and his age, all the while staring hard at the young English boy, forcing eye contact. Picking up a stick he started drawing lines on the heaped rice, seemingly at random, scrutinising the grains carefully.

'Your parents were not born in this country but in a foreign land towards the sunset, you know more than one language, know how to wrestle and you feel safe in the jungle.' Jason involuntarily stiffened. *My friend can't have told him, surely?* The old man cleared his throat noisily, turned his head and deftly spat out some phlegm. 'You and a younger brother of a different race will often work together under difficult and dangerous conditions ...' Something seemed to trouble him. He drew some more lines, again seemingly at random and studied them before continuing. 'You will be hunted by a *kalo gulab*' – 'black rose', what does he mean? – and the shaman repeated the name in Malay, *mawar hitam*, which Jason also understood.

Jason made as to ask what that meant but was nudged by his Gurkha friend so stayed silent.

'You wanted to ask me a question,' the shaman said, surprising Jason by such insight. 'I'll tell you the answer. Not only a *mawar hitam* but three more like it. Four in four years and after that three more at ten-year intervals with different names.'

Jason sat riveted, almost dazed, hardly knowing what to think or believe.

'That is all I have,' said the old man, wiping the board clean. 'Leave me in peace.'

The two friends got up and moved off, both in a chastened mood. They were just out of sight when they heard a commotion and saw a man carrying an unconscious woman over his shoulder making towards the shaman. 'Let's watch,' said Jason's friend. They crept back and sat, hidden, in earshot.

A coconut had dropped on the woman's head, knocking her unconscious, and her husband was worried in case she would lose her memory. Laying her gently on the ground, he pleadingly asked for help. Rheumy eyes looked at the woman and gently stroked her battered skull. 'For her head a poultice of hot, ground-up rice flour must be applied, for her mind ...' and, to the watchers' surprise, the shaman lay down beside her and spoke softly into her ear, for her alone. After about ten minutes they saw the strained look on the woman's face relax. The shaman stiffly got up and told the man that his wife's mind would not be affected.

Soberly Jason and his friend left and back in the house, the two boys tried to unravel what they had just seen. 'It can happen if you have trained for such an occasion,' was the slightly unsatisfactory answer his friend offered. Jason then asked, 'how much do you believe in what he said to me?'

His Gurkha friend answered soberly, 'my parents tell me that since they were children every prophecy he has ever made has come true,' and left it at that.

PART ONE

PART ONE

1

10 April 1938: For two senior Intelligence operators from two countries on opposite sides of the world shortly to be at war one against the other to accidentally meet in a third country is such an unlikely event that not even the most optimistic punter would lay any odds on it happening. Yet happen it did a day or so after Jason Rance had returned home and the seeds it unwittingly sowed in two otherwise unconcerned young men's minds were not harvested for seven more years.

It came about in Kuala Lumpur, Muddy River Junction in the vernacular, Malaya's capital city, when Peter Mason, Britain's Secret Intelligence Service's senior Asian Affairs Desk Officer, was out on his final inspection of his 'men on the ground'. He and his deputy, due to take over from him on their return to London, had been allowed to travel by air as the journey by sea would have taken too long. At first-stop Delhi they had talks with the Viceroy and the Intelligence fraternity before going on to Calcutta by train where they caught one of Imperial Airway's Short Empire flying boats to Sydney and from there to a high-level meeting in Canberra. On their way back, again by flying boat, they had stopped off at Singapore, where the deputy would stay for an in-depth briefing, while Mason himself visited his 'man in Malaya', Philip Rance.

Philip Rance spoke Malay like a native and was virtually fluent in Chinese, keeping this latter skill as close a secret as possible. Peter Mason, apart from a rudimentary knowledge of Hindi and Malay, was a Japanese interpreter. After a couple of working days together in Rance's house, Hibiscus Cottage on Golf View Road, the senior man said, 'I'm due to return to Singapore on the night train tomorrow. I haven't "sniffed the air" in this part of the world for a few years and now, before retirement and pension, I'd like to revive old memories. I doubt I'll have another chance. Also I'd like to stretch my legs.'

'So would I,' answered Philip. 'My wife took her camera to the Cameron Highlands when we went up recently for a cool weekend and I need to give her roll of film in for developing. Let's go a little later when it's cooler. The shop is in Batu Road. That walk will do us good.'

Philip was a 49-year-old, untidy-looking man with a 'lived-in' face who would never have been taken as an intelligence officer. That and a first-class brain were the reasons why he was rated so highly by his colleagues in London and ignored by those elsewhere who were his legitimate targets, the disassociation of ideas working in his favour. People do not normally think of such men in that category, a great asset in the Intelligence world as few would recognise or remember him again. He wore a white, open-necked shirt, khaki shorts and long grey socks that turned down below his knees and on his head a pith helmet. His companion, older by several years, was tall, gaunt, lined of face with white eyebrows, a clipped moustache and a cleft chin. Dressed in long trousers, a white cotton coat over a silk shirt, he wore a straw hat with an old Etonian ribbon round its brim covered his thinning hair. He radiated sincerity and kindness.

They reached the Nakajima Photo Shop, managed by one Sugiyama Torashira, a Japanese. A bell sounded as they opened the door and went inside. There was no one at the counter. 'Unusual,' said Philip laconically, 'I expect he'll be out in a moment. It won't hurt us to wait.'

It was, one could suppose, a great shame that neither Philip nor Peter could have been 'flies on the wall' and so been able to overhear an earlier conversation in the stock room between the shop manager, another Japanese, and an Indian. Both Japanese were Intelligence operators: Sugiyama, a strong, slightly obsequious, good-looking man in his late twenties, was one of a network of agents all over Southeast Asia working in many activities from the mundane, for example bicycle repairers, café managers and shop keepers, to the more highly qualified, such as dentists and doctors. Their task was to report back to Tokyo on the state of affairs, especially matters military, in the vicinity where they worked. At his real job Sugiyama was keen, alert, cold, observant, detached, manipulative, ruthless and formidable. The other Japanese, Yonai Karechika, thirtyish, fleshy-cheeked, wide-eyed, pursed lips and well built, was on a tour of various Southeast Asian countries. He wore his authority with a bland goodwill that masked a subtle intelligence and deep cunning. His main interest was in airfields and their means of defence, military camps and the capacity of roads and bridges to withstand armoured vehicle movement over them. Before the two Englishmen arrived he was authoritatively holding forth on the future; 'When we attack, as we surely will – but when is still being considered – the military here will not be ready to resist us, even if there were enough of them. That means that the British will reinforce numbers with Indian troops and that is where you, Akbar Khan-san, will play your crucial part.'

'Happily, happily,' almost crooned the Indian, waggling his head from side to side and hands a-flutter. He was a lawyer, originally from Peshawar, whose native tongue was Pashto. He was a burly, squat, overweight, quick-witted, affable man with a heavy moustache, untrustworthy eyes, pinched lips and a head of thick, black, oiled hair. He was the Kuala Lumpur representative for the above-board and so lawful Indian Association that, in turn, was cover for the unlawful anti-British Indian Independence League, the IIL, with its headquarters in Tokyo and branches all over Asia. Akbar Khan gave a throaty chuckle and a lop-sided grin. 'My boss in Penang, Nedyam Raghavan-san, will also be happy.' Yonai Karechika had close links with the IIL, hence the meeting. Interestingly the conversation was in Japanese.

On hearing the shop doorbell ring Sugiyama stood up, bowed his head to his superior and, asking to be excused, made his way to the counter.

'So sorry to have kept you waiting, Tuan,' he said in English, bobbing his head in politeness. As Philip handed his roll of film across the counter he said 'If you haven't finished developing my last roll I'll call back another time.'

'Please wait, Tuan, while I go and check. I think it's ready.'

He went back to the inner sanctum but neglected to shut the

door fully. Both Philip and Peter caught sight of the two men already there and Peter, whose hearing was acute, heard him say, 'I have my doubts about the *gaijin* barbarian with the pith helmet. When they leave, follow them discretely. It may pay dividends.' Gaijin, *yes. Barbarian? No. Hostile!* Peter thought, hackles rising.

'*Ah so desu.*' Yes.

'*Domo.*' Thank you.

Yonai and Akbar nodded, Sugiyama bowed and returned with Philip's photos. 'So sorry for the delay. Here they are, Tuan. You seem to have had a pleasant holiday in the Cameron Highlands.' His English was surprisingly good.

'Yes, it was fun and the weather blessedly cool for a change. I'll call back for the new photos in a week or so. Put both lots on my bill, please, and I'll pay you at the end of the month' and the two Englishmen left the shop. Once outside Peter repeated what he had heard. 'Obviously I'm not known to be a Japanese linguist and I think we should take evasive action. You lead the way.'

'We're back with our basic training with escape and evasion,' prattled Philip. 'Follow me.'

They moved off normally. After a few hundred yards Philip bent down as though to tie a loose shoelace and saw that their two followers were about fifty yards behind them. Two teams of schoolboy footballers, riotously happy, approaching them temporarily blocked the pavement. Philip and Peter, moving smartly across the road and causing a horse-drawn buggy to slow up, reached the far pavement, dodged round a tree and went down Jalan Petaling some fifty yards farther on. Their pursuers lost sight of them. Down a side street at No. 150 was a restaurant-cum-bar, cryptically named PS 150. They went inside, closing the door behind them and made for the bar. 'We may be followed. We'll hide for a few minutes,' Philip warned the barman and the pair of them disappeared into one of the three curtained booths. Drawing the curtain, each man took one of the four chairs set by a table and, placing them with their backs to the side wall, sat down, feet tucked underneath. 'The barman Ah Hong is one of my agents,' explained Philip, 'and I may be over-reacting by our trying not to be seen by any casual observer.'

Shortly afterwards they heard two men come into the bar. Philip peeped through the narrow slit at the curtain's edge and saw the Indian and the Japanese. *So I was right after all!* Putting a finger to his lips, he looked at his companion and nodded.

'Did two Europeans come in here just now?' the Indian roughly asked the barman in bazaar Malay. 'There were no other Europeans about, only those two who we were following. We had a good look down the road and didn't see them so presume they came in here. I think the one you work for works in the tax office and the other I don't know.'

'One I work for? I work for myself, thank you, and always have done. There's no one here so your friends' – sarcastically – 'must have gone on down the road. *Orang puteh* normally don't come here. I don't know what Englishman works where. How can I? And how do you expect me to know who you know or don't know? In any case I was facing the back wall polishing some glasses and didn't see you until you spoke.'

'They're not in one of the booths are they?'

'How can they be if they haven't come in?' Ah Hong answered

in an exasperated tone of voice.

'I'll check,' said Akbar Khan. He pushed back the curtain of two of the empty booths with both hands and saw a table and four chairs in each. He did likewise to the third, neatly blocking his own view as the curtain shielded the two Britons. He saw a table and two chairs and nothing else.

'All empty. Both of us would have been angry if you had told us an untruth.'

The two Asians went to the table under the fan and the Japanese brusquely ordered a small Tiger beer for himself and a lemonade for his Muslim companion. 'Bring us your coldest.' While the barman was putting the bottles and glasses on the table, the Englishmen were horrified to hear the Japanese say to him in bazaar Malay, 'Your government will stay as it is now for only a few years longer. Then we Nipponese will get rid of all such people as you. You'll find out that death knows neither pardon nor pity. *Bakayaro!*' Ah Hong didn't react at being called a bastard as he didn't understand Japanese. Glasses were heard to clink and the Japanese toast *Kanpai!* Peter Mason quietly took a notebook and pencil from his jacket pocket to jot down notes on the two men's conversation.

Philip Rance had, by now, recognised the Indian as Akbar Khan in both his guises but not the other man. Talking to his companion, Yonai Karechika included the words '*Hakko ichiu*', '*Kodo*' and '*Kokutai*' to which Peter gave a start of incredulity on hearing them. Ah Hong did not outwardly react at the Chinese '*Sook ching*'.

As they drank their cold drinks Akbar Khan said, 'Yes, you

are quite right, Sugiyama-san. Just a few years more and then your country will look after east and south Asia and my India will get rid of the British once and for all. One danger that needs countering here is the Malayan Communist Party but I don't consider them all that strong. As for the Malay military, they have two battalions. Immensely smart on parade, I don't believe their training involves the soldiers "going those last few yards" and the British officers they have are not credited with being the calibre of those in the Indian Army.'

'I've heard that already. As far as the two British battalions are concerned, they have long been the target of our people and we know a damaging amount about them, their capabilities, their few strengths and many weaknesses. For instance, they have to carry thick overcoats, respirators and steel helmets when they go on exercises, which is not very often. It's unbelievable military stupidity. In real war fatigue and heat will have killed them before we'll be able to do it for them,' exclaimed Yonai Karechika, laughing immodestly. 'They'll be no problem for us, only to themselves.'

They continued talking about airfields with no supporting military defence, how all attention was given to any hostile attack coming from the sea at Singapore and not overland, then on to how the rubber and tin would benefit Japan. 'And not only here. In the Dutch East Indies as well.'

Behind the curtain chairs were heard to scrape as the two men got up.

'Give me money,' demanded Ah Hong, naming the amount required.

'Never.'

'Yes. You must.'

'Never.' *Slap, slap.* Two resounding smacks were heard and it was all Peter and Philip could do not to go out and remonstrate.

The door was shut with a bang and Ah Hong could be heard clearing the table. After waiting a short while Philip and Peter emerged, glad to stretch their legs. They sat down at the same table under the fan, both mopping their brow as it was stuffy inside their booth. 'The Japanese shouldn't have hit you. We'll pay for their drinks. Can't have you out of pocket,' Philip told the barman. 'Please bring us two cold beers.'

Ah Hong's cheek was red and swollen and he was silently seething but Philip's kind gesture calmed him down, at least temporarily. Did he want to report it to the police?

'Tuan, you know as well as anyone else, no Malay policeman takes any notice of us Chinese. I have other methods.'

Sipping their beers, Philip told Peter who the Indian was and what he did. 'I didn't recognise the Japanese but he must have something to do with Akbar Khan's unlawful side of life'.

'Yes, it certainly seems so. I'll tell you what I heard when we're back in your house.'

Philip paid for three beers and the bottle of lemonade and told Ah Hong to let him know if the Japanese or the Indian came back, together or separately.

From a shop a little way down on the other side of the road the two Asians saw Philip and Peter leave. 'Your hunch was correct. That was smart of you. How did you guess?' the Japanese asked appreciatively.

'Something nagged at me and only now has it occurred to me why: two booths had a table and four chairs but the third, with the curtain drawn, only two. Let's go and check.'

'Those two *orang puteh* were with you the whole time. Why did you lie to us?' Yonai Karechika roughly asked the barman. He noticed that the Chinese now had a dagger in his waistband. *No slapping this time!*

'They came and sat at the table under the fan and had a beer each after you'd left,' replied Ah Hong angrily and truthfully. 'And they paid for them.'

'Liar! We've been watching from outside, saw no one go in but saw two Europeans leave. They could only have been here the whole time. If I had my way that would earn you something more permanent than having your face slapped. My friend here thinks you are an informer working for the shorter *orang puteh*. We'll deal with you later, not now,' and he glowered menacingly at the silent but furious Chinese. 'You've had your last chance. *Kinjiru*. Forbidden.'

Back at the photo shop they held a council of war. 'My son will be here soon,' Akbar Khan told the others towards the end, 'he and two of his friends went to the Odeon on Batu Road avid to see a widely-advertised film that has somehow showed parachuting …' The door opened and in came his son. He greeted the three men politely and burst out, 'Father, that parachuting. I and my two close friends feel that that is something for us.'

Akbar Khan's son, born with a jet black rose-shaped birthmark on one side of his forehead, had been named Tor Gul, Pashto for Black Rose, was fit, strong and a slightly overweight, dour-looking eighteen-year-old lad. Standing at around five feet and ten inches he had the north Indian's paler skin with shifty, pale green eyes that showed his ancestors came with Alexander the Great's eastward thrust from Greece more than two thousand years earlier. He was clever and crafty and could be vicious and malignant. He was, if anything, more anti-British than was his father who rejoined with, 'Good, that's for the future but for now sit down, keep quiet and listen. We were talking about Mr Rance and a visitor he has.'

Akbar addressed both Japanese. 'I know how much my son dislikes Mr Rance's son Jason. He hasn't met him all that much as they were in different schools but they played football and cricket against each other as well as having sports days. He says that Jason Rance never has time for us Indians, only for the Chinese and because of that we have watched him, secretly. Likewise, I don't trust his father, the one who wears the pith helmet. To prove your suspicions of his undercover work, I will get my son and his gang to plan a bit of burglary. It will also show how strong we are. That's why I want to use my son and his friends here and now. I'm sure they'll be up to it, learn lessons from it, enjoy the challenge and also be of use to you.'

The Japanese hissed their respects.

'What and when have you in mind, father?'

'I want to make war on that *orang puteh* Mr Rance. We think he works secretly for the Colonial government against us. I want to hurt and humble him for real so it's up to you and your gang to plan and act. When? Tonight as ever is. Do you know where the Rances live?'

33

'Yes, they live in Golf View Road so there's an easy approach.'

'Good. There are two sheds in the garden at the back of the house and I have learnt from his gardener …' and he went into details of what he wanted his son to do, using English '…and I want that box,' he finished off.

His son smiled lasciviously. 'Father, this is the first time you've given me what I believe is known as an operational order for my Tor Gul Gang. You'll excuse me, please, I'll be off to make my plan and alert my gang members.'

He had three men in his gang. Two were who he had been to the cinema with, both Muslims whose fathers were also members of the IIL working under legal cover. They were cousins, somewhat confusingly named Abdul Rahim Khan and Abdul Hamid Khan, both tough and useful with knife and rope. The former had one ear larger than the other, the latter's Adam's apple was protrudingly triangular and his feet were turned out as he walked. All three were braggarts who always thought they knew best. The fourth member was, surprisingly, a Gurkha, Rabilal Rai, whose father was the chief clerk on Bhutan Estate, one of three rubber estates whose labour force was Gurkhas. The first group had been brought over from the Darjeeling tea estates in India in 1904. Rabilal had never been particularly anti-British until he had met Jason Rance there on one of his earlier visits. His antipathy was caused entirely by chance because of a mistake Jason, who had only recently started to learn Gurkhali, had made when talking to him. Feeling a sneeze coming on, he had tried to warn Rabilal who was close to him. But instead of saying 'Go, thou, a sneeze,' he had said what sounded like 'Pubic hair, go fuck thyself.'

'You round-eyed devil,' had been the answer as the furious Gurkha stormed off. What had gone wrong was a couple of misplaced nasal 'n's and a 'chh' where 'ch' was needed. *Say that to me, would you?* Rabilal fumed and the dye was caste. A pall of hatred for all British overwhelmed him from then on. He'd come up to Kuala Lumpur with his father who had some legal rubber business with Akbar Khan: one thing had led to another and he joined the Tor Gul Gang.

Back at the Rance household, host and guest bathed and changed into long trousers and shirts with sleeves rolled down, anti-malarial fig, before going to sit on the verandah on bamboo chaises-longues where the house boy brought them each a *stengah*, whisky and water. A welcome breeze came from the golf course but, even so, a joss stick had been lit and put on the floor under the rattan table between the two men to keep mosquitoes at bay. From where they sat they could just see the two small sheds at the back of their small garden. The one in front was used for garden tools and deck chairs and the other was Philip's private work office, *well camouflaged,* Philip always thought. Both were securely locked when not in use.

'Before you start to tell me what the two men said I'll tell the Mem to leave us alone for about half an hour and then we'll eat,' and so saying Philip Rance stood up, put his head through the French window and called out to his wife that they had to talk shop for a while and they'd eat later. 'Say in half an hour from now.'

Both men pulled out the leg rests and relaxed comfortably. Peter Mason looked at his notebook and told Philip Rance what he had heard being said. 'Philip, I'm worried by that man saying he had his doubts on you. I heard the Indian call the Japanese you gave your film to at the Nakajima Photo Shop Torashira-san and that immediately started bells ringing at the back of my mind. I think his main job is intelligence and the photo business is his cover.'

'Peter, that's worrying to say the least. As for the name Yonai Karechika, which we heard when we were in the shop, it also rings a bell with me. I'll have a look at my card index file tomorrow.' They had known each other long enough to be on Christian-name terms and not the more normally accepted method of using surnames.

'He used four Japanese words that the Chinese would not have understood,' continued Peter, almost didactically. 'The first two were *hakko ichiu* which simply mean "eight corners of the world under one roof", in other words making the world one big family, a moral goal; the third word was *kodo*, "loyalty to the Emperor", the road which implements that goal. *Does that presage an increase of fighting from Manchuria?* I ask myself and answer, Yes, I think it well might. The fourth word was *kokutai*, which is the notion of Imperial Japan as a unique nation by virtue of the sacred Emperor. Those four words point to something brewing and almost indubitably coming from the very top. By the way, did you hear what the Japanese said to the shop owner in Chinese?'

'Indeed I did, Peter. He said "*sook ching*" which has the

unpleasant meaning of "purification by elimination". It is what the Japanese said in Manchuria when they slaughtered so many Chinese men, women and children so its use now could, surely, only refer to where there are overseas Chinese. That blatantly means more Chinese deaths and from where else except south from Japan? Even the way the Japanese slapped the barman was strongly indicative.'

'Let me dilate a bit.' Peter's memory was pointillist, a series of dots which, when joined and filled in, was encyclopaedic in its details. 'The Mukden Incident that led to the invasion of Manchuria on 18 September 1931, with more attacks on China proper expected shortly, are seen as the latest manifestation of *kodo* as indeed was an insurrection only last year involving Japanese officers and over a thousand men. It points to a mood of unhealthy, certainly to us, Japanese government in-fighting. Now your turn tell me about the IIL, which I'm a bit hazy about.'

'The other half before I tell you?'

'Good idea. Can't hurt.'

Philip called his house boy for a refill and said nothing until both drinks had been refreshed and the servant dismissed. 'As you well know, there have always been Indian anti-British movements. There was the Revolt Movement, *Ghadr* in the vernacular, that started life in 1907 and was defeated in 1917. It flourished, strangely, mostly in North America and the Far East. Musicologists would have described the IIL as a "variation on a theme". Its virtual founder is one Rash Behari Bose who fled to Tokyo in, um, 1915, and has been there ever since. He has married a Japanese woman, has Japanese citizenship and is fluent in the language. He'll be around forty years of age now.'

'So Tokyo is at the root of both movements, it seems.'

'Can't fault you there.'

'That certainly fits with Delhi and London's thinking.'

They sipped their drinks as they ruminated on the unfavourable and unfathomable implications of what they had heard. 'Do you think that Yonai is more than likely doing what I am but in a deeper, more sophisticated and threatening manner, action rather than British *re*action?' Philip queried.

Running his fingers through his thinning hair in a pathetic gesture of weariness and puzzlement, Peter said, 'I'm afraid so and on a much larger scale than yours. I served in Asia for a good many years, including Japan before having to work in London and I miss it horribly. But I've developed a nose, if I can use that word, for sniffing, um, below the surface tensions and I fear that, more than likely, something drastic will occur in Asia …'

'War?' Philip interrupted, in a shocked tone of voice.

Peter put his glass in the hole provided in the arm of the chair, put his hands into a steeple on his stomach and stared at his host before replying, 'I hope not but I fear it's rather more than less likely and,' with a sad, sad look in his eyes, 'one we probably won't win.'

Philip almost choked on his drink in surprised disbelief and spluttered, 'You're not being serious are you?'

Shall I tell him? Yes. 'Intensely so. I am one of a small band of people who have never believed that the big guns make Singapore an impregnable fortress or that an overland route for the capture of Malaya and Singapore is impossible. We were told to shut up or we'd lose our jobs so you must also keep your mouth shut. There's no need to foul your nest.'

'Lips tight and mouth shut. Thank you for telling me. Frightening. So what is London saying?'

A look of disgust crossed Peter's face as he took his drink out of the hole in the arm of the chair and looked at his host over the rim of his glass, smiling sourly before he gave his answer with the pity which only the Irish keep for drunks, spoiled priests and congenital idiots. 'Oh dear! Oh dear! The majority of our service, especially those in the Colonial Office, most politicians except for Churchill and the top brass hats seem to have no idea other than "not enough money for this, that and the other",' this last mockingly offered in a mimicking, mincing tone.

'So that really boils down to all our work and reports either meaning nothing or having us put down as jingoistic exaggerators,' countered Philip. 'So what can we do about it?'

'What indeed? Sadly nothing much if anything at all. The future is never easy to foretell, never black and white, open and shut. But I believe there could well be grave trouble within five years by which time we'll both be too old to make much difference.'

'So, rather than us, within five years our sons will be ready to fill our shoes, your Hector my Jason.'

'My boy Hector is eighteen and reading Japanese to take over from me. He is at the School of Oriental Studies in London.' His father was obviously proud at the thought.

Father Rance's views on his son were longer: 'Jason, who'll be sixteen next birthday, is my only child. He is fluent in Chinese having adopted my Chinese counterpart's son Ah Fat as his brother. He also has a good working knowledge of Malay. He is doing well with his studies at the Victoria Institution and is in the First XI football team. He also spends time during the holidays with the children of the all-Gurkha labour force on a rubber estate not far from Seremban, to our south from here. They go camping in the jungle whenever possible. The estate is run by a Mr John Theopulos whose father or uncle, I can never remember which, brought the original labourers over from Darjeeling way back, so Jason also has a fair knowledge of Gurkhali, if that is its correct name. He's a wonderful linguist for a lad of his age and his mother and I are proud of him.'

'And what has he in mind for the future?'

'If I had my way I'd have him work in our job, in the Firm, but some years back we were visited by a stray cousin who, apart from being the company commander of the first Gurkha winner of the Victoria Cross in the Great War, filled young Jason with some thrilling yarns about them and since then he feels that life in the Indian Army serving with Gurkhas is what he wants to do. His visits down to the Gurkha labour force have intensified that resolve. I have agreed and have managed, with considerable difficulty, to get him accepted as a late entry into the Army Class at Wellington College starting this coming autumn ...'

'... I'll keep an eye on him. I know the headmaster, Bobby Longden.'

'... thanks indeed. He has never been to England. He'll find it strange, certainly to start with. Getting him there took a lot of doing I can tell you. From there he'll try and get a place in the Indian Army's equivalent of Sandhurst, the Indian Military Academy, IMA, at Dehra Dun. There I believe they have GCs, Gentleman Cadets. I'm working on it for him.'

'I've had a spell in Delhi and have some powerful army contacts. They should be able to help.'

Mrs Rance came out onto the verandah. 'You've had more than your thirty minutes. We can't wait any longer or the cook will go on strike. If he doesn't, I will. You men don't half gossip.' Her smile robbed her words of any vituperation. 'That's where we women learnt how to. Swallow what's left in your glass and come on in. Jason's also ready.'

Earlier on Jason had come back from a game of squash and now, bathed and ready for his meal, he joined them. Tall for his age, not much off six feet, his body was lean and taut. His penetrating, clear blue eyes and his features were almost hawk-like and stern until he relaxed them with a wonderful open smile. *A potentially tough nut*, mused the man from London as he noticed the boy's ripple-like movements.

After their meal all four of them sat together on the verandah with a cup of coffee, the two men, neither of whom smoked, also with a glass of kummel. 'Jason, your father has told me that you are going to study in the Army Class at Wellington and want to go to the IMA for a commission and serve with Gurkhas. How come you have that desire? Gurkhas haven't served in Malay since … can't remember exactly but I've read somewhere that it was some time in the 1870s.'

'Sir, your history is better than mine. There are three estate labour forces comprised of Gurkhas here in Malaya and in the summer holidays I go on camping jaunts with some of the lads from Bhutan Estate. I have come to like and admire them' – *except that anti-British Rabilal Rai, whose father is staunchly pro-British, always going on about how backward Malaya is compared to India but how much more advanced India would be if Indians were given a fair chance and 'we Gurkhas in Darjeeling'. Where does he pick that stuff up from, I wonder.* The slight pause before he continued was hardly noticed. 'I take my Chinese friend, Ah Fat, with me and we go into the jungle and practise jungle lore such as tracking each other. Say it who shouldn't, I can track one man through jungle by using ground signs and top signs and I can even speak enough of their language for simple conversations.' He looked over at his father and said he hoped joining the Indian Army would not be thought a waste of his other languages. 'But I don't think my father's job would attract me, working in a tax office doesn't sound all that much fun.' *So he doesn't know my real job,* Philip Rance thought. 'Going to Wellington College will be my first time in England and my first time away from home.' He hesitated and Peter saw a shadow of doubt in the young man's eyes. 'But it'll be a tremendous advantage and one I'm trying to get used to the idea of,' he finished off hesitantly.

The man from London, struck by the lad's slightly clipped speech with no verbal tics, looked steadfastly at the young man who sat stone-still in his chair as though lost in contemplation. Sensing his moment, he said, 'Jason, none of us are thought readers or particularly clever at reading the tea leaves but part of my job in London is trying to advise people in high places about developments.' Jason nodded his head, not having been told what his father's guest's job was. 'My gut feeling is,' Peter continued with a lift of his eyebrows, 'you are doing the right thing. Also I can be on hand when you are at Wellington and I have contacts in the Indian military, too, so could be of help. Also, no language learnt should ever be regarded as wasted.'

'Oh that would be wonderful,' Jason beamed happily, 'but I could never repay what you are doing for me, sir.'

'Don't consider it.'

Jason excused himself to go to bed. Philip looked at his watch. 'Yes, one way and another it's been a long day. Time for us, too, I think. Bed tea at half-past six too early, Peter? That's when we have ours.'

'No, that's just when I like it.'

'Good. Then after breakfast we'll go to the office. There are still some bits and pieces to discuss and there'll be time as your going on to Singapore is by the night train.'

'Suits me fine, Philip,' and they bid each other good night.

Before Jason dropped off to sleep his thoughts once more turned to that strange session he had had with his Gurkha friend. *Before I am much older, but how much? Four quite-whats? People I suppose will try and kill me, then, at ten-yearly intervals, three more.* It had frightened him. He hadn't dare tell his parents who, broad-minded thought they were, did not have minds as broad as all that.

The warning had made him cautions, more so than one of his age normally would be. Ah Fat had not found any esoteric message in *hak mui gwai*, Chinese, Malay or English. 'Best to keep it to yourself,' he had advised. 'You people have lost so much of what we Orientals still hold as part of our inner life ...' and Jason dropped off.

Sleep also came slowly to Peter Mason: the Rances were an uncommon couple. Obviously devoted but not quite top drawer? He was wonderful at his job and had great empathy with the natives. Her background was highly unusual, almost controversial for an Intelligence operator's wife. Her father used her to help him run a Punch and Judy show. She was also a trained ventriloquist and had taught her son how to be one. *I wonder if he has his own puppet. Better not ask him! Such a versatile lad, what with also being a superb linguist. It'll be his first visit to England all on his own. I must find out if he has any relatives there. It is a pity I can't take him back and settle him in ...* and he fell into a deep sleep.

Jason had drunk three large glasses of ice-cold lime juice after his game of squash so unusually, around two o'clock, he got up to go to the lavatory. It was full moon so there was no need to put on a light. The bathroom had a view over the back garden and on to the golf course. Looking out of the window as he was washing his hands he saw four men climbing through the wire. He stared at them and saw they were moving along a small path towards the two sheds. *Thieves!* He quickly dressed in slacks and a dark shirt and, putting on his squash shoes, went downstairs. He picked up one of his father's heavy walking sticks, quietly unlocked the kitchen door and went out to investigate. As he approached his father's office shed he saw a couple of torches flashing around inside. *Father's office! How had they got in? Forced the lock with a jemmy or something.* Seeing they were about to leave carrying something, he slipped round to the back of the sheds and stood in the shadow of a bush ahead of them, waiting for them to go back the same way as they had come. *Four men and I'm only one* flashed though his mind. They came out into the moonlight. *Not Malays or Chinese. Indians, they look like.* One of the men carrying a torch flashed it in another's face and Jason recognised the birthmark on the side of the man's forehead. *That's Tor Gul, blast his eyes. What the hell's he doing here?* Unused to carrying one, he had, unthinkingly, put the walking stick to one side. With a spurt of rage and a face that could have curdled milk, *I'll tackle the whole lot of them.*

The four of them walked towards him, Tor Gul carrying the box was second in line. Just before the first man reached him Jason dashed out in front and, with an expert rugger tackle, knocked him backwards and, as he fell, he knocked over Tor Gul, causing him to drop the box. '*Suareñke bachcheñ*,' sons of pigs, Jason unthinkingly damned them with the worst Muslim insult he could think of that he had learnt at school from a Muslim friend as he picked the box up and, using it as a bludgeon, hit one of the third man's kneecaps hard. With an ear-splittingly loud scream he fell down on top of Tor Gul, pinning him down on the ground. Jason's impetus carried him into the last man who seemed to be frozen with horror at the unexpected encounter. With the hard edge of his rigid right hand Jason struck him on the brachial plexus nerve bundle at the base of the neck. The man went limp and slumped. So unexpected was the attack the intruders were struck with raw, sickening fear which Jason could actually smell.

Jason quickly retrieved his father's stick. Winded, the first man was trying to get his breath back. Tor Gul was trying to get to his feet. The other two were *hors de combat*. 'If either of you start to move,' Jason warned them chillingly in Malay, 'I'll savage you both. I have a superb weapon in my hands,' and he showed them the heavy stick, 'and I know a trick or two as well.' He was astonished to see that the man he'd hit on the back of the neck was Rabilal Rai.

The noise had awoken the rest of the family. Philip and Peter, carrying torches, came out in their dressing gowns to find out what the trouble was. Philip, who, because of his job, was allowed to own a revolver, had brought it with him.' Jason, what is this?' he asked curtly.

'Father, these four were burgling your office and I found them carrying out a box. I took action against them and the box is safe. Here it is.'

'That was good work. Well done indeed. Go and get the keys to the potting shed and find a rope. Peter, take my revolver and cover them until Jason has tied them up. I'll go and phone for the police.'

Peter Mason's torch shone on the captives' hands as Jason tied them up and sometimes on Jason himself. The captives saw his penetrating, clear blue eyes and hawk-like features which they would never forget. Likewise, they felt they could recognise their assailant's voice in the future as his words were unusually clipped. For his part, Jason did not pay attention to the facial features of the other two Indians and, come the morning, would have forgotten what they looked like.

The police soon came to take the dejected and hapless quartet away to put them under lock and key. As they were led past Jason, Tor Gul said, 'Swear at me like that, would you, you bloodless ape? Next time I won't fail,' but as he spoke in Pashto, Jason didn't understand him. As Rabilal Rai passed, he muttered 'I'll get more than even with you yet,' which Jason did understand. *God's Law for me and Sod's Law for you if we do,* Jason thought to himself. The other two Indians, the cousins, said nothing. As the group got into the police vehicle a hoarse cry came from their leader, 'Jai Tor Gul'.

By then it was three o'clock. 'Time for another couple of hours shut eye,' Philip prompted. 'Jason, you for one have certainly earned it. I didn't know you were so skilled in such a rough house. Where did you learn how?'

'Ah Fat taught me, Father,' he replied, rubbing a bruise.

Next morning, after having checked Philip's office and finding no damage had been done, Philip and Peter discussed their final points. Then it was time for Philip to refer to the previous days' and night's activities. 'I don't at all like the way that Japanese was meeting up with Akbar Khan. There was, on the surface, nothing illegal about it but, even so, I don't like it one little bit. Give me your views, please.'

'I don't like it either. As an inspired guess, apart from Japanese Intelligence work, I'd say that the two are hatching some kind of plot with the long-term aim of rendering any future Indian

Army unit that is posted to Malaya, Singapore or Hong Kong come to that, so dissatisfied with their colonial British officers, comparatively meagre pay and below-normal standard conditions generally, how best to penetrate them to render them ineffectual in war and, God forbid and Heaven forfend, even to side with any Japanese forces,' the man from London answered with a rasp in his voice. 'That's a terrible scenario, the worst case I can think of and which scares me rigid. Also what I can't understand is why bother to track us in the first place. They seem suspicious of you but surely not of me and yet I was in Japan those many years back. I can't see what they thought they'd gain by chasing us. And why did they make for where we went rather than somewhere more obviously suited for us to make for?'

'Initially I also pondered that and I now wonder if they suspected or even knew Ah Hong is related to my Chinese counterpart. But they did not strike an anti-Chinese blow by meaning to attack his son, Ah Fat, Jason's friend, but an anti-Colonial against me. That's one possible scenario. It certainly can't have been against you, surely?'

Peter thought that over, rubbing his chin as he did, and stated, 'What they don't know is that we know we were followed, that we heard what they said to each other and what the Japanese said to Ah Hong and that the Chinese had his face slapped. Can we work on that to our benefit, you, rather, as I won't be here?'

'In my bones I feel sure that Dame Fortune has given us the advantage, if the old adage "forewarned is forearmed" is true. I can't yet see how we can use our information ...' He was interrupted by his phone ringing. 'Rance here.' He listened

48

intently. The line crackled and the voice was faint. 'Mr Mason? Yes, he's here. Hold on a second.' He handed the phone over to Peter. 'It's from Singapore, for you.'

'Mason speaking.' A clouded look came over his face. That's a terrible shame. How bad is he?' He covered the mouthpiece with his hand and turned to Philip. 'My relief has had a serious motor accident and is critical,' then back to the phone, 'Look, keep him under sedation in hospital and I'll be down tomorrow morning.' As the person on the other end talked Peter remembered the final thoughts before he went to sleep. Before he rang off, 'Look, this is probably going to put a few backs up but make a point of going to the Imperial Airways office as soon as we've rung off and change the name of my fellow passenger to that of Mr Jason Rance. I'll fill in all necessary details on arrival tomorrow. Got it? Good,' and he rang off.

Philip's mouth was agape as he heard what was being arranged and, as soon as Peter had hung the speaker on the phone's column, asked him what that was all about.

'Philip, I'm sorry to take you so much by surprise but I think it is better to get your son out of the country soonest. Also, once he gets to England, he'll become part of my family and I'll not only take him to Wellington College and settle him in myself but also a little advanced briefing on the quiet, "no names, no pack drill", will sharpen him up if ever the balloon really does go up in this part of the world.'

'That's really decent of you, Peter. As you know the stock market for rubber and tin has not fully recovered after its collapse in the early '30s but my father-in-law was no slouch with money and I can assure you, you won't be out of pocket. Now let's go and tell his mother and the lad as we haven't got all that much time. If the worst does come to the worst and there is a war with Japan, however unlikely it might seem here and now, your help will never be wasted. And, with him not here, although we'll miss him dreadfully, as will his friend Ah Fat, he'll be safely out of the way to escape any repercussions from last night.'

'And you and your missus?'

Philip grinned. 'I have ways and means to look after both of us.'

Next morning whilst under lock and key, the four young captives vowed vengeance on Jason Rance, 'with that unthinkable abuse which we can never forget, wherever, whenever and however. From what that Japanese Yonai Karechika was talking about there'll be a war soon and we'll get a chance. When we meet him we will mount an operation to be known as Operation "Tor Gul",' promised the gang leader, 'and try to kill him.'

There was a thoughtful silence then one of the cousins said, 'Much as I'd like to, it will be risky trying to get him again here in Kuala Lumpur and in the future there's not a chance in many, many millions of meeting him ever again. Can't you extend our search to any Mat Salleh "wherever, whenever and however" we can wreak vengeance on?' Mat Salleh, Malay slang for an Englishman, was a legendary Malay who always thought he knew more than he actually did.

Tor Gul sniffed: he did not like anyone to contradict him but even he saw the logic of that remark. 'I agree. Let's swear an oath on that, whether we work as a group or as individuals.'

There and then swear an oath they did, grimly and evocatively.

The two Japanese and the Indian were deeply worried by the non-return of Tor Gul and his three supporters. The answer came at eleven o'clock when Akbar Khan was called to the Police Station to claim his son. There he met the fathers of the two cousins. The whole affair was a most distressing loss of face. It took a couple of days for Rabilal's father to come and fetch his son. As all the boys were juveniles they were not sent to prison but given a strong warning, with the matter being settled by the four fathers paying a hefty fine.

Before they left the house for the station Philip Rance called his son over to him. 'Son, I want to tell you something which you must keep very, very tightly under your hat, on oath, until you feel you simply have to break it. If you can't manage that I can't tell you.' Jason stared at his father in surprise. 'Father, when have I ...?'

'Never,' his father broke in. 'My accounting tax job is a cover for undercover work, secret stuff. Of course you know I speak Chinese fluently and I never let it be known except to my sources. Nor have I ever spoken my faultless Malay in front of you.'

Jason looked at his father almost pleadingly. 'Father, on oath' and they solemnly shook hands.

'Before you go, I will give you a list of the names of the three Indians you so nobly captured. It may turn out useful, it may not, but in my real job there's no telling what is of no importance now will be of great importance later.' He handed over a list to Jason.

'Skim read it and ask questions.'

Jason read 'The person named Tor Gul because of a birthmark in that shape on one side of his forehead, has the north Indian's paler skin with shifty, pale green eyes. He is about five feet ten inches in height. He is clever and crafty, and can be vicious and malignant. He is strong and, if anything, more anti-British than is his father, Akbar Khan of the IIL. There other two are cousins, named Abdul Rahim Khan and Abdul Hamid Khan, both tough and useful with knife and rope. The former has one ear larger than the other, the latter's Adam's apple is protrudingly triangular and his feet turn out as he walks.'

'No questions, father. As you put such so much importance on this I'll keep it safely.'

Before they loaded what luggage they had into Philip Rance's car Jason had the good sense to put the fourth man's details on the same piece of paper, lest he forgot them: Rabilal Rai, a well-built, good-looking youth, tall for his age with a passively set brown face, with a firm chin, strong white teeth and unusually bushy eyebrows. His back is straight and he holds himself well. When he thinks he has been insulted his face becomes a blaze of anger and his temper quickly reaches boiling point. He has a grudge against the British and seems unnaturally politically inspired.

They drove off to the railway station where Ah Fat, previously warned, came to see his friend off. Jason told him about the attack. 'Watch your back, my friend,' he warned. Talk was cut off as the guard waved his green flag: the two friends waved and shouted to each other as the train started to move off and his friend answered. Neither boy noticed two slightly older Chinese lads looking first at Ah Fat then at Jason. Both had studied at the same school as had the two friends but had been kicked out for open anti-British behaviour. One of them was later to be a Political Commissar and the other a barman in a nightclub. Both were near enough to hear the boy in the train shout out Ah Fat's nickname, *P'ing Yee*, Flat Ears, and Ah Fat to answer with Jason's, *Shandung P'aau*, Shandung Cannon. It was to be fifteen years later that Jason's parting was to be remembered, with gruesome results for Ah Fat.

After Peter Mason, Jason Rance and Yonai Kaechika left, risibly on the same train, life in Kuala Lumpur returned to its peacetime torpidity and an uneasy peace reigned once more ... not to be broken for just over three years. The seeds of a return match for Operation Black Rose, having been sown, would take longer to germinate but had started, ever so slowly, to come to fruition, aided by what had been tattooed in Pashto on all four youths' left shoulder, لورگوط. A Malay Special Branch man who knew the script spelt out Toye Wau Ray Gaaf (with a 'pesh' on top of it showing that the pronunciation was Goo) Lam, that read 'tor gul', recognised it as the name of a gang but, not knowing Pashto, could not translate it, nor could Philip Rance when told about it.

2

Mid-April 1938, England: From the moment Jason left his parents and Ah Fat waving to him as the night train to Singapore drew out from Kuala Lumpur station, his world started to change irrevocably. Something told him that however churned up by the frantic events of the past twenty-four hours, he felt he must behave as though he were in complete control of his feelings and show no weakness. A phrase he had recently heard came to mind as he lay in the upper bunk of the sleeping compartment, *we are our own shop window. That's as good a motto as any to start off with*, he thought, drowsing off in fits and starts as the train clattered and rumbled its way south.

Everything was new, Singapore itself, the visit to the hospital to see the badly injured man in whose place he had a seat in the flying boat, the hotel where the two of them stayed and the hustle and bustle of the differing vistas of a vibrant and busy city. In the inside of a week they were airborne in Imperial Airways Short S 23 Empire flying boat 'Challenger' and after seven night stops with the weather growing decidedly cooler in the last three they landed in the Thames Estuary. He had reached England.

Peter Mason, whom Jason called 'Uncle Peter', had a flat

not far from Cambridge Circus where he worked – Jason did not know what his job was – and his eldest son, Lance, was living there. A camp bed was put up for Jason in Lance's bedroom. 'I will be busy at the office until the weekend when we'll all go home together. What you need to do first thing tomorrow is to get kitted out with something suitable to wear as even summer here is not as hot as it is in Malaya. Come the winter we'll get you fitted out with even thicker clothing. Oh yes, once I get a spare moment I'll open a bank account for you. Your father has arranged funds for that. He told me to tell you not to spend too much too quickly and make it last as long as possible.'

Jason stammered his thanks and next morning he and Lance went to the tailors – 'off the peg' – and a draper's shop for underwear, socks, shirts and ties. They spent the rest of the day on foot or in a bus 'exploring' and on the morrow they opened an account at a National Provincial Bank. Jason found London stranger than he had somehow expected it would be. Apart from being endless, he was overwhelmed by everybody having a white face and white people doing 'coolie' labour. Also he was forcibly struck by how most people so slurred their words when they spoke they were difficult to understand. Odd glances were made at him when he didn't immediately understand what had been said to him.

On the first Friday after their arrival Peter took his car out of its garage and the three of them motored the sixty odd miles down to his house at Aston Tirrold, halfway between Reading and Wantage. It was a pleasant village, nestling at the foot of the Berkshire Downs and promised some good walking. As they were stretching their legs on the Saturday, Uncle Peter said, 'Jason, term time doesn't start for about four months. What I have arranged is that until then the School of Oriental Studies, part of London University, will coach you on improving your knowledge of writing Chinese characters.' He was interrupted by a gasp of delighted surprise. 'Yes, your father told me how many characters you already know and now's a really good chance for you to learn many more. You never can tell when it will pay you dividends.'

'Uncle, that's truly wonderful,' Jason enthused then hesitantly asked if his bank balance would allow it.

'Don't worry about that. I'll look after it and, if payment really worries you, you can think of repaying me once you've started earning your own money.' Jason was not to know, nor would he ever, that funding for such unplanned and short-lived requirements was met by his sponsor's organisation's budget.

Jason quickly got used to the routine and found that he was missing his parents less and less. When he told his Uncle Peter that he planned to put his enhanced knowledge of Chinese characters into writing letters to his close friend Ah Fat, the answer surprised him: 'Don't post them to him directly but in an envelope addressed to your father. It might be suspicious if other than Ah Fat's friends were to see a letter with an English stamp on it and so detrimental to him.'

Jason looked perplexed. 'Uncle Peter, that is something I had never imagined necessary,' he said, not exactly querying what was said but worried, nevertheless.

'The fewer people who know about it the safer it will be for Ah Fat,' and, with a grin, his 'Uncle' added, 'a grown-up's world is never as straightforward as one might think.'

At the end of June Uncle Peter said, 'It's half term and Speech Day at Wellington College next weekend and as I know the headmaster, Dr. "Bunny" Longden, but "Sir" to you, I think it's a good wheeze to go over and introduce you. Of course he knows you're going to start there in the Army Class come September but it'll be good to meet up with him and have a look around. We'll motor over, it's at a place called Crowthorne not all that far from here and you, me, my wife and Lance if he's free. It'll give you a feel for the place.'

The visit went well although the headmaster was rushed off his feet so had little time to spare. It was much grander than the Victoria Institution. While there they went to the school tailors and he was measured for two sets of school uniform, to be ready when term started. He was glad he'd seen the place. By the time he was due to start the term his knowledge of Chinese characters was much better than before.

Jason wondered how he'd fit in to his new school and, after an uncomfortable few days, he started to get the hang of living with English youth, till then something he had not experienced. His peers were not unkind but he was surprised at their ignorance: initially Malaya meant nothing to most boys and only 'postage stamps with the picture of a tiger' to one or two of them. He joined the Officers Training Corps, which, unremarkably, was attached to the Duke of Wellington's Regiment. He quickly assimilated the drill and weapon training. When on fieldcraft parades those summer holidays spent with his Gurkha friends in the jungle near Bhutan Estate paid dividends as there was no one to touch him. Until then his peers had been on the slow side to accept the 'colonial' but from then on, accept him they did as he had something they did not.

Apart from having to use some 'strong-arm' tactics against the school bully in the showers one evening, his first year, on the whole, went smoothly. Studying hard for his army exams, political developments passed him by but, in the 1939 Easter holidays when he visited London, he was surprised if not mildly shocked to see trenches and air-raid shelters being dug and filled sand bags stacked outside important places to limit any damage from bombing, to say nothing of Searchlight troops and Anti-Aircraft guns being sited in Regents Park and other open spaces. *Will they ever be used for real,* he wondered ... but four months later on 3 September Britain declared war on Germany so the answer was 'Yes' with a capital Y.

Army cadets due to be commissioned in 1941 had that date brought forward to 31 December 1939. Jason found that his final exams were also brought forward to that date. Working flat out, he managed to pass out top. He was already over the minimum age when he volunteered for service in India and was overwhelmingly relieved to hear he had been accepted as a Cadet, to be posted to the Indian Military Academy. With about fifty others he was posted to a battalion of the Queen's Regiment, the holding unit for Indian Army cadets awaiting a passage. The boat taking him and his draft out sailed from Southampton and he found that his good friend Hector Mason, now a qualified Japanese interpreter, was also a passenger. Their voyage was the last through the Mediterranean before Hitler gobbled up most of Europe and shipping had to go to India by way of the Cape of Good Hope.

March 1940, India: Bombay! The gateway to India! To Jason it had always sounded romantic but, on arrival, he found it to be the opposite, especially when compared with the cleanliness of Malaya. Even when it was pointed out to him that Malaya's daily rain was a blessing India did not have, what upset him were the teeming crowds of depressingly poor humanity, to say nothing of the pitiful, the blind, the beggars, the wheedling children, the laden women, the scavenging dogs, the bare-ribbed horses pulling over-loaded gharries, their bulb horns honking mournfully, the old and rheumy-eyed, the young prematurely shrivelled, ever eddying and swirling in kaleidoscopic patterns. The raucous black crows and cows wandering in the streets with an air of indifference were the only living creatures seemingly unaffected by the heat, the clamour and the squalor.

A railway journey to Dehra Dun by way of Delhi let him see much of the countryside. As doors on Indian railway carriages open inwards it was fun to sit on the steps in a cooling breeze watching the landscape go by. At dawn on the second morning the rails were too slippery for the wheels to get any traction so the train could not get up a gradient. Everyone was ordered out and pushed it up, another world for the passengers coming out from England.

At the IMA, now to be their home only until 10 December 1941 because the three-year course had been shortened following the outbreak of war, they were met by their new officers who wore unexpectedly different cap badges and shoulder titles. The expressions on their faces as they regarded the draft of travel-worn, pale-faced, long-haired and badly turned out cadets showed as much enthusiasm for them as had the Bombay crowds had for Jason. There was silence until a gorgeously starched wonder, the Company Commander, a major, leisurely strolled over and drawled rather than spoke, 'If you want a pee, go behind that hedge there.' Not the welcome as Gentlemen Cadets they had expected.

The camp was superb, set in spacious grounds made wonderfully green by pre-monsoon rain. After the cramped conditions on board ship, the accommodation – and being looked after by a bearer – was palatial. They were issued with bicycles and the words of command for communal riding amused Jason: 'walk march, prepare to mount, mount.' That, apparently, stemmed from orders to mount horses.

Once training started the new cadets found what the old lags had said was true, 'the scene changes, but the music never'. For drill, weapon training, physical training and route marches the new cadets were taken in hand by gnarled British warrant officers and sergeants who told them that 'when in Rome you do as India does. Get it?' And get it they did. The cadets from England were surprised at how antiquated most of the weapons were, and how few of them. When one of them asked why there were no Bren LMGs, Light Machine Guns, only one of the sergeant instructors had heard of them. Until a few Bren Guns were issued towards the end of the course, last war Maxim guns were toted around but not fired. When Jason did get to fire the Bren, he most unusually fired a 'possible', full points, both for single shots and rapid.

Officers taught tactics and ran exercises. Civilian *munshis* taught the cadets Roman Urdu, the *lingua franca* of the Indian Army. It had not occurred to many of the cadets from monolingual England that the sub-continent had many other languages besides Urdu until, some months into the course, soldiers of various Indian Army units were introduced and their language explained: Punjabi, Pashto, Bengali and a whole raft of others. Jason, of course, knew that Gurkhali was different but was thrilled when a Gurkha NCO, Havildar Rahul Dura of the 1st Gurkhas who had recently been called back from the Reserve as a Company Quartermaster Havildar, was introduced to the course. He was a man unlike any Jason had previously met: time and determination to overcome a dull hurt in his shoulder sustained in the 1905 earthquake that had spoilt his face, with its hard eyes, its determined jutting chin and of a darker than normal hue, with furrows that resembled the marks of a leopard's claws on a tree trunk. A British officer of Gurkhas told the cadets about Gurkhas and afterwards Jason Rance managed to meet him.

'My name is Quartermaster Havildar Rahul Dura, Sahib, and I am happy to meet you.'

'I am happy also to meet you, Quartermaster Havildar. I have learnt a little Gurkhali from Gurkhas who work in Malaya,' Jason answered haltingly but understandably.'

'What regiment will you join when you are an officer?' There was authority in his manner and iron in his voice.

'Oh yours, I hope. The 1st Gurkhas.'

'I hope so too, Sahib,' replied the NCO, making an indelible impression on Jason.

Jason wanted to know why his name did not end in 'Bahadur' as most other Gurkha names seemed to so asked, 'Rahul, not Rahul Bahadur?'

The older man tried to answer in simple Gurkhali. 'Rahul. Meaning is "be wise when old".'

They shook hands and separated. 'I heard you talking in Gurkhali,' said a captain of the Directing Staff. 'Fine for now but you must realise that you will not speak anything but Urdu until you have passed the Elementary Urdu Examination.'

Jason had no option but to accept the rebuke. Nevertheless, 'exercise enemy' and demonstration troops were Gurkhas from one of the three Regimental Centres in Dehra Dun, the 2nd, the 3rd and the 9th: having ascertained none of the Directing Staff was watching, he was thrilled to get a chance of talking to them in their own language. They too were happily surprised. It made him try all the harder to pass out as high as he could so be commissioned in a Gurkha rather than an Indian regiment. In fact he never had had anything against any Indian as his detractors in Kuala Lumpur had alleged.

It was on close-country exercises in the Tons Valley that Jason came into his own. All that he had learnt with the Gurkhas at Bhutan Estate paid great dividends. Although there were no 'cuckoo-calling' birds in Malaya, he had learnt to 'cuckoo' with his hands. On one exercise as a platoon commander in fairly open country he kept in contact with his sections by imitating cuckoo calls. This fooled the opposing 'enemy' commander, one

Gentleman Cadet Ranjit Singh, who remained baffled by real live cuckoos answering, so *Drat it! Where is this elusive man?*

In thicker country he was yet more effective and even managed to better the Gurkha 'exercise enemy'. He thoroughly enjoyed himself and the Directing Staff watched his progress with much enthusiasm. However, rapid German conquests eastwards and the fighting in Africa meant that those in High Places in India looked towards the barren North-West Frontier as the danger spot. Events in the northeast of India were seen as remotely unreal. 'Jungle? In no way! Japan attack? Don't be ludicrous and if they do, Singapore's impregnable, isn't it? The jungle is impenetrable.'

Wrong, wrong, wrong! But I'm too junior to argue with them.

2 July 1941. Emperor's palace, Tokyo, Japan: Forty-one-year-old Emperor Hirohito sat silently, stiffly and solemnly at one end of two long brocade-covered tables, before a gold screen on a dais. In front of him his civil and military chiefs faced each other across those tables, almost ready after years of planning for a final decision to go to war other than against the Chinese. In early 1936 a group of officers, seeing what Hitler and Mussolini were getting away with in Europe and Africa, wanted to plan the same in Japan so had murdered enough ministers and high-ranking politicians who were against military action to form a 'military' cabinet. Momentum had been slow to build up, but it rapidly increased its impetus when General Hideki Tojo, nicknamed 'Razor', came to power the following 17 October, heading a militarist government.

The meeting was the climax to many less formal but equally important ones held during the previous weeks and the final one to decide how an impending war would be waged. Already their traditional enemy, the Soviet Union, was engaged in a life and death struggle with Germany so their northern flank was safe enough, certainly for the foreseeable future. That meant that all effort and attention could be directed south into tropical Asia – but first east to Pearl Harbour.

Western economic sanctions had deprived Japan of many raw materials, oil, of which there was already a marked shortage, being only one of them. Oil there was aplenty in the Dutch East Indies and that country of many islands was Japan's primary goal, so the major effort was to be directed thereto. Then on to Malaya for tin and rubber, both commodities sorely needed. As a first step, Japan would implement previously made plans for the domination of Siam and French Indo-China 'with the purpose of strengthening our advance into the southern regions'. Strangely, as matters turned out, Singapore was not mentioned although the Japanese would 'not be deterred by the possibility of being involved in a war with Great Britain and the United States'. The Showa Dynasty was fiercely proud, sensitive and far from logical.

However, the President of the Privy Council, Yoshimichi Hara, a thin, willowy past master at intrigue, was troubled by the willingness of the others to risk war with Great Britain. 'I think that such a war will occur if we take action against Indo-China,' he stated bluntly.

But he was overruled and the Emperor, at one-thirty exactly, immediately after lunch, speaking for the first and only time, gave his consent. Although he had an introverted personality, Emperor Hirohito was an extremely intelligent man with a remarkable memory. He had served as regent for his mad, politely referred to as 'mentally incapacitated', father from the age of twenty-one, four years before he became Emperor, and had taken a keen interest in matters military from an early age, too keen some of his staff sometimes felt. Ironically, he was still, for a few more months, an honorary Field Marshal in the British Army. He was sixteen years younger than his youngest adviser. His innate caution made him rely on his advisers rather than on his own instincts. Emperors did not lead, they only symbolised the legitimacy of Japan's wars.

However, the Imperial Army Chief of Staff, General Hajime Sugiyama, a square-jawed man whose right eye never opened as much as did his left, knew that the consent would indeed result in war, not only in the Dutch East Indies but in Malaya and Singapore as well, so a new, Southern Army, under Field Marshal Count Hisaichi Terauchi, was formed. 'My Headquarters will most certainly have to be in Singapore, which I will rename Shonan, "Brilliant South",' he declared, with a delicate cough, 'but, of course, not to start with.' It was the nearest to a joke anyone had heard him try to make.

Having studied maps of the terrain and had reports from the plethora of spies Japan had had in Malaya and Singapore for more than ten years, working in all sorts of professions, he had already made his outline plans. 'We will approach Singapore from the north by land,' he pontificated, 'working our way from an invasion of Malaya on its east coast but first being involved in Siam. That way the fortress guns in Singapore will not be able to fire on us when we make our final attack, not that they could stop us if they did. In Bangkok, so I have learnt, is a powerful Indian

Independence League office also working to get the British out of India. The Indian Army will be sent to Malaya where there are also anti-British Indians who plan to help our victory by subverting the Indian soldiers against the British and for us. Such, to be a success, has had to be prepared well in advance.'

He then unexpectedly waxes lyrical as the flow of Shintoism glides through him: 'Who surveys a force of Nature? Who applies his eye to God's keyhole? What fool thrusts his hand under the skirts of the Inevitable? Who can sidetrack the fidelity of Fate? Destiny and Japan have made a love match: Dame Fortune has, after many experiments, found her bedfellow.'

His audience knew how to show appreciation of such remarks by looking suitably stunned. It was, of course, another way of talking about the Greater East Asia Co-Prosperity Sphere, known in private as Southern Resources Area, with Japan its instigator, leader, mentor and chief beneficiary.

'After our victories we will have our two thumbs in the eye sockets of the western world,' and he raised his thumbs, 'and I shall put this hand on the throat of white-skinned humanity everywhere we find it. It will be up to us to make where we sit the Head of the Table.'

Now there was a man who already had strong links with the Indian Independence League, a Major Fujiwara Iwaichi, a good and sincere man, and he was the obvious person to send back to Bangkok, hot foot. From there he sent orders to the IIL's branch in Malaya, headed by the round-faced Penang lawyer who had eyebrows like hairy caterpillars, was small-bodied and hirsute as a man-eating spider, named Nedyam Raghavan. His spies would be sent down into Malaya to discover as much as they could about Indian civilians who might be used in trying to turn Indian soldiers, who assuredly would be sent to defend Malaya, against their white officers. This was not so fanciful an idea though no British officer would ever have considered such an eventuality. Certainly Nedyam Raghavan and Akbar Khan knew that Malay-domiciled Indians were opposed to British rule.

Three of the many places visited by Indian agitators were rubber estates where Gurkhas comprised the labour force. Their frosty rebuff was 'We are Gurkhas, not Indians. Leave us alone. Go away.' And, crestfallen, away they went, having drawn an uncompromising blank, except for one man, Rabilal Rai, who, not in the hearing of his peers, told the IIL representative that he would do all he could against the British - *pubic hair, go fuck thyself* still heavily rankling him.

Still later that year it was decided that the 25th Army would be used for the ground offensive. The General Officer Commanding-in-Chief was Lieutenant General Tomoyuki Yamashita. He was days short of fifty-six, a forceful and imaginative officer with extensive experience in command, mostly up in Manchuria, but little in combat duty. Round of face, he had dark, close-cropped hair and a neat moustache. Although he often seemed passive and stoic, he was ruthless and ambitious. He dared not fail in such an important operational command. Later he became known as 'The Tiger of Malaya', so brutal was he, indifferent to danger and pain, alert and selfish, and cold-blooded as a cat.

He expounded his views to his senior staff. 'Our training is based on loyalty to the Emperor and the warrior values of courage, bravery, obedience, frugality and self-discipline. Compared with our Imperial Army, our adversaries don't start as none of their pamphlets or manuals put any emphasis on those attributes which we Nippons see as of over-riding importance. Our adversaries are weak in spirit and training, even if superior to us in numbers. British troops are indolent, effete and out-dated. In fact the normal state of all white foreigners is one of extreme caution. The British could be an irritant, as could the Australians, but not much else. As for the Indians and those men of Nepal' – 'Kulaka' as he tried to pronounce 'Gurkha' – 'they are cowardly and many are disloyal to their white-skinned masters. Field Marshal Hata Shunruko, who as a major was in Delhi in 1911 at the English King-Emperor's durbar, once showed me a letter written by one of our monks, Ekai Kawagushi, written in 1905, to the Maharaja of Nepal after visiting that country. In it he suggested that Nepal had a better army than was the case. The Field Marshal said that in 1911 the King-Emperor told him that the Kulakas had a famous name and were smart – but,' and here he sneered – 'famous name and smartness do not mean brave or efficient. Our name is famous already and, once the war has been won, it will be more famous still.

'There is a Malayan army, a rabble from all accounts,' he continued, trying not to sound superior but failing. 'Even defending their own soil they are two-faced and cowardly. There is nothing to fear from them either. As for the Overseas Chinese, they're no better than that troop of monkeys in the north where we have been working up till now. A heavy hand is their best medicine. I have been given an order to be in Singapore in one hundred days.'

He made the figures one and two zeros with forefinger raised and then forefinger joined with his thumb, not in Kanji but in Roman, to emphasise the foreign enemy against whom the struggle was to be. 'It will bode ill for us and a national shame to boot if we are even one day late,' he finished off threateningly, knowing that anything in the world is better than shame ... and leaving the implied threat hanging in the air, the conference broke up.

30 September 1941, Indian Military Academy, Dehra Dun: Shortly after feeling vexed about being told that the jungle was impenetrable, Gentleman Cadet Rance got a letter from his parents letting him know that they were folding up their affairs, shutting up their house and going back to England. After their due leave his father was going to work in Head Office in London. *So they will be starting a new life like I've already started on mine.* In the letter was a reference to the Pashto tattooed on the left shoulder of all four youths he had so successfully managed to capture that time: they merely read 'Tor Gul'. That was news to him and he wondered what it meant. *I'd only recognise him again by his birthmark. As for the other two Indians, their faces never made much of an impression on me.*

The Directing Staff were so impressed with Jason that when, six weeks before the end of the course, it was time to ask each cadet what regiment he would like to be commissioned into, his answering 'First Gurkhas, Second Gurkhas, Third Gurkhas,' was not quarrelled with. In early December they were told their future: Jason, the senior Under Officer and top cadet, was to be commissioned into the First Gurkha Rifles and, having passed his Elementary Urdu, would be able to concentrate on learning Gurkhali as soon as he reached the regiment's centre at Dharmsala.

After the last exercise held against the Gurkhas they held a party. Normally only British officers attended but, as Jason was to be commissioned into the 1st Gurkhas and a 1st Gurkha officer was one of the staff, he too was invited. First of all came the obligatory glass of colourless 'country spirit', *raksi,* a great tongue loosener, and new to top Gentleman Cadet. Jason found himself talking to a platoon commander, Jemadar Buddhiman Dura, also a 1st Gurkha. 'Sahib,' the Jemadar said slowly. 'I am a 2/1 GR soldier. We had to provide two hundred of our NCOs and riflemen for the raising of 3/1 GR in January 1940 and another eighty when 4/1 GR was raised in March 1941. That left us weak and we were made even weaker when our new recruits did not get their full share of basic training. To make up numbers one of my relatives, Rahul Dura, who is really too old for active service, was recalled from the reserve and promoted from Quartermaster Havildar to QMJ, Quartermaster Jemadar. We have heard nothing from him since the battalion went to Malaya. His family pray all is well. His shoulder was badly hurt in the severe 1905 earthquake that hit Dharmsala. It won't be easy for him.'

'Jemadar sahib, I met him when he came here and we spoke with each other. If I hear any news of him when I get to Dharmsala I'll ask the office to let you know.'

Jemadar Buddhiman Dura smiled. 'Thank you, sahib,' he said, indicating to an orderly to fill up the sahib's glass with more *raksi.*

10 December 1941, Indian Military Academy, Dehra Dun: On this day thirty-five new British and fifty new Indian Army officers were commissioned as war-time, not regular, Second Lieutenants. All were ignorant, as was everyone else outside Japan at the very highest level, of what had taken place there just over five months previously. The pre-war necessity of British officers destined for the Indian Army having to spend a year with a British battalion had been suspended so Jason went directly to the 1st Gurkha Rifle Regimental Centre at Dharmsala, in north India.

Late December 1941, Jitra, North Malaya: Relentless Japanese attacks that outflanked the road-bound 2/1 Gurkhas soon showed up the paucity of their battle readiness. Movement became snarled, fluid, concentrated and split up. Within twelve hours, the battalion had virtually ceased to be a coherent unit so successful had Japanese tank action been. Led by a Major Saeki and a Captain Yamani, it managed to scatter, capture or kill over three hundred officers and men. Two men, Havildar Parsuram Thapa and Rifleman Manbir Gurung, suicidally tried to jump up the side of the tank that carried a pennant so obviously carrying the commander. Both fell off and Parsuram was squashed flat by the next tank. No one would have recognised his mangled corpse nor did anyone know what had happened to Manbir.

But one man the triumphant Japanese neither killed nor captured was Quartermaster Jemadar Rahul Dura. Rationing the troops was an unending nightmare for him. He well knew that the forward troops were wet through and probably tired out so he decided to bring an especially cooked hot meal and rum: he never let on how he got it but it was from an Australian transport unit's stocks that were 'no longer needed'. He himself was already over-worked and tired; orders and counter-orders had resulted in inevitable disorder. Enemy air strikes and infiltrating snipers, or maybe spies, had caused delay after delay and problem after problem. So he was well pleased when eventually he did reach Jitra just before dark that same day, almost being swept off his feet by the blinding rainstorm and its gale force wind as he got out of his vehicle. He splashed away to report his arrival and find out where to take the hot food at exactly the same time as the Saeki surge engulfed the area. The crash of guns, the staccato chattering of automatic small arms fire, the yells of derision from the crewmen of Japanese tanks roaring down the road and destroying practically everything, left those still alive stunned. The leading tank squashed his vehicle almost flat so ruining the food and a round of tank fire threw him to the ground onto his bad left shoulder that had already started to hurt him, what with the bumpy journey and all-pervading dampness. Hitting his head hard, he passed out, lying in some long grass.

As the battalion evacuated its position to move south, no one noticed him. When he eventually came to the rain had stopped but trees still dripped water. Groggily he stood up and called out, 'Can anyone hear me?' his voice hardly audible still so shaken was he. He saw burning buildings and smouldering stores. The severely wounded lay there, some with arms torn off, others sightless, others with faces drenched in blood, some squirming and writhing, others too dazed to move, all of them waiting to die as quickly as possible. There was nothing he could do for them except hope they died before any more Japanese arrived. Shaken voices from the lightly wounded greeted him, asking for help he could not give. 'All those who can walk come here,' he called out, his head still aching. About twenty men gathered. 'Quartermaster Jemadar sahib, what now?' one asked. 'I am hungry. Is there any food left?'

'Go and see if there is. That goes for the rest of you. I'll give you a quarter of an hour.' The men were back before then having found nothing edible.

'We move south. The battalion must re-group somewhere near the main road. We can't move through the jungle at night in this state, so we'll walk on the road. Single file. Spaced out.' His voice was shaky and he felt unbalanced. 'Move and hope to live: stay here and die.'

'Where are the Japanese now?' someone asked.

'I'll only be able to tell you if we meet up with them, from behind, on a flank or in front, and then you'll know as much as I will. I'm off. Follow me.' The QMJ moved over to the main road, turned south and started walking. There was something about this old Gurkha that crushed protest and curtailed discussion. He saw a mangled corpse and instinctively felt for the identification tabs. He tore them off, thinking to look at them when he reached Battalion HQ, then tramped off down the road, still shaken and head in a whirl, despondent at the dashed hopes of feeding the battalion after so much effort to say nothing of other unending difficulties he had had to cope with.

He thinks savagely of what he would have to indent on Brigade for now that everything seems destroyed. He gropes for details but his mind refuses to stay clear. His thoughts wander ... 'I brought up rice to eat,' he mutters, 'long-grained, short-grained, the kind that tastes almost like honey, spring rice, autumn rice, padi rice, hillside rice, unhusked, cooked ... with meat ... and vegetables and dal pulse, yellow, black, red ... and spices. Spices: aniseed, cumin, coriander, pepper, nutmeg, cinnamon, ginger, turmeric, chillies, the long hot kind, the shorter, even hotter kind' – and he licks his lips in anticipation because none of the food he has brought up had been eaten ... and ... his mind switches to equipment – web, canvas, boots – *how long will our boots last?* – laces for the eyelets of boots, studs for the soles of the boots; hammers to knock the studs in and pincers to wrench the studs out ... iron feet for the use of anybody who mends boots – wooden stands for the iron feet; handles for the hammers ... and socks for the feet to fit the boots ... and wool to darn the socks and needles for the wool and thimbles for the needles and housewives for the needles and thimbles and wool. And thinking of wool –threads for the buttons, buttons for the thread – shirt buttons, fly buttons and the pants to which you sew them. And the shirts worn above the pants ... and the vests under the shirts ... the underpants worn below the vests ...

By now Rahul is wretchedly weary as he drags one foot after the other, his shoulder hurting him so much he cannot hang his rifle from it and even the straps of his equipment are a penance that has to be borne. He says, out loud, 'Rifles to kill the Japanese with ... shovels to bury the *shaitans* with – it's a wonder I don't have to conduct their funerals – or give them rum in case they faint.' ... rum, tea, armbands for the Regimental Police, or do they not matter anymore? Ground-sheets, helmets, straps, buckles, spoons ... waterbottles, corks for waterbottles, metal tops and screws and strings for the tops of the corks of waterbottles ... nuts to screw on the screw-eye things that hold the strings that attach the corks to the waterbottles. Covers for the waterbottles. Covers for the covers of covers ... Verey light pistols. Anti-tank ammunition. 'Ammunition! .303 alone has broken my heart,' the QMJ says in a mumble. 'Ammunition has shortened my life by ten years, even if I don't have that long to wait.' He thinks of tracer, of ballistite, of Tommy guns, Bren guns, Lewis guns ... and magazines for them. He is almost asleep on his feet, this most loyal of loyal men. Then he says, 'Blankets,' but finds himself thinking of oil-skin wallets, of camouflage nets and covers for helmets; of Regulation Flannelette, otherwise known as 'four-by-two' to clean out barrels, of pull-throughs, oil-bottles, pencils, hand-grenades, First Field Dressings ... cotton waste, carbon paper, bayonets, ink-powder, salt, pepper, spices, chillies which burn the mouth ... 'Fire buckets,' he sighs and, as though walking down the dumb, dark corridor of infinity, without beginning, without end, without perspective, without horizon, the Old Soldier falls down fast asleep.

The man behind him, also in a semi-coma, trips over him and falls across him. That wakes the QMJ up. But it's no good. He staggers to his feet and calls out, 'Rain or no rain. Let's sleep here for a while ...' and, crawling under a bush, sinks down asleep before his sentence is fully out of his mouth. Those bringing up the rear see him, a black shadow under the bush which suddenly becomes sparklingly alive with a mass of fireflies and they too sink down and are asleep as soon as their head touches the ground, sleep so deep that the unending stridulations of cicadas and incessant burping of bullfrogs go unheard. The Gurkhas become 'old soldiers' overnight. Luckily no enemy pass down the road as they sleep.

Next morning, when Japanese aircraft, their engines making an ecstatic sound like gulping laughter, fly low over the rubber estates on either side of the road, the QMJ's remnants move under the protective covering of the rubber trees, staying put against the trunks, regardless of the fire ants that search and probe and sting and nip, regardless of the giant black spiders with their coarse-fibred webs ... then there is silence above them and they continue their harrowing walk.

From one Chinese house where they ask for food the occupants run away, thinking that the Gurkhas, whom they have never seen before, were Japanese. They try again, at a Malay house this time, and are given a bite each. Not much, but it helps. The glum, sullen stares and silent, shut mouths of others they meet tell their own tale of disillusion and disenchantment beyond their dreariest dream, by now a nagging nightmare. The end man looks over his shoulder from time to time and once only, along a particularly long, straight bit of road, manages to shout out, croaks, in fact, but loud enough for the message to be passed up the short column in time to disperse, that he sees Japanese cyclists approaching. The Gurkhas hide and see with amazement as their enemies ride past that they are lightly clad and wear a bandolier around their shoulders rather than being weighed down with cumbersome equipment as they themselves wear.

Back once more on the road, the Gurkhas pass abandoned trucks, three burnt-out Japanese tanks. No survivor remains and the nauseating stench, foetid and foul, lies heavily on the air, with the sickly smell of roasted flesh still pungent – the men try to spit out the lingering taste but without much success – bits and pieces of equipment strewn around the place and, sometimes, the anguished look on a dead comrade's face. They recognise Havildar Som Bahadur Dura, who was overdue pension, killed while trying to rescue one of his men being bayoneted. Half a body of a once-living soldier hangs from a branch, having been catapulted there by high explosive. They can't leave it there. They pull it down to put in a ditch – why? – cover it under some branches they hack off but search its still-worn haversack. Joy! They find some biscuits and raisins, which they share out before moving off. On the way they are joined by more stragglers. They avoid eye contact with any local they come across. Forty-eight hours later and thirty miles farther south, a sentry of the nucleus of the battalion on the northern outskirts of the small town of Sungei Patani, sees a party of men holding each other and staggering in, the last lot, as it turns out, of scattered, tattered, battered groups to re-appear. Looking over his shoulder, the sentry calls for help. Willing hands take hold of them. They are taken to a place to eat then to sleep and, even before taking their footwear off – those who are still wearing any – all of them are out to the world. But they are alive, which is more than can be said for more than a quarter of 2/1 Gurkha Rifles.

'How wrong, very wrong indeed, we were to think that the Japanese were second-rate soldiers,' said the CO to the Adjutant.

'I hate to say it but in every way they seem better prepared for war than are we. Who in Hell would have thought it would turn out like this?' The question needed no answer: there was none to give. The CO was dead shortly afterwards, as used up and lifeless as a piece of chewed celery.

2 January 1942, 1st Gurkha Rifles Regimental Centre (GRRC), Dharmsala: 2nd Lieutenant Rance travelled from Delhi by rail to Ambala, changed on to a narrow-gauge line that wound its way through low hills to the railhead at the small town of Pathankot. From there to 1 GRRC at Dharmsala Cantonment, now also occupied by the 1st Battalion, was a road journey of about fifty miles. It started along a gently rising valley until a steeper climb for the last three thousand feet into the clear, crisp air running through thick groves of pine, rhododendron and deodar with patches of wild cherry, not yet in bloom, glimpsing families of black-faced langurs swinging in the branches or on the ground picking inquisitively at anything that caught their fancy. Overhead lammergeyers and eagles drifted effortlessly and gracefully in the thermals. To the southeast ridge after ridge of undulating hills gradually lost themselves in blue haze where, about a hundred miles away, lay Simla; to the north were twenty-thousand-foot-high snow-covered mountains, the Himalayas, the snowline high. In the middle distance were tea gardens dotted with shade trees.

The soldiers' barracks, situated at about five thousand feet above sea level, had been started in 1880 and had long been condemned but finance, that age-old bogey, stalked with deadening effect here as in so many other places in the Army of

Hind. There was no electricity or running water and all conditions were rudimentary.

On his arrival Jason was interviewed by the Adjutant before being taken in front of the Commandant, an elderly, white-haired man, heavily wrinkled with a drooping moustache. He had started his commissioned service in the Inns of Court, a regiment with a history stretching back to 1584. It had its own Officers Training Unit at No 10 Stone Buildings, set in a quiet backwater on the fringes of the City of London, sandwiched between High Holborn and Fleet Street. There, unusually, 'experience in the colonies' was seen as a mark of approval. He had fought from the beginning of the last war as well as in a number of frontier skirmishes. Jason, standing rigidly to attention, saluted him. The Commandant looked up at his new officer before dropping his gaze to a book on his desk and unexpectedly asked, 'Did you know that when, in 1893, fifteen hundred Mahsuds attacked the 1st battalion at Wana they were chased away? Eventually they headed for home near the frontier with Afghanistan and were last seen in a valley known as Tor Gul, Pashto for black rose ...'

Tor gul means black rose! That black birthmark on one side of that man's forehead is like a black rose. So that's *why* ... Jason's fingers gripped his trouser creases and his head spun as suddenly all the pieces of the little linguistic jigsaw fell into place. He gave a little gasp. *Now I understand what the astrologer meant.*

'Come now, Mr Rance, that was only a minor action but I do insist on a new officer learning our regiment's history. Most important. However, I'm sure the battles to come will be harder but we don't really know, do we?' The Commander needlessly riffled the pages of the book. 'You've a background the regiment would not have accepted in peacetime but we have accepted you because there's a war on. Don't get any ideas of speaking to the men in Khaskura' – a name Jason had not heard before – 'as officers are not meant to become too intimate or familiar with them. Talking to the Gurkha officers in Urdu is quite sufficient.'

Jason trying not to show his surprise and disappointment, ventured to say, 'I understand, sir, but in fact I already speak enough to get by well enough.'

The Colonel, normally a reticent man and one of the 'old school' who thought subalterns were not worthy of being spoken to, was, however, intrigued. *Would never have happened in peacetime.* He had a son Jason's age. 'How on earth did that come about? And having lived in Malaya did you pick up any of the heathen languages there? If you did, as I suppose you might have done, I consider it most unusual and hardly sahib-like. Tell me your background,' and he leant back in his chair, rubbing his eyes.

Most unusual and hardly sahib-like! Deep inside him Jason bristled. *I must be rather a culture shock for the Old Man.* Hesitant at first he described his childhood years and that he was to all intents and purposes bilingual in Chinese, could read and write many characters and also was a fluent Malay speaker. Feeling he was already being looked upon as 'not like the rest of us', he kept his being a ventriloquist a secret.

'All right,' came a grudging answer, 'but don't make your being able to talk Khaskura too obvious as some of the senior majors might disapprove.' A thought struck him, 'A great pity you did not come a year earlier when the 2nd battalion was sent to Malaya. You'd have been a most useful Intelligence Officer.' He called in his Adjutant. 'Did you know Mr Rance is bilingual in Chinese? No, nor did I. Do you think there's any chance of his being allowed to reinforce the 2nd battalion or is it too late?'

'That's a fast ball, sir. It'll take time for anything like that to be answered. It'll have to go all the way to GHQ and I'm sure they're busy enough with more important matters.'

'Yes, I suppose so,' and without any more ado, he dismissed his new reinforcement.

Jason was posted to a recruit training company to learn the rudiments of all that which is needed to be a commander of Gurkhas. He had to come to terms with that quintessential aspect of the Indian Army, namely *kaida*, the proper way of doing things in a tightly knit, well organised, extended family that a good unit is. Each unit has its own *kaida*. In the battalion it was stiff and reeked of pre-war snobbery. Officers with 'temporary commissions' were known as 'temporary gentlemen' and the toast to the King Emperor on Mess Nights was prefaced with 'Gentlemen and Temporary Officers'.

Contact with the soldiers was only during parade hours. A new officer was never quickly accepted by them. He was minutely observed, much more than he realised. Quirks and foibles were watched and, provided nothing untoward was noticed, acceptance came sooner or later – sooner in Jason's case – with a nickname that was seldom known by the officer concerned. In rare cases when the Subedar Major saw that a particular officer's chemistry simply was not in sympathy with what the Gurkhas were used to or would accept, the CO would be told that, if the officer remained, the Subedar Major could not accept responsibility for any mishap. Such an officer was normally posted away.

Rifleman Hitman Gurung, a loyal pre-war soldier too old for promotion, became Jason's batman and helped him out when 'military protocol' stumped him. He'd had an unusual experience on the North-West Frontier in the 1937 campaign. At a ten-minute halt on a route march he had slipped off to one side to have a pee but had been knocked unconscious so had to be taken back to Battalion HQ. There the Muslim doctor found out from those who had brought him back where the incident had been and, after treating his patient, visited the place. He found that it was a Muslim graveyard and the jet had landed on a place holding a dead man. Hitman was now thought to be invulnerable to any *djinn* so an added safeguard for the new sahib.[1]

Jason had not realised that none of the recruits had ever worn boots before. One of them made the mistake not only of putting his boots on the wrong feet but of lacing them together. The first step he tried to take saw him crashing down on the ground, bursting his nose open. He was taken to the hospital, admitted and issued with a shroud as well as pyjamas. The Irish doctor in charge did not think he would die because of a sore nose but he had been found deficient of shrouds on the last inspection and was determined to leave nothing to chance. Every person admitted to the hospital had to sign for one – just in case. This practice had

---

1 A similar incident is recorded in the regimental history of the 4th Gurkha Rifles.

to be stopped soon afterwards as it was having a depressing effect on morale.

There were several other newly joined British subalterns, the only Indian officers found in Gurkha regiments were the doctors, and one worry they had been told about was that the 1st and 2nd battalions had been 'milked', 'bled' some said, of so many of their long-service NCOs for the two new battalions that they could not be as good as they had been, to say nothing of the normal time needed for training recruits had been so foreshortened it was secretly hoped no first-class enemy would be met up with before more training had been done in battalions.

'And', the Senior Subaltern added, 'I hear from my friends in Indian regiments that the problem there is just as bad, if not worse. The Indian officers also seem to be worried about having to fight England's wars for her. They find it difficult not having the same rates of pay, of not being allowed into white men's clubs so have a chip on their collective shoulders and foster feelings of resentment. I hope relations don't go sour because of it.' His listeners nodded their assent but there was nothing they could do about it if matters did deteriorate.

Wartime officers were excused buying expensive peacetime mess kit and were allowed to wear service dress for Mess Nights. For the first time there was such an occasion after he had arrived, Jason was 'dined in', thereby sitting on the Colonel's right. The long ebony table was spread with white damask on which silver and crystal floated and a row of candlesticks seemed to march in stepless union. The centrepiece was a silver rendering of the fort at Malaun, taken by General Sir David Ochterlony from the Gorkhas in 1815, and the regiment was born then. In the flickering candlelight the sides of the fort were craggy, creased and crinkled. The regimental history had it that was a hard-won fight and if Ochterlony had not had artillery the Gorkhas would never have been beaten. The food and the drink; white wine with the oysters – how *did* they get here? – sherry with the soup, champagne with the fish, claret with the roast, port with the cheese and Madeira with the fruit. As course followed course, the servants, Indians not Gurkhas, who stood outside that magic of golden light, stepped in with a plate or a cradled bottle and stepped back almost as though they did not exist.

Before the coffee, liqueurs, cigars and snuff, three decanters – always pushed on their passage along the table and never lifted – one each of port, sherry and marsala, were put lovingly in front of the officers sitting at either end of the table, the senior major as President and a junior lieutenant as Vice President. Both filled their glass with their choice of tipple before sending them to his left and after all glasses were filled, the decanters stopped at the far end of the table from where they had started and stoppers put on again.

The Second-in-Command of the 1st King George V's Own Gurkha Rifles (Malaun Regiment) Regimental Depot, an aging major dressed in ceremonial mess kit with medals, rapped on the table, stood up and, a glass of port in his right hand, surveyed the assembled diners. The buzz of conversation died down: all was quiet as the Mess Havildar had already ordered the band to stop playing.

Raising his glass, the President loudly intoned, 'Mr Vice, the King Emperor!'

At the other end of the table, Mr Vice stood up, glass in his right hand raised to the level of his mouth. 'Gentlemen and Temporary Officers, the King Emperor!'

Chairs were pushed back as all stood, glasses in right hands. 'The King Emperor' rippled out and the toast was drunk. The pitter-patter of glasses being put back on the table mingled with gruff voices announcing, 'God bless him,' the privilege allowed to field officers. Seated again, coffee in small cups appeared.

A while later, decanters having circulated once more, the President rose to his feet for a second time, replenished glass in hand. 'Mr Vice, the Regiment.' 'Gentlemen and Temporary Officers, the Regiment.' 'The Regiment,' and another toast was drunk. As glasses clattered back onto the table, the field officers added their privileged amen, 'God bless it!'

Seated once more, from either end of the table the three decanters were once again religiously started on their left-hand journey and glasses were refilled. Cigars were cut and lit, snuff was sniffed. Then, pleasantly relaxed, the President leant back in his chair, head slightly turned, and the Mess Havildar standing behind him bent forward, although he knew the order would be for the pipers and drummers to enter and play. At a sign through the open door at the end of the room there was a drone and squeal as the pipers, bags full, started piping. Seven Gurkhas, four pipers and three drummers, two tenor and one base in his leopard-skin apron, dressed in rifle-green jackets with medal ribbons peeping through and trews, black leather belts and Highland pattern shoes with white spats, entered the room and what little talk there was dried up. In step and with slightly swaggering gait, they orbited the table. Their passively set brown faces, high cheekbones and slit, almond eyes, gave an added majesty to the occasion. After the second circuit the lead piper, the Pipe Major, on whose banner was the CO's personal family crest, swayed gently from side to side as a signal for a change of tune. After two more circuits they halted **behind** the Colonel, turned towards the table and continued playing.

Some officers nodded their head in tune, some strummed on the table and a few sat stock-still. The Colonel turned to his right and caught the eye of his newest officer, 2nd Lieutenant Jason Percival Vere Rance, *strange background so obviously not a proper sahib* he mused, drawing on his cigar and watching the pipers and drummers march out.

Right hands beat acclaim on the table and cries of '*shabash*', well done, ended when the Pipe Major came back, marching at the quick, rifle-regiment pace, to just behind the Colonel's chair, halted, turned inwards and saluted. The Colonel stood up, took the quaich of neat whisky from the silver salver held ready by the Mess Havildar and handed it to the Pipe Major.

'Well done, Pipe Major. You played well. Drink this with our special thanks, tonight of all nights.'

The Pipe Major took the quaich with both hands, raised it to the level of his mouth and gave the formal toast, '*Tagra rahau*,' May you remain strong.

'*Tagra rahau*,' answered the officers in a base rumble, words neither formulaic nor perfunctory; they expressed everyone's wish at this most exacting of times. The Pipe Major drained the contents in one, gave the empty quaich to the Mess Havildar, saluted, turned to his right and marched away to more applause. Outside, out of sight and out of hearing, the drummers and the other pipers were also drinking their tipple.

They rose from the table at 10 o'clock and moved back into the anteroom. Talk continued, with the mood serious because of the bad news coming from Malaya precluding any untoward frivolity. Near midnight the Colonel left and only then could 2nd Lieutenant Jason Rance leave with the rest of the officers. It was after midnight when he got back to his room and turned up the lantern his bearer had left dim. It being a new day he moved the calendar on his table to Friday, the 13th of February. Two days later, on Sunday the 15th, Singapore fell to the Japanese.

PART TWO

PART TWO

1

15 February 1942: The news of the surrender of the impregnable fortress Singapore by the British to the Japanese, following on the sinking of HMS *Prince of Wales* and HMS *Repulse*, came as a devastating shock to the Allies, great rejoicing to the Japanese, Germans and Italians, huge satisfaction and glee to all anti-British Indians.

How and why had it come to this many people asked themselves and one another. The real reason was the apathy of the British to the defence of their eastern empire over many years, doing nothing till too late like a frog in boiling water which simply stays where it is until it boils to death. The strong-looking but brittle exterior of British supremacy was unable to bear the strain of a force about which much negative propaganda had been disseminated: squint-eyed, buck-toothed, round-shouldered men who could not see properly to fire straight or to fly aeroplanes so were unable to fight a 'civilized' army. Oh how different it had turned out for the defeated men who were led away into captivity, under appalling conditions none had expected nor had been trained to withstand.

The shock and horror at the thought of their second battalion was keenly and miserably felt in the three Regimental Centres of 1 GR, 2 GR and 9 GR. Jason Rance sadly remembered CQMH Rahul Dura and wondered if he'd ever see him again. *I feel sure I'd recognise him if I do, however remote such a chance be.*

'Cease fire! Surrender! Show a white flag to every Japanese soldier you come into contact with.' Apart from there being no white flags, the orders were short, understandable and irrevocable … but, even so, unbelievable. Surrender? Disgraceful!

The Gurkhas looked at each other wide-eyed, shocked and horrified. Some of the elder men wept. No one had ever envisaged anything remotely like this. Hadn't reinforcements to make up losses only recently arrived? They hung their heads, mentally paralysed, not knowing what to do next. Sure, the fighting had been hard but none of them believed that the Japanese soldiers were the better. *Was all we have done and been through for this wasted?*

'It was the British, Australian and Indian soldiers who have let us down, who we have seen panicking and running,' was uttered more than once. 'We have never lost any war we have fought with our British officers leading us, have we?' one man asked rhetorically, 'even though there have been setbacks to start with.'

'No,' came the answer. 'The last time we lost a war was against the sahibs, not with them, and that was more than a hundred years ago.' His features seemed to spring to attention at this historic announcement.

'True,' someone chimed in, 'but this time we never saw any of our own aeroplanes, only Japani ones. And were they accurate!

Maybe ours were flying and fighting somewhere else.'[2]

The world of all those captured fell apart. As prisoners-of-war under the Japanese everyone's life changed for the worse, with death a merciful release for far too many innocent people. The worst cruelties, indignities and deprivations were inflicted on the hapless Chinese population who suffered agonies from a fury of hatred, rage and terror the like of which none could have imagined, even though news of Japanese atrocities in China were well known about. Up in Kuala Lumpur both Ah Fat and Ah Hong escaped into the jungle to join the anti-Japanese guerillas.

'Banzai!' – May the Emperor to live for ten thousand years! – was the word heard more than any other that day and for quite some days to come. Congratulations were, no doubt, well earned even though future historians would ask if the Japanese won because they had the better army or because their adversaries the worse?

'Although we had fewer men than our enemies had, we beat them hollow. Of course we sustained casualties but that was right and proper in the service of the Emperor,' exulted Major General Tomoyuki Yamashita. 'Our Chief said that we expected to be in Shonan, Brilliant South, as brilliant as our victory, within one hundred days. We are here after a paltry seventy. That means we have thirty days to spare,' and he allowed himself a rare smile of self-congratulation.

---

2 Examples of what Gurkha prisoners-of-war felt about the behaviour of other troops are to be found in *Gurkhas at War*, edited by J P Cross and Buddhiman Gurung, London, 2002 and London, Singapore, USA and Canada, 2007, as well as in the J P Cross Archives in the Imperial War Museum, London and The Gurkha Museum, Winchester, England.

'From now on we are unstoppable: Burma, India to our west; the Philippines, Dutch East Indies and Borneo to our east; Australia to our south will be ours – and, on the other side of the world Pearl Harbour and the American navy have already been severely dealt with. Asia is ours, now and forever.'

And indeed it could seem like nothing else that Sunday afternoon, especially as Lieutenant General Percival had signed that total surrender document earlier in the day.

No British officer in the Indian Army was allowed to stay with his troops. Every Indian Army soldier felt bereft and unbalanced though none would have used those words because they were not common parlance; 'numb' or 'brain heavy' they might have said. The recently arrived reinforcements who had done no fighting were, if anything, even more perplexed. But there was nothing anyone could do about it. Uncountable miles from home, not knowing any language of any of the locals, incarcerated on an island with no familiar British sahibs to tell them what to do or where to go because the Japanese had insisted they be separated, spelt an unimaginably bleak future with individual dignity shattered and a plunge in morale.

Rank and file sepoys of Indian units, mostly uneducated country lads, had been brought up to believe in the British sahibs' supremacy if not invincibility and were now as thunderstruck as everyone else. As villagers and as soldiers their whole upbringing was obeying their seniors and the great majority of them had feelings of utter wretchedness, weariness and woe.

The backbone of the Indian Army, the Viceroy's Commissioned Officers (VCOs), Jemadars, Subedars and Subedar Majors, mostly wanted to remain true to their 'oath of salt' but almost all those with King's commissions had a deep, unquenchable, emotional urge to do anything, which even in their more serious moments they would have considered as treason, to rid India of the British. These feelings were exacerbated by, compared with British officers, their lesser pay, below normal standard conditions and, sadly, often a colour bar, implied or explicit. Major Fujiwara's long-term planning and the machinations of people like Nedyam Raghavan and Rash Behari Bose of the IIL were paying enormous dividends, as Philip Rance, Peter Mason and the subalterns in Dharmsala had foretold.

Although Queen Victoria had promised Indian independence, her words had yet to germinate into anything positive. The British just didn't realise that people would rather govern themselves badly than be governed better by outsiders. It took the war, with the British bled white by debt and fed up with Indian politicians' intransigence, for such to happen because that was still an undated 'pencil entry' having no bearing on the here and now, and an eventual Japanese defeat which seemed a near impossibility. So surely, thought the Indian officers, the most effective way of being successful in their struggle for an 'Indian' India was to fight with the Japanese army who, seemingly, could rid India of unwanted colonialists as it had so done in Malaya, the Dutch East Indies and the Philippines and by May would have in Burma.

Escape for Europeans was impossible. For Indians, especially those whose 'oath of salt' to the government was overriding, a gleam, a glimpse and a glimmer seemed to offer themselves when plans were made for going to Burma for a 'March on Delhi'.

'Brother, do you think there'll be a chance of rejoining our army?' was often furtively whispered one to another.

'Perhaps so, brother, perhaps it will happen if the gods have written it in the inside of our foreheads,' came the answer, forlornly and without conviction.

A Captain Mohan Singh of 1/14 Punjab Regiment, an unstable unit having had four COs in three years, had already joined the Japanese Army near Jitra so had done no fighting himself. The Adjutant of 2/1 GR and both his Gurkha escorts had seen him either shake hands with a Japanese officer or give him something before going off into the jungle with him. The Sikh Captain, a bully with a short fuse, could be persuasive but not being a 'natural' commander liked to have 'yes-men' around him. After hostilities ceased, he and Major Fujiwara Iwaichi, who had formed the *Hikari*, Light from the East, *Kikan*, Agency, to deal with the IIL, had a meeting to discuss how best to get the Indian Army POWs to 'March on Delhi'. With them was the founder of the IIL, Rash Behari Bose, now so old his limp skin looked as grey as a worn-out dishcloth and his hands brown and fragile, like last year's leaves. Even with a common aim the meeting was not wholly propitious.

Indian rank and file POWs were instructed to forget their oath of loyalty, the cement that keeps an army together as a fighting force, taken when enlisted. From now on they were to regard the Indian Army as their enemy and the Imperial Japanese Army as their unshakable ally for the 'reconquest' of India from the British. Once again the age-old ploy of the plausible versus the gullible would end in tears for one or the other – or, maybe, even both. The plan that was hatched was to form an army of four regiments of eleven battalions from the defeated soldiery whose numbers were to be swelled by as many civilian Indians living in Singapore and Malaya as the IIL could encourage to join. Its obverse Hindi name was *Azad Hind Fauj* while its English version was the Indian National Army (INA) by those for it with '*Delhi chalo*' – 'March to Delhi' – becoming the over-riding and unappeasable impetus for action. The reverse term was Japanese Inspired Fifth Columnists, 'Jiffs'. For the rank and file as POWs under the Japanese there would only be degradation. Rather than staying doing fatigues for the Japanese for the indefinite future, not an exciting prospect, joining the INA would be an adventure and a chance to get one's own back after such vast dishonour and disillusion. If there had been an Indian Hobson, his choice could not have been starker.

The Gurkhas were first herded to Farrer Park with the Indians and told to wait. But what for? And wait they did. They could not have known or even guessed of any seeds of sedition that had been planted, wittingly by Indian agents and unwittingly by certain insensitive and arrogant British officers of Indian units who, for the life of them, were completely unconscious of their failings in Indian man management, but successfully planted such seeds had been. Never having been particularly friendly with Indians, the Gurkhas kept to themselves, disregarding the clamour and recriminations emanating from the Indian part of the camp over the ensuing weeks.

Later the Gurkhas were separated and moved to a less

cramped camp in the River Valley area. This small bonus was offset by diminishing rations and harsh working conditions imposed by officious Japanese commanders who slapped the Gurkhas' faces as they slapped their own soldiers' faces and, in turn, had their own face slapped by their superiors, even a major slapping a captain's face in front of their own troops. Any who remonstrated were more harshly dealt with. They heard rumours of what was happening to the British and Australians in Changi jail. Malays, whom the Japanese did not consider worth bothering about and still on the mainland, were ignored. The Gurkhas saw for themselves the way Chinese civilians were treated, wincing at the bestialities perpetrated on them but, of course, there was nothing anybody could do except carry on as ordered. Japanese behaviour acted like a slow poison in the heart of their imperial aspirations and their quest for imperial grandeur.

Discipline became more severe. Recalcitrant soldiers were kept even shorter of rations, beaten, put in solitary confinement, put into small cages like animals, with the Gurkha officers being treated even more harshly and many wanton acts of cruelty, if not exactly torture, were commonplace.

On 21 August, after being cooped up for six months, every Gurkha, even the cooks and the sick, were ordered to fall in for an important parade. Of the three battalions' more than two thousand strong to start with, there were now a few less than three hundred men, including the reinforcements, so severe had been the casualties during the fighting. Overseen by Japanese NCOs, the senior Gurkha gave the order for 'right dress', then, at attention, reported to a Japanese officer, whose thin lips were corrugated like the edges of scallop shells. Then 'stand at ease' was ordered, both commands given in English as was Indian Army custom.

Four Japanese soldiers, each armed with a submachine gun, took post at the four corners of the three ranks and the senior Japanese officer handed the parade over to Officer Mohan Singh who had been strutting about on the fringe of the parade ground, slapping a swagger stick against his leg. He marched up to the front of the parade, followed by an Indian woman, waddling like a broad-based duck and finding it hard to keep in step. She had the air of a great man's poor relation, smug pride mixed with anxious humility. Those near the Sikh could see that he had slighting pouting lips and shifty eyes, and his uniform and rank badges were unfamiliar. Behind him was another Sikh officer.

'*Saudhan*!' No English words of command now, only Hindi ones.

No one obeyed the order to stand to attention. The Gurkhas remained as they were.

'Listen,' the Sikh began, in Hindi. 'I am Major General Mohan Singh. I used to be a captain in 1/14 Punjab Regiment but now I am a major general in the newly formed *Azad Hind Fauj*. I want all you Gorkhalis to join it. You will be able to beat any army the British will put against you in Burma – look how pitiful was their effort in Malaya! I will tell you what has happened since then,' he continued, gloatingly. 'The British have lost Burma as they lost Malaya and here Singapore. An all Gurkha brigade was almost wiped out trying to cross the River Sittang in south Burma after a foolish brigadier ordered a bridge to be blown too soon. Most were drowned, shot, killed or captured while trying to cross. All their stores were captured by our allies, the Japanese. That was in February. Then in March, Rangoon fell. By May, chased all the way by our victorious allies, the British had completely evacuated Burma and were back in India, trembling with fear at more to come: not enough men, not enough stores, not enough weapons and not enough rations. If they try and retake Burma, we, the *Azad Hind Fauj*, and the Imperial Japanese Army, will drive them back. We have sent messages to Neta-ji, Subhas Chandra Bose, now with another victor, Adolf Hitler in Germany, to come and lead us back to India. Until then I, Major General Mohan Singh, am the army commander and your leader. You will therefore obey every order I give you.'

The Gurkhas listened, they had no other option, but with no reaction. *True or false? Who could say?* Mohan Singh sensed that his words were having no effect. Despite his high rank, he was easily waterlogged beyond the shallows of the commonplace.

He turned and called the other Sikh officer over to him. 'Captain Dhillon sahib.' Gurbaksh Singh Dhillon had failed medical college and, although over-educated to be a sepoy, had enlisted as one. He was full of resentment and scuffled with those he thought had slighted him. He too was an officer of 1/14 Punjab Regiment. 'Dhillon sahib, join me here. Lakshmi Swaminadhan Sahgal-ji,' he called out to the woman, 'please take notes for our history.'

The woman took a surreptitious bite at a thumbnail then clenched her hands. Her watery eyes blinked in the sun.

Mohan Singh faced his front and tried again. 'There is no

point in your staying here. Join us and have an easy victory, then freedom, comforts and cash,' he coaxed. 'And after victory you'll be your own masters.' After more of the same, he ordered, 'Hands up those who will join me and my army.'

Not a hand moved.

Mohan Singh had been haranguing Indian troops for several days past and now he was so hoarse he sounded more like a dog barking than someone talking. He chewed his sentences between gritted teeth and spat them out with disgust. Nobody could fathom what this angry bore was ranting about.

Again, a call for volunteers. 'Step forward, brave volunteers.'

Again, not a hand moved nor did any man step forward.

Pursing his lips as though someone had put alum on his tongue, his vicious temper snapped. Exasperated at making no headway he turned on one man in the front rank. 'You are nothing but a lump of shit. I'll deal with you first in your own coin.'

He looked behind and shouted out to some of his own soldiers. 'Bring the communal shit pail from the nearest block.' These, when full, were heavy, needing two strong men to carry. 'If there's not enough in one block's, put two together in the one pail. Bring a couple of stools from somewhere and a long stick. Hurry!' Mohan Singh's face was ravenous and full of unworthy glee.

While the two men were away, Mohan Singh ordered a soldier, Balbahadur Rana of 2/2 GR, to come out in front of the parade. 'I won't punish you if you'll join my army.'

No answer.

'One more chance.'

Again no answer.

'Undress.'

No movement.

'I repeat my order, otherwise I'll get a Japanese machine gunner to kill you.'

Balbahadur complied, choking back rancour as bitter as the gall of a musk deer.

A full bucket of night soil, hanging from a pole carried by two men with another man carrying two stools, was carried onto the parade ground. The stench was repugnant. 'Place the stools either side of that man.'

'No, you can't do that,' came the voice of the senior Gurkha officer.

'Can't I? Keep quiet. All the Japanese machine gunners need to kill the whole lot of you is an order from me.'

Seething inwardly, the senior Gurkha officer, spoke again. 'No, you can't do that.'

'Your turn later.'

The man at either end of the long pole stood on a stool, grunting with the exertion that was needed to lift the heavy bucket and a third man was called over. Given a stick he tilted the bucket over, deliberately slowly, pouring the whole contents over Balbahadur … who fainted … and was left, unaided, to recover. He was a shocking sight and a worse smell.[3]

Balbahadur regained consciousness. 'You will not be allowed to wash until you volunteer to join my army,' called the Major General, standing well back. 'Now will you volunteer?'

3 The incident of the night soil bucket is on p 40, Cross and Gurung, *op. sit.*

'You have no right to do that. Let him go and wash,' called out another Gurkha officer.

'How many of you will volunteer now?' was Mohan Singh's riposte.

No reply.

'Why not?' Mohan Singh went vituperatively 'ape' at being made to look useless in front of his own men and particularly the woman. He gritted his teeth and flecks of foam oozed from the corners of his lips.

'Because we are not Indians,' came from over a hundred throats. 'We are from Nepal. We have our own government. We serve the Raj with our oath of salt. We are not turncoats,' called out the senior Gurkha officer. 'We will never join you.'

'Then I have no other option but to convince you the hard way.'

He told the Japanese officer with him to call one of his soldiers forward. One came and stood in front of the parade. His flat, reptilian eyes were almost blank and he had the vacuous smile of the mentally under-nourished if not the truly idiotic. He loaded his submachine gun, drooled and licked his lips in anticipation.

'Make ready to fire,' Mohan Singh said, slowly and deliberately, 'on my order,' and an interpreter standing behind him, translated.

After walking around the parade Mohan Singh ordered three men to go to the front. 'You are to be shot. If you don't, I'll have the whole lot of you killed.'

The three condemned men came out in front and stood to attention. They declined to be blind-folded ... and were shot in cold blood. The three corpses lay on the ground, twitching and oozing blood. What a tragic waste of small, heroic lives.[4]

'Now I am sure you will all join my *Azad Hind Fauj*. Step forward those who will, or rather step back those who won't.' By now his tone of voice indicated that his command was more a matter of aspiration than a hope of achievement.

The whole parade stepped back like one man.

Almost crippled by anger the Sikh knew he had been beaten by Gurkha hill manliness and sense of togetherness.

The senior Gurkha officer darted a glance at the Indian, which might, like sunlight through a lens, have burnt a hole in his cotton shirt, then dismissed the parade and told off a section to get digging tools from the stores to bury the dead.

Balbahadur slunk away to wash, everybody keeping well clear of him as he went. He sat under a tap of running water for as long as it took to feel clean, longer than just getting clean. His hair was his main problem. It took him the whole of his only piece of soap to feel almost human once more and it itched for a long time afterwards. He felt within himself the stirring of primitive passions which normally lurked beyond a normal man's memory. Gurkhas who suffered never forgot their ill treatment or forgave the perpetrators. INA behaviour towards some of their own men was almost, at times, as egregious.

As the Sikh Mohan Singh walked away, defeated, vowing that he would catch up on the Gurkhas on another day, the unwarranted and cruel killing of the three men and the indignity

---

4 Witnessed by then Rifleman, 2/2 Gurkha Rifles, later Captain (Queen's Gurkha Officer), Gurkha Military Police, Parbhu Thapa.

of Balbahadur being so treated, Jemadar Rahul Dura reacted by calling out in a loud voice, 'Eh Boké. You're nothing but a coward, a bully and a traitor. You would never have dared to do anything like that one-for-one. May your soul rot in Hell.'

The Sikh turned abruptly, his face a mask of rage at that unbelievable insult made worse by all those Gurkha officers on parade who clapped and shouted, 'Yes, yes. QMJ sahib, correct, correct,' in Nepali.

Japanese soldiers were called and the Gurkha officers were frog-marched away and put into separate cells. For the next six months they were beaten, starved, made to work till they dropped of exhaustion and humiliated in front of their men. But for the QMJ the treatment was special: he suffered the horrors of the water treatment, a Japanese torture gloatingly improved on by the INA bullies who applied it more than even the Japanese did.

'Will you apologise?' he was asked again and again.

'No, never,' the older man insisted.

So more pressure was applied as was the unbearably painful 'finger press' torture, also a Japanese creation, that broke all his fingers. In agony he passed out and when he came to, he was unable to use his hands for anything, eating, washing, wiping.

Once more he was asked if he would apologise and once again a brave answer came: 'Even if I will be reborn a hundred times, never.'

The Japanese, in their extraordinary way, admire stoicism and four months after plaguing the Gurkha officers so badly, they suddenly relented. Nobody ever understood quite why but six, two from each battalion, were taken to Penang and lodged in a bungalow in Northam Road, a continuation of Gurney Drive. It was not far from the Penang Club, which the Japanese Military had taken over for their Headquarters. They were looked after by a 'batman', an Indian stool-pigeon, given good rations and sheets for bedding. The Gurkhas, always rigidly correct in all matters of protocol, were polite but never obsequious. When they went on their afternoon walks they were surreptitiously followed. After a while a Hindi-speaking Japanese officer took the QMJ to one side and told him that as Gurkhas and Japanese had a common ancestry he ought to join the Imperial Japanese Army, 'not the Indian National Army who are inferior and worthless'. Even though his broken fingers were properly set by then, the QMJ declined to be persuaded by such blandishments. Yet the seed of an idea was sown in his head when one day his interlocutor said, 'Dura–san, we understand that you have experience in the commissariat branch. One job we would like you to do for us is to escort a trainload of stores from Singapore up as far as the railway goes. On your return we will commission you into our army.'[5]

The old Gurkha had the instinct of the poker player: he did not let his burning and implacable hatred for the Japanese show in his lined face. *First play it their way then later mine. Come what may, I could escape!*

'Your kind offer intrigues me but protocol means I must

5 This bizarre occurrence is vouched for in the regimental history of the 1st King George V's Own Gurkha Rifles, Volume II, 1920-1947, page 145. It is not mentioned in the 2nd King Edward VII's Own Gurkha Rifles history. Your author has not read the history of the 9th Gurkha Rifles.

accept through Major Fujiwara Iwaichi when I get back to Singapore. Once the job has been ratified, I'd like to take Subedar Narbahadur Gurung, the other 2/1 GR Gurkha officer here, as he and I are great friends and with the responsibility you are likely to give me, two are always better than one.'

'I like it.' The Japanese put his hand up in front of his mouth to smother a wolfish grin. 'I'll let Iwaichi-san know you'll be speaking to him.'

Spring 1942, 1 GRRC, Dharmsala: In every army there is never a 'school solution' that happily separates those needed to lead in battle and those needed to train soldiers for battle so some people become disappointed. 2nd Lieutenant Rance certainly did when, because of his excellent weapons shooting ability and general physical fitness, he found himself detailed as WTO, shorthand for Weapon Training Officer and PTO, Physical Training Officer for the recruits. It might not have happened that way had not some Bren guns unexpectedly been issued: the Adjutant looked through his young officers' records to see who would be the most suitable for the task of giving training on the new weapons and somewhat naturally picked on Jason Rance. When he was called to the Adjutant's office, that worthy straightway said, 'It doesn't matter how much you want to go to an active battalion. This job is what matters so like it and lump it for a couple of years. With our two new battalions now on the North-West Frontier most likely being sent to Burma at any time, both COs need to send some NCOs to learn the Bren so when, rather than if, they are issued, there'll be no need for any *ab initio* training on operations against the Japanese. So the better you handle this job the more Japanese will die,' and gave his new officer one of his rare smiles. The rumour among the rank and file was 'if the Adjutant smiles, it will probably rain.'

Jason said he understood what he had to do, saluted smartly and left the office, bitterly disappointed not to be going to an active battalion but determined to try his best, hoping the job would not last for two whole years. Indeed both COs did come to see their NCOs training on the new weapon, both were impressed by how well their NCOs were being trained and both made a mental note to try and get the WTO on their battalion strength.

Initially Jason found Gurkhas more like Chinese than Malays in that it was they who decided when to become friendly rather than showing friendliness, often without meaning it. He impressed his seniors and his peers by his obvious dedication and quite soon after he started his job he was 'given his head' in how to organise events. His ability in the language soon put him in the forefront of Gurkhali speakers but he tried never to show off. That meant never giving it full force in front of senior officers.

Apart from training NCOs for both battalions and his own staff on how to use the new Bren guns and supervising normal weapon training, he was busy arranging details for firing on the 30-yard ranges and the long range with the provision of suitable targets, the firing of 2-inch mortars, the throwing of grenades and even of ensuring relevant pamphlets were up-to-date. The physical training aspect also involved allocating pitches and grounds for football and volleyball matches. It was an unwieldy jigsaw puzzle and a full-time job, exhausting but interesting.

At the end of one batch of recruit training, before the by-now trained soldiers and no-longer recruits went to an active battalion, the Commandant held a ceremonial 'passing out' parade, complete with inspection and march past. In the evening there was a party. Men sat on mats on three sides and the officers sat on chairs at tables on the fourth. The area was lit by 'Petrolmax' lamps that had to be hand pumped when the light grew dim and the pre-meal delicacies included goat's testes and chicken's heads. Drink was the almost colourless *raksi*, 'country spirit', which to the unwary in the dim light, looks like water. Jason, unwary of its potency and not having a good 'head' for alcohol, soon had more than enough.

It was after the Commandant and senior officers had left that Jason's natural exuberance for working with Gurkhas got the better of him. All new officers were pulled out and made to dance. In Jason's case, as he didn't know how to, he pretended to show reluctance by putting his two hands in front of body and had them 'talk' to each other, the one in easy English and the other in Gurkhali, his face looking at them in mock surprise and making up 'the script' as he went along. After the initial and total shock had passed, shrieks of unprecedented laughter overwhelmed him and from then one he was accepted. He was induced to drink more and ... he passed out.

The subedar in charge ordered a lance-naik and four riflemen to carry him back to his quarter. There they properly undressed him and because he was an officer the lance-naik stood his squad to attention and gave the order, 'Officer on parade, dismiss!'

At that moment the Adjutant appeared and was aghast at

what he saw. With a winter chill in his voice he upbraided the squad commander for bringing a drunken British officer to the wrong room. Jason came to his senses and, once he had realised the enormity of the lapse, was showed where his clothes were, picked them up and stumbled back to his own. The Gurkhas went back to their lines.

2nd Lieutenant Rance was awarded a week's extra Duty Officer.

However, it turned out that the enigmatic and opaque ways of the military, wanting his Chinese language ability that saved him from having to stay in his job for the whole two years, not his lapse from grace making him 'unacceptable to the regiment'.

June 1942, Kathmandu, Nepal: It was late afternoon and the two-horse buggy, outriders to the fore, splashily drove up to the imposing front door of the British Residency, a large two-storey villa over a hundred years old built in a style unlike others in Kathmandu. It had a handsome pillared portico, was shaded by trees and surrounded by a garden and a park. Buildings for the two British diplomats and their servants were in abundance. An early monsoon deluge was slackening off. A servant emerged from the front door, unfurled an umbrella, and went to the nearside door of the buggy. The Minister Plenipotentiary and Ambassador Extraordinary to the Court of Nepal, Sir Geoffrey Bethem, KBE, CIE, heaved himself out of the opened door, ducked under the umbrella and stepped into a puddle, splashing both himself and his servant. Inwardly cursing, he hurried inside where he gave his elongated, feathered hat to another servant before going to his room to change into more comfortable fig. He was a middle-aged man, pompous and prickly, his red face not sun-tanned but just medium-rare, his trimmed military moustache and straight back sure signs of an earlier life as a regimental officer. He had been called to the Singha Durbar, 'Lion Palace', by the Maharaja, Juddha Shamsher Jang Bahadur Rana, hence his formal uniform.

'Bearer! Whisky pani,' he called out as he entered the drawing room where his wife was sitting waiting for him. 'And give Beamish sahib and memsahib my salaams,' he added, in the time-hallowed way of asking someone of status to 'Attend the Presence'.

'How did you get on, dear?' Lady Bethem cooed, anxiety in her watery eyes.

'I'll wait until Victor and Frances come over before going into details, dear,' he answered, 'but I can tell you that the Maharaja is grumpy, frightened and seems lost. With me he was trying, sticky and difficult.'

'Oh dear,' his wife sympathised. 'How awkward for you.' She had the lank, haggard face that went with a sick stomach and not enough exercise. Kathmandu was not her favourite place but she valiantly made the most of it for dear Geoffrey's sake.

Bethem took a cigarette out of his case and a box of matches from the small table in front of him. Before trying to light up, he carefully rubbed the corrugated side on his trousers to dry the perpetually dampened surface to get some friction otherwise it would not ignite: monsoon weather put mildew on leatherwork overnight and nothing was ever properly dry. He lit his cigarette with his third match.

Lieutenant Colonel Victor Beamish, the only other British officer in the residency, was the First Secretary whose main task was dealing with leave men and pensioners, paying out the latter himself, sitting next to a clerk with a long nominal roll. He was a small and bouncy man with a round face tanned by the tropical sun, bushy browed and clean shaven, breezy without being glib and original without being eccentric, a good choice for Nepal and a foil to the other man.

The bearer escorted him and his wife into the drawing room and Lady Bethem offered tea 'or something a little stronger perhaps?' asked with a perfunctory giggle.

Requirements fulfilled and the bearer out of the room, the Minister said, 'First of all, as is so often the case, what I am telling you must go no further. I will send it by post, sealed, to the Viceroy personally as it is of the gravest portent. I doubt nothing as serious as this has happened for well over a hundred years.' He coughed delicately.

'Of course we will keep this utterly secret, Your Excellency,' ventured the First Secretary, agog to find out what the trouble was.

'I was summoned to the Maharaja's palace and quite frankly he is an exceedingly frightened man. He has, he told me, always trusted the armed might of Britain ever since the sepoy mutiny of 1857 that has, indirectly, bolstered the rulers here for so long it is now taken for granted. But the tragic and inexplicable loss of Malaya, then the impregnable Singapore followed by being drubbed out of Burma have made him believe that the Japanese are invincible to the extent that, and here's the rub, if "my subjects in the Indian Army's Gurkha Regiments" are allowed to take any future counter-offensive operations in Burma, he believes that Japan will not only crush India but colonise Nepal. His strict edict is, therefore, that he forbids all Gurkha units to go across the Indo-Burma border.'

The First Secretary gasped his disbelief and was about to say something but was prevented by, 'However, to show good faith, he is allowing four regiments of his own Nepalese Contingent into India to help us. One is due to go to the North-West Frontier and three "reinforcement troops" he called them for our eastern-facing armies.'

'And do you think the Viceroy and the Commander-in-Chief will adhere to such an edict?' From the look in his eyes the First Secretary obviously didn't think so.

The Minister pursed his lips, shrugged and made a small gesture with his hands, brooding for a few seconds before answering. 'Of course I can't say what either will do or how they'll react, but Juddha is sending his son Bahadur, who has the rank of General I believe, to Delhi where he will presumably be ensconced in the Nepalese embassy. May I refresh you drink, Colonel?' using the tone of voice that expected a negative answer. 'Then thank you for coming round. I must now write my letter to Delhi.'

June 1942, New Delhi: On receiving the Most Secret letter the Minister had sent, the Viceroy read it and sighed. *As if I hadn't enough problems without this new one* and asked the Commander-in-Chief to stay behind and confer with him after their next meeting. Seated, he was shown the letter, which he read in silence. 'What is your reaction, General?'

'Your Excellency,' said General Wavell with a slight frown, 'at first blush it looks serious but I feel that unless the Maharaja recalls all the men we have recruited, something I believe he simply won't do, we merely let the Minister in Kathmandu know that his letter has been received. We will not tell him that we propose to do absolutely nothing about it. How does that strike you?' The General instinctively knew by now, having had to deal with many more difficult problems during the African campaign, how to let matters cool themselves down.

The Viceroy smiled and after a long pause said, 'a sensible answer. And what will you say to General Bahadur?'

'That we will honour his father's word about the four battalions His Highness has sent to help us in the hour of our need and fully welcome them. Of course we won't mention anything about our paying for their use, except rationing them.'

The Viceroy agreed and that is how matters stood.

General Bahadur was the Nepalese Contingent's senior representative after its arrival in India. The battalion sent to Kohat on the North-West Frontier felt so far from home and in a place the men just didn't like, refused to obey orders. The Nepalese General went to sort matters out and help quash the 'Kohat Mutiny' as the Indian Army top brass certainly viewed it although such euphemisms like 'serious discipline' were used by the diplomats. Juddha felt frustrated that the British were not treating his son with as much consideration as he would have liked and he told the British Minister in Kathmandu in March 1942 that, since Bahadur was being kept out of the political side of affairs, he would be more useful back in Kathmandu. He was therefore replacing him in India with Krishna Shamsher, a more distant relation of his.

Meanwhile, in northeast India each of the three Contingent battalions, *dal*s, were given special training for combat before being employed in defensive operations in Assam. Weapons and rations were standard for the Indian Army. Most of the soldiers took to these conditions without any difficulty although there were isolated cases of some men finding the life strange to an extent that it bothered them and their performance was not up to standard. In the main nobody outside the battalion realised they were not a Gurkha battalion of the Indian Army. When the Japanese made a push west, in 1943, the Mahindra Dal, was ordered 'with white-hot priority' to advance south to Silchar but no one had no idea why, even until the unit was still thirty to forty miles from any action. The CO and his men could hardly believe it when higher formation gave them a lot of fireworks and the battalion's job was to get close to the enemy surrounding Imphal and let these fireworks off, up to twenty minutes at one time. Some sounded like rifle fire, some like machine guns and others 2-inch mortars, while others looked like flares. The aim was to give the Japanese the impression that the spearhead of the attack was coming from that direction. The battalion did not take part in any action at Imphal.[6]

---

6 The CO supplied these details to the author.

July 1943, Singapore: The proposed relevance INA under the recently and over-promoted Major General Mohan Singh that was formed on 1 July 1942 and had its HQ near the Bidadari multi-faith Cemetery in Upper Serangoon Road clashed with the Japanese idea of Indians only being support troops to the Imperial Japanese Army. There was, however, one point both he and his chief Liaison Officer, Major Fujiwara Iwaichi, did strongly agree on was, if possible, Gurkhas recruitment in India should be interrupted and made more difficult. By that time Nedhyam Raghavan had made Singapore his base, there being not enough work in Penang to warrant him staying there. His suggestion was that, if there was a 'Malayan' Gurkha he should be sent to India, preferably by submarine, and contact Congress Party 'sleepers', including members of the anti-British All-India Gorkha League, especially the Darjeeling Branch, who were able to put pressure on Gurkha recruiting. By then Tor Gul had ingratiated himself with Nedhyam Raghavan so when asked if he knew of any such person he gave his answer at once; yes, he did: Rabilal Rai of Bhutan Estate. The result was that the Gurkha was fetched and a proposal put to him: will you go by submarine to India and start an anti-British movement among the Gurkhas, aiming at the recruiting depots? The answer could only be 'yes', so Fujiwara put a case forward for such an operation and Rabilal stayed in Singapore, waiting for an answer.

However, before any news came through bad relations between the major general and the Japanese came to a head and on 29 December 1943 Mohan Singh was arrested and the INA was dissolved. It was not to be resurrected until July '43 and the request for a submarine went into limbo. There now being no INA Rabilal went back home.

August 1943, Ramgarh, 375 miles west of Calcutta: After victories in Africa a camp for twenty thousand Italian POWs was built for them there, well away from the town itself. The Indian Army's own major training and holding area was to its north, at Ranchi.

That part of Generalissimo Chiang Kai-shek's army that was in Burma, Major General Sun Li-jen's 38th and Major General Liao Yuan-hsiang's 22nd Divisions, had also fallen back at the Japanese onslaught and they, too, had limped into India, battered, hungry, torn and listless, weak from dysentery and malaria as had all the others. Their American commander, General 'Vinegar' Joe Stillwell, wanted them to be rehabilitated as far away from the clutches of the Generalissimo as possible and trained ready to go back to north Burma to prevent the Japanese from closing the one overland route for supplies for the Chinese Nationalist army in China itself. In the event Chiang Kai-shek squirrelled all American supplies away to use against the Chinese communists, feeling that the USA would the better take on the Japanese without his wasting his military hardware on them. This had nothing at all to do with Britain's campaign for the re-conquest of Burma.

As part of the Lend-Lease deal between Britain and USA, the Italians were moved to other, smaller camps and Ramgarh camp was handed over to the Americans, not without considerable objections from GHQ in Delhi, for training Chinese troops. The camp was at the edge of an extensive elevated area, mostly open but thickly wooded enough in parts to emulate jungle conditions.

It was ideal for training large formations of troops.

The Chinese soldiers were flown the first short part of their journey. Packed thirty-five to forty into cargo planes, some of which had no doors, they only wore underpants. 'You'll be given new uniforms in India so why bother to clad you for a three-hour flight?' stated the senior Chinese officer in charge. 'Cheaper for us that way.' Several died of the cold. Train and truck took them the rest of the way. The one weapon missing for training was a good, reliable light machine gun. The Indian Army liaison officer who met the Chinese on the border somewhat rashly said he'd see if he couldn't get some of the newly issued Bren guns to learn on before any general issue was available or the US Army produced an LMG better to its liking.

The wheels of any General Headquarters turn slowly but a Lieutenant Hector Mason, working there as a Japanese interpreter, saw the paperwork asking for a suitable officer to be a Bren gun instructor. He wrote a minute that it would also be a great advantage if the officer commanding the group who took the guns to Ramgarh were also a Chinese speaker and, knowing all about Jason's Chinese language ability, gave his name. He wrote 'I do not know the whereabouts of this officer' at the bottom of the minute, signed it and sent it on its journey round the HQ. It was eventually read by an officer senior enough to give the executive order and authority to promote 2nd Lieutenant Rance to acting captain to be in charge of the undertaking and to go there with a small team of Gurkhas as instructors.

Jason was sent for, 'now', and was half-perturbed at being so peremptorily summoned. No junior officer liked being called to the Adjutant's officer without knowing why so he thought back to any possible indiscretion but could think of none, even so a small cold worm turned in his gut. He heaved an inward sigh of relief when the Adjutant had briefed him. 'Go and see the Colonel now and on your way out the Chief Clerk will give you your squad's authority for movement and for you personally written authority to meet the Director of Military Intelligence in person in GHQ Delhi.'

Jason knocked on the Commandant's door and was called in. 'You've been here a year or so and, apart from a couple of thoughtless slip ups, Rance, you have done well. I'm pleased with you. Your relations with the men and officers are good. I can tell you now that the CO of 3/1 GR, Lieutenant Colonel Wingfield, whose battalion is on the North-West Frontier, has seen you at work and wants to poach you. I didn't let him. Now you are off elsewhere on a difficult job. Once you have fallen into the maw of the Higher Planners there's no knowing what will happen to you. You and your team will take all your kit to save you coming back here in case the Americans want to take you with them to Ledo or some other God-forsaken place such as Chunking at the end of their training,' and leaning his head on one side like an amiable parrot, he gave a throaty chuckle.

'Sir, I understand. I apologise for having to be carried back after that party' – *military 'growing up'* – 'and I now know better. No excuse but I had just heard that my father and mother were being posted to New Delhi and I was stupidly happy to think I could be seeing them when I had any local leave.'

'The Commandant stood up. 'Understood, forgiven and

forgotten. Settle both your Mess and Contractor's bills before you go. I am sure you'll look after your men in the Chinese camp. Goodbye, Rance and good luck. That's one thing we all need.'

Captain Rance left Dharmsala cantonment for GHQ Delhi on 7 August, about the same time that 3/1 GR was ordered to Ranchi for jungle training prior to being sent on to Burma. Apart from his batman, Rifleman Hitman Gurung, he had a team of ten men under Havildar Dilbahadur Pun, called back as a Reservist. They went by truck with loaded personal weapons as the Quit India disturbances made all travel dangerous. They arrived safely without incident as the monsoon had dampened the enthusiasm of the Quit India revolutionaries. Jason took his men to the transit camp before being taken to meet Brigadier Lambert, a squat affable man with wavy black hair, the Director of Military Intelligence, DMI.

'Sit down, Rance. This is an unusual task we are sending you on and if it had not been for the Bren guns neither the Americans nor the Chinese would have allowed you to go anywhere near their camp. The Colonel in charge of the training is ...' he looked at a sheet of paper in front of him, 'ah, here it is, Colonel McCabe. There is a Chinese speaker, a Colonel Boatner. The American staff regard themselves as a closed shop and your Bren guns are the "open sesame" for you and your small team to go there. There'll be no other British officer there so you'll be on your own. Think you can manage? A feather in your cap if you can.'

'Sir, it won't be me if I don't try my best,' answered Jason with an engaging smile, his penetrating, clear blue eyes almost sparkling. 'My only worry is that my Chinese may not be compatible with what the troops speak. They will have come from the north and despite being completely illiterate will have a language more like Mandarin than my Cantonese. Rather sadly, I gather that the southern Chinese are looked down on by the northerners but maybe the senior officers will understand me. How many of them understand English is something I'll have to find out.'

The Brigadier nodded. 'Now, I am the DMI, not the DMO, O being Operations. I have been told to brief you because the C-in-C and I want to know just as much as we can about the set-up, their standards including those of morale. We've let General Stillwell know about this, couldn't not have,' he added slightly ungrammatically, 'and he is as anti-British as Satan would be anti the Pope. If he visits while you're there, don't cavil at his rudeness. Ignore it. Men with power and no love are a menace.'

That's an unusual remark. 'How long will I be there for, do you think, sir?'

'Just as soon as you think you have nothing more to do, let us know and we'll get you back. I can't see you being there for more than a month or six weeks at the very longest. You won't have any chance of getting any money there so I'll write a note to the Camp Commandant authorising you and your men to draw a month's advance of pay. I have a subsection working in Calcutta. Once you're in Ramgarh, ring them up. Here's their number,' and he shoved a piece of paper with it written on over to Jason, 'and get them to help you make arrangements when it's time to come back. I've told them about you.' He called in his Chief Clerk and told him to make out the necessary paperwork for the advance of pay for his signature.

'While we're waiting, can you tell me anything of what you picked up when you were still in Malaya?' Rance gasped. 'Oh, we have your details, don't you worry and do not ask how we got them. Now, what can you remember about the IIL operating in or near Kuala Lumpur or even on that Bhutan Estate' – another gasp – 'and any personalities?'

Jason's mind flashed back to the four people he had arrested on his last night in Malaya, 'Ye-es, sir,' he started hesitantly. 'Do you want some names?'

'If you have any, yes.'

And so, blessing the habit of carrying the names and descriptions of all four men in the same wallet as his ID card, Jason took it out and gave it to the DMI as he told him about the Tor Gul Gang, how angry the four men had been when he'd prevented theft, who Tor Gul was, his father, Akbar Khan, the other two Indians and Rabilal Rai –*something stirred at the back of his mind* – and how he had prevented their looting his father's office.

'That's all of five years ago but once such dedicated youths get the bit between their teeth they don't let go so your list could be of great interest,' said the DMI. 'Who knows but maybe we'll be able to use that information sooner than later. Thank you. Have you any questions for me before I tell you where to collect the six Bren guns from?'

'Sir, apart from having to admit I could only recognise Tor Gul and the Gurkha again and not the other two, I have a request. My parents have been posted to Delhi and I haven't seen them since I left Kuala Lumpur for England in 1938. May I stay with them while I wait for the Bren guns? I have their address but I don't know their phone number.'

The DMI, a good family man, said 'Wait a moment,' and buzzed his Chief Clerk. 'Please look up the phone number of ...' He looked at Jason. 'Has he a rank?'

'Sir, I last heard he was a captain.'

'... Captain Rance.'

On being told, Jason joyfully jotted it down as he did the details of where to collect the Brens. He stood up, saluted with obvious satisfaction and left to join his men. Busy during the three days it took to get the LMGs he spent three happy nights with his father and mother before he and his Gurkhas were ready to move off. It was during this time that Jason's mind-stirring thought clarified itself. *My Gurkhali is now good and I realise that when I spoke to Rabilal that time in Bhutan Estate, instead of saying 'Get out of the way I'm going to sneeze', I had said what sounded like 'Pubic hair, go fuck thyself.' No wonder he is so against me.*

Once Jason and his men had settled in, Colonel McCabe, with the official interpreter, Colonel Boatner, took them all on a tour of the facility. 'We do things in a big, big winning way,' he boasted. 'After Pearl Harbour we're in this till the end, till we win and win we will.'

That remark was made complacently. The failure of the recent Arakan operation had not shown either the British or Indian army in a particularly flattering light and the Colonel wanted to show Jason the Americans' superiority in fighting.

The Chinese soldiers' interest in all weapons was obvious. Their keenness to learn was a trainer's joy to behold. That was evident to Jason and his instructors as they were taken around the large camp – there were six thousand troops and many more were expected.

'We get things weaving. Look!' and the Colonel pointed out where two US Army instructors and a Chinese NCO were teaching a class of two hundred Chinese soldiers how to fire the rifle. Jason, used to having one instructor for ten men, gazed fascinated at troops squatting around a large metal turntable. Lesson one on the rifle, he presumed, was being taught. One American, in the kneeling position, had the rifle tucked into his right shoulder while the second American, standing armed with a long pole, was pointing out various parts of the rifle and how it was being held. The interpreter, holding a loud hailer to his mouth, was describing what was happening and the names of various parts of the weapon. The turntable slowly rotated so everyone could see what was what. No excuses for ignorance! But it was only when, having pointed out that the firer's left eye was shut and the troops were told, to many giggles and smirks to shut their left eyes, did it become apparent that hardly any of them could do so.

'How will we deal with that?' Jason asked, as an aside to his men, as they watched fascinated, wondering indeed how to overcome such a disability when firing the Bren gun. It was as though Colonel McCabe read their thoughts. 'Every Chink has to be able to fire a rifle to keep the enemy's head down, not necessarily to kill him,' he weakly covered for them. 'Only one or two in each rifle company need to know how to fire an LMG. The turntable method will only be used as a general demonstration after you've done your job.'

The training went better than expected. Colonel McCabe arranged with both Chinese Divisional Commanders for a demonstration team to learn how to strip the guns for cleaning, quickly re-assemble them, fire them on the range, practise changing the barrel if a stoppage occurred and how to alter the gas pressure, first in daylight and later at night. Again everything took much more time than any of the team from Dharmsala expected: venues and times for training were either changed without being notified or days would pass before the next lesson would start.

Once it was found that Jason's Cantonese was virtually word perfect, a captain who could speak it was 'found'. Although all southerners and their languages were looked down on, there was an Intelligence cell in Major General Sun Li-jen's 38th Division and two of its members had been sent to Hong Kong to 'test the political waters' there so speaking Cantonese had been essential. Jason had no difficulty in his teaching.

The curved magazine of the Bren gun looked to the Chinese like a cow's horn so the proper name for the weapon, Light Machine Gun, with 'Light' not required, *bo leng gei gwaan cheung,* was not used but 'cow horn weapon', *ngau kok cheung,* was used instead. Towards the end of August the training was almost complete and on the 28th the tall, raw-boned and ill-mannered General Stillwell, whose charges the two divisions, now known as X Force, were, paid Ramgarh a visit during a three-week tour of India – which he loathed with a deep, bitter and malicious loathing. Bespectacled, with a long, narrow face, brooding eyes under the thatched brows and the granite moulding of the inflexible jaw, he was a man of ascetic and at time violent character, with an alert mind, grim, self-contained and formidable. He saw himself as a 'soldier's general'. He had, of course, been told of the Indian Army's Bren gun training and he asked to see some being fired on the range. He had a shot of rapid fire in short bursts after a magazine of single rounds and liked what he found. He asked where Captain Rance was and Jason was pointed out, talking vivaciously with some Gurkhas.

'Call him over here,' ordered the General, standing with the two American Army Colonels and the Chinese Generals. A man was sent to fetch him. Jason came up to General Stillwell and saluted. 'Hey, Limey Captain,' he drawled. 'I don't like Limeys. Never have and never will and the only reason I like the Bren guns is because they were not made in Limey-land but by the Czechs.

'You Brits don't know how to fight. Look at Burma. We got the hell of a licking there. Look at your fumbling in the Arakan. Useless. I'm going to take these Chinese back and there, in the wild, jungle-covered mountains of high, steep sided ridges separated by deep river valleys, kick Japanese ass.' He had a far-away look in his eyes as his mind had gone back to the devastatingly hard exodus from Burma he had made the year before.

Jason, whose salute had not been returned, said nothing: it was better to stay silent than commit an indiscretion.

'Sulking, eh?' said the General as turned to go. Jason muttered a Cantonese proverb, not realising that 'Vinegar' Joe spoke excellent Mandarin Chinese. *Drink poison to kill thirst? No.*

Stillwell's Executive Officer was, it so happened, the Cantonese General Luo Shuo-ying. 'What was that?' Stillwell asked him. General Luo translated.

Vinegar Joe turned back and put his hand out to shake Jason's. 'God damn it son, you win!' he said with a smile, all ice broken. 'If ever you come Chungking way when I'm there you're welcome,' and returned Jason's salute.

Later, talking to the DMI during his visit to GHQ, although fulminating about most aspects of the Indian and British armies, offered that 'that captain of yours down in Ramgarh. Gets on well with Asians and speaks their language. I told him he'd be welcome up in Chungking. He's good enough for the US Army.'

That last remark went down like a pork chop in a synagogue. *Just as well Vinegar Joe doesn't know that in our military parlance, US is the abbreviation for 'unserviceable'.* A year later, on 8 August 1944, the acerbic American General left Chungking forever.

3 September 1943, Singapore: By now there was a new Commander-in-Chief of the Indian National Army, a Bengali, one Subhas Chandra Bose. He was a thoroughbred scholar as well as being a politician of the first water, first as Mayor of Calcutta and later leader of the Congress Party, but his over-zealousness had landed him in jail several times nor did his ideas how best to overthrow the British accord with those of Nehru or Gandhi. Bespectacled, fleshy-cheeked and taller than average, one side of his character showed him as serious, courteous and always dressed tidily while the other side saw him as tough, resolute, ambitious and non-swerving in intent. He was wise enough to know that no taskmaster is harder than one's own self-expectations. He had done some military training when he was in university but now he declined to get involved either strategically or tactically.

In the mid-1850s Lord Macaulay had written that Bengalis were a race of deceitful cowards, schemers, intriguers and not honest. Those and other deleterious remarks both about Bengalis' shortcomings allied with a breath-taking and all-inspiring desire to rid India of the British had led Bose, by way of Germany and Japan to Singapore. Once there his one aim was to make the INA into a victorious army fighting with the Japanese in Burma then 'on to Delhi' to cause every Indian to rise up against the hated, and now because they had been so easily beaten by the Japanese, despised 'Britishers', as he knew them. Not only was he 'eaten by racial hatred' of them, he had put himself beyond the law in India. Now he was his own law and woe betide any, Indian or Japanese, who didn't accept it. The fatal flaw in the weave was that whatever he said or did and however he said it or did it, the name and fame of the new INA was personal in origin and transient in quality so making it rinsed but not laundered. Even though his ideas turned out to be 'fool's gold', he was, none the less, scratching the itch in the crotch of Indian society. However, he never realised two points: although belief becomes fact after a lifetime of professing it yet remains but a belief; and that nothing lingers longer in the mind than a bad idea. Pies in the sky and castles in the air were no substitute for rations, clothing, ammunition and other sinews of war on the ground. In the long run the slow defeat of nothing done properly was a mind-deadening constant and resulted in total military failure bought most expensively and uselessly in men's lives: eventually reality proved itself over perception. The INA became rotten without ripening but politically there was victory of a sort and Subhas Chandra Bose went into the history books as one of the few people more useful dead than alive.

After convincing the Japanese to use his men as a fighting army rather than regarding any INA's potential as support troops, Bose formed an Intelligence Group for planning, a Reinforcement Group to collect deserters and prepare them for service in the INA and a Special Service Group for infiltrating men among the Indian Army proper, those in action and those in India. Some were to be parachuted in and others taken by submarine. Such were later known as the *Bahadur*, Brave, Group and some of the first to apply for training in it were Tor Gul and the two cousins. *We must be true to our oath and now we have the chance.*

The INA was re-raised into various regiments, named Gandhi, Nehru, Subhas and a woman's, named Rani of Jhansi, formed into the 1st and 2nd Divisions.

After their dismal performance five years previously, the three Indians of the Tor Gul Gang had stayed together for a while. They had been thoroughly politically indoctrinated by their fathers and now they wanted to be given an operation role, together or separately. 'Holding their noses', they had joined the Volunteers and learnt how to shoot rifles and practise minor tactics, then disappeared. When they got to Singapore hoping to be enlisted in the INA, they didn't know it had been disbanded. Once they knew that the new INA C-in-C wanted action, Tor Gul, volunteered for the Nehru Regiment as it promised action sooner than being a parachutist. Also he was encouraged to volunteer as his superiors thought him to be of NCO material. The two cousins, almost bursting at their seams as they remembered that awe-inspiring film of parachuting so long ago that time in KL, implored their Operations Officer to make them into parachutists so they could be infiltrated into an area for their anti-British work with any Indians, but preferably military ones.

Having appointed himself as the 'non-operational' C-in-C, one of Bose's first tasks on his arrival from Japan had been to galvanise those waiting to be trained, military men and Indian civilians in Singapore and Malaya, ready to go on operations as a conquering army. When the second call for men trickled down to Bhutan Estate Rabilal Rai told the recruiter that he had already given his name in. The recruiter had been briefed about the aborted submarine task and said 'Your name has been recorded. Are you still willing, if we can get you to India by submarine, to go to Darjeeling and get the All India Gorkha League people there to try and prevent Gurkha recruitment?'

A hungry look of anticipation came into the lad's eyes. 'Yes, please take me back with you,' he said, *'Pubic hair, go fuck thyself'* still resonating in his memory. 'It's a job I'd really like to do' *and get my own back on people like that*, he sought for the name … *Jason Rance*. In any case, after that insulting failure at that Englishman's house, more and more he felt he had need to prove himself, if only to himself.

Bose broadcasted on Radio Shonan, as the Japanese had named their communications station in Singapore, in English and in Urdu, unaware that his hated adversaries were able to monitor both his and the Japanese broadcasts. This gave the 'listeners' in Delhi an untold increase in knowledge of enemy activity, to the enemy's disadvantage.

The INA Operations Officer called the Gurkha in and approved of what he saw. 'Sit down and listen.'

Rabilal sat down and did listen, all sorts of thoughts chasing one another as he did. Came the inevitable question: 'Are you still willing to go to India in a submarine? There has been a delay in the original request and I have been asked to confirm your willingness to go so the original request for a submarine can also be confirmed.' Willing or not the answer simply had to be 'yes'. *I have sworn an oath, haven't I? Operation 'Tor Gul'.*

Not having met any of the Gurkha POWs he decided to go and visit them in their camp and he asked the other three gang members to go with him. He found them singularly uninterested when he and his friends tried to encourage them about service with the INA. None of the four had any idea that service in the Indian Army was the only honourable occupation open to Nepalese hill men, with enough red velvet cloth taken back on their first leave to entice the most nubile lass into matrimony and, at the end of their service, a pension, pay for no work, so when they started sneeringly inquiring why they had joined up in 'the oppressors' army' the reaction was the last they had expected. There was a strangled yelp of dismay when Balbahadur Rana, the victim of the night-soil buckets, came close enough to listen to what was being said. 'Who are you?' he demanded. 'None of you look like soldiers, you don't talk like soldiers and you don't seem to have the courtesy of one to his elders. Are you spies? If so, we'll have to kill you.'

A furious row arose and there was nearly a set-to. Jemadar Rahul Dura, sitting one side still thinking about how to get away, said, 'I'll never forget your faces, come what may. I always have a sharp kukri with me.' The four extricated themselves, inwardly cursing and frightened, muttering how they would not forget the gnarled Gurkha and when Rabilal, who had stayed behind, tried to explain his own background he was jeered. 'Get out of our sight or we'll cut you up here and now.' His face became a blaze of anger and his temper quickly reached boiling point. Their attitude made him all the more keen on trying to make his task in India a success. He was not to know that the Gurkhas were not allowed to carry their kukris and left with indecent haste.

'Major Fujiwara, my intelligence group, resurrected from the first attempt, tells me that Major General Mohan Singh and you decided to send an agent to India by submarine on a special task but nothing happened. I want to reactivate that operation immediately so that means we must have a submarine to get him there.'

'I am willing to help you, Bose-san, as I was before but I still need higher authority's permission. Please give me the details of what and where to.'

Bose swallowed his impatience and, under the table out of sight of the Japanese, he clenched and unclenched his fists in frustration. He wanted an answer there and then. 'Why can't you order one when it comes to Singapore? Quick and easy that way.'

'Neta-ji,' he had heard the other Indians use that term and now was a time to be tactful, 'So sorry, please let me explain the background. The Imperial Japanese Navy's Intelligence Department, *Chuo Kikan*, has overt intelligent tasks and covert ones we call *choho*. Your request is *choho* and there are priorities so I need exact details of what you want.' *Bose does not have the tact we Japanese have cultivated.*

'It's like this. You know how the Gurkha captives have refused to join the INA. Among the British-Indian Army are Gurkhas who do not come from India but from Nepal. Only one or two who were born and brought up in India, known as line boys, are open to suggestions and then probably only to escape, not to serve us. I want a Gurkha, and I have one, Rabilal Rai, to be infiltrated into India. He is not military. He was born and bred in Malaya. His task will be to get the All India Gorkha League, which is controlled by Congress and has its headquarters in Darjeeling, to try and prevent all Gurkha recruiting, both at the eastern depot in Darjeeling and the western one at Gorkhapur. Come, I'll show you on the wall map.'

Both men wore spectacles so had to peer at it with eyes screwed.

Back at his desk Bose said, 'I don't know how many Gurkha battalions are in Burma but I believe there are more there than in any other theatre.'

'If the Imperial Navy allows this, when do you want it to happen? Only one man, you say.'

'When? As soon as possible. Also, if the sub is big enough I'd send quite a few more. Indians to the Indian recruiting depots on the same task.' He passed an impatient hand over his forehead.

Fujiwara, eyes guileless, continued the conversation at his own pace. 'So sorry. If the Imperial Navy agrees, it will have to choose the point of disembarkation. Have you any ideas?'

Bose had it thought out. 'Yes, I must have it as near Calcutta as possible, in Orissa. Any farther south my man, who has no English, only Nepalese and Malay, will find himself in a Telugu-speaking crowd, so be utterly lost.'

'Let's have another look at the map,'

Back they went to it and closely scrutinised the eastern seaboard. 'Let it be somewhere between Berhmapur and Vishakhapatnam, at, say, here, opposite the small town of Haripur. From the colouring of the water it is deep until quite near the beach. What say you?'

The Japanese smiled. 'In early April 1942 our navy made an attack on the British navy almost opposite where you're pointing. That means that in the naval Record Office there'll be details of that area already. But I repeat, it's not up to me.'

Both men stayed quiet while they considered the implications. The Japanese broke the silence. 'One major point, Bose-san, how will the submarine captain and the navigator know when to put their man overboard? What you'll need is a fishing boat to meet the sub and,' here he paused to make the point, 'that is your responsibility, nor ours.'

Bose was not fazed. He put his head around the door and gave someone the Japanese could not see an order. 'Get Mr Nedyam Raghavan here as soon as you can. If he's not available, get his next one down.'

Mr Raghavan was available and was told the problem. He was, by now, rising sixty years of age and, to his shame, deaf. In his haste and with the noise of a whirring fan, he misheard his instructions. He left thinking that a British submarine was on its way to Malaya to drop agents, something that had, indeed, happened already. 'I may have an answer. I must look at my records as the name of a person I think can tackle the job is not at my tongue tip.' He excused himself and the major asked what Bose had in mind.

'There is an Indian Association, legal and on the level, in India. They are mostly Congress men. They are "sleepers" for any job like this. Each has his individual code name. If one has to change the code word stays the same. What I'm thinking of is for me to make a broadcast, use his code name and tell him to wait details and only when I have a yes or no from you will I make another, coded, broadcast. The landing will be in Orissa so I'll have one of my men who comes from there to send the message in Oriya.'

'Is there no other way?'

'If I can think of one I'll let you know. Thank you for your time,' and imperiously the Japanese was dismissed. *After all, I am the leader of Free India and he is only a lowly major.*

Nedyam Raghavan came back. 'I have all the details ready, Neta-ji. Just tell me when you want me to make the broadcast.'

Bose gave him the date. 'It's up to you. I don't speak Malay and you do so just get on with the job and tell me when you've done it.' Incompetence and complacency are always a fatal brew.

Raghavan got hold of Rabilal and told him what was wanted. 'Are you ready for this task? Neta-ji thinks you are.'

By that time Rabilal, who got around Singapore as much as he wanted to, was becoming more and more displeased with Japanese behaviour as, indeed, were many sepoys of the defeated

Indian Army. The Japanese had brutally forced the Chinese to clear up the town but it was still dirty. Rations were not good and Japanese manners were appalling: they'd take their organs out in front of women and piss against lamp posts. They even bathed in the nude. INA officers were clearly working hard but it was obvious, even to those who didn't know anything about military matters, that they were captains and majors trying to do generals' jobs so of course there were many incidents of inefficiency and unhappiness. The English tuans he had met at Bhutan Estate had never treated him quite as arrogantly as some of them here – *except for that appallingly rude what was his name again? Got it, yes, Jason Rance.* And surely India couldn't be worse than here, whether he wanted to go there by submarine or not was not at the top of his mind. *I have a chance, at long last, for Operation 'Tor Gul' and to prove myself to myself.* 'Yes, I was ready before so of course I am ready now,' simply had to be his answer.

2

4 September 1943, GHQ New Delhi: India's grandly spacious, tree-shaded capital built in the 1920s as an imposing setting for the British Raj had never been planned to accommodate the paraphernalia of wartime needs so expansion for more offices and living quarters resulted in congestion. During the hot weather a pall of lethargy heavier than usual overhung the place. Tempers became strained and leaden heads from nights without enough sleep did not enhance the speed of inter-departmental liaison. One heavy-handed joker, feeling what he had read in a minute to a file being circulated for comment was really a waste of time and being too polite to write the improper word 'Balls' beside the offending paragraph, wrote 'Round objects' instead. A month or two later he was amused to see a comment written by a bemused Staff Officer asking, 'Who is Officer Round? I can't find him in my directory and to what does he object?'

However, reaction to work was at the other end of the scale at the innocuous-sounding Wireless Experimental Centre, the WEC. Its security was of the tightest. Its provenance was the code-breaking centre in England's Bletchley Park: its branch in India was located outside the town on top of Happiness Hill,

Anand Parbat, where reception was good, in an unobtrusive and heavily protected building, topped by tall antennae. In happier times Ramjas College, one time part of Delhi University, had had its being there.

Those few who worked there were the only people, apart from a small group of senior officers (not even the Viceroy), who knew about it. Those working on receiving and sending transmissions were from the Royal Corps of Signals and linguists who translated those sent in Japanese into English were scrupulously vetted and top quality operators in the Intelligence Corps. Everyone who entered the building was always escorted, even those permanently working there coming on a new shift: at the outside gate he rang a bell and someone came to unlock from within, first always asking to see an authenticated pass. The gate would be opened and a silent escort who, beckoning the new entrant to follow, led him along a short concrete path flanked by two wire barricades to another gate where another bell was rung and the visitor wordlessly handed over to a second escort. Again, no word was ever spoken, only a finger beckoned him to follow. Reaching the main building, the outside door of which had no handle, the escort rang a bell. Through an opened Judas hole an eye peered at them. The escort left and the door opened. The visitor would be taken down a passage to another door where the third escort would knock. The door would open, the pass shown and only then would the visitor be invited inside.

'Magic' was the highly guarded code word given to the breaking of Japanese codes and only those who had the security grading even higher than that of Top Secret had been sworn into silence about the system. 'Need to know' said it all. There was a cipher machine, Alphabetical Typewriter 97, known as 'Purple'. The British had been given two, one was in England and the second, given in June 1941 to Singapore, had found its way to New Delhi by way of Colombo and East Africa. A Royal Signal's Wireless Company that had been in Abbottabad had moved to Delhi to join forces with the British Combined Operational Intelligence Centre where the cryptanalytic work was being done. The psychological gratification of all intelligence work lies in knowing more than your adversaries but also more than your allies. It says much for America's tolerance that in this case the latter gratification did not pertain.

After lunch that day in the WEC, sweating, although the rains had broken some weeks before and the fans were rotating at full blast which made anyone trying to rescue paperwork as effective as a one-armed wall-paper hanger, a red light winked. The duty corporal, a war-time 'call up' from a university, immediately snapped to attention and put on his headset. Red light meant that a Japanese transmission was being sent. Japanese Morse, code-named Khana, a local word for 'food', had seventy-six symbols to be learnt so immense concentration was needed thus taking it down was a skilled task.

A second burst of coded message began. *An answer? Abnormally quick if so.*

As an experimental backup there was a novelty, a wire recorder, but as it was 'moody', all broadcasts listened to still had to be more than carefully manually copied down. If not, the message could not be translated properly.

Headset off and wiping the sweat from his brow, the operator rang a bell which sounded in the translator's office. On duty was Lieutenant Hector Mason; a quiet, observant, intelligent, red-haired, freckled-faced and perhaps a little religious linguist in his early twenties who looked younger than his years. After qualifying as a Japanese interpreter, he had been trained in code breaking at Duchess House, Broadway, London, W1. This was the first time he and his sidekick, an equally intelligent and sapient officer, had been alerted since coming on duty that morning. On hearing the bell Mason went to a small counter set in one wall, knocked on it and, window opened, signed for the message recently received.

'Hard work?' he asked socially.

'Yes, it is. But it has let me travel the world and,' with a mischievous grin, 'the King has paid for it all.'

'Same here,' said Hector as he took the paperwork away to work on it. It took the two men more than two hours to translate the transmissions. The first message, in outline, was a request to the Imperial Japanese Navy's covert, *choho*, Intelligence cell in Tokyo from Singapore asking for a submarine to infiltrate a man to India to be dropped off at Haripur, map coordinates given, on the night of 15 September or, if conditions did not allow it, the next two nights, between 0100 hours and 0230 hours. The stated reason was for a pre-war member of the IIL, a Malay-domiciled and pro-Japanese civil Gurkha, Rabilal Rai, to go to India to try and prevent Gurkha recruiting so make victory in Burma even easier. This task was considered one of the highest priority by the INA. Once approval for the operation had been given the submarine's signal of arrival would be notified to Tokyo. Likewise a coded message would be broadcast by the INA to one of its 'sleepers' in Oriya to be ready to meet the man being infiltrated.

The second message was the authority for the operation. A Sentaka type submarine, I-203, carrying a midget submarine of the *Ko-hyoteki* class, M-19, was available. It would depart from Shonan on 12 September. The recognition signals were three long flashes, followed by three short ones then three long ones if all was safe. A similar answer would confirm safety for the passenger to leave the submarine and go to the shore. If that was unsafe for him six short flashes, a gap and six more short flashes would be shone and the mission would be aborted till the following night or the night after then totally. All activity would be confirmed to Tokyo.

A message from the INA was also included. It was in Urdu and Hector, having passed his Elementary Urdu exam, could understand it. 'There's something wrong here,' he observed. 'The INA message doesn't seem as if it were meant for India. That'll have to be pointed out to the DMI. I'll make a note of it at the bottom of the translation. It's code word Mauve so it must be hand-delivered by an officer.' The code word, although it, too, was classified as secret, was almost insecure as mauve merely meant deep purple. 'I'll ring him up now and ask when he'd like to be briefed,' Hector decided.

Brigadier William Lambert, the DMI, was having tea with his wife when his secret red telephone rang. He was still in uniform having had an unwanted session with the C-in-C. 'Blast it,' he muttered, 'can't it wait?'

'Darling,' objected his wife, 'it must be urgent because it so seldom rings. Tell the person on the other end to ring back whenever it's convenient to you.'

'Oh, all right,' and he went to the phone. 'DMI here. Who are you and what do you want?'

His wife saw her husband grow tense. 'Have you transport?' Obviously a negative as 'I'll send my staff car round in,' he looked at his watch, 'figures twenty with my ADC armed as escort.' So secret were Mauve messages that an armed escort was a necessary precaution.

'You military men,' his wife teased him, 'why "figures twenty", why not just "twenty minutes"?'

The DMI yawned, 'Habit and I'm going to put on something more relaxing after alerting George.' George was Captain Riggs, the Brigadier's long-suffering ADC.

The ADC, staff car and driver were permanently at the Brigadier's quarter and nine minutes later off they went. Evening traffic was not thick and by half past five, Captain Hector Mason was closeted in the Brigadier's study. The DMI had himself a whisky water and the captain asked for a cup of tea before handing the translations over in a sealed envelope.

The General read them avidly. '"Will you come into my parlour", said the spider to the fly',' he remarked blithely as he finished. 'Have you anything you want to say about them?'

'Yes, sir. The INA transmission doesn't read as if it were meant for India. Something's gone amiss somewhere. If we hear nothing in the next few days that will mean I'm correct.'

'Has it, indeed? How lucky I debriefed Captain Rance in the

detail I did. Look at that name, Rabilal Rai. Action stations! We'll have to do this in fine style. It is not often that we can catch those traitorous Jiffs red-handed. One of our key players has to be Captain Rance. Thank you. Off you go back with my special thanks.'

The Brigadier finished his drink and muttered to his wife, 'There's one more thing to do,' as he dialled a number.

'ADC to the DMO,' came the answer after a long, long delay.

'DMI here. Tell your Lord and Master I have a Mauve message for him. I must come to see him tomorrow – there's still time for an early morning gallop but not for a round of golf. I'll be at his quarter by nine o'clock.' Without waiting for an answer he put the phone down.

'Lucky we were in the same platoon at Sandhurst, m'dear, or I couldn't get away with a message like that,' and he smiled at his wife as their bearer came to tell them that their supper was ready.

Brigadier William Lambert and Major General Albert Arnold, sitting comfortably in the latter's study, had been discussing this latest case of an INA- planned infiltration by submarine by a Jiff. They'd already had one session, then a leg stretch and were now back again for a final 'going firm'. One point of discussion had been on the treatment of caught infiltrators: the policy was 'work with us and we'll be lenient, don't and we'll string you up'. Some had refused to work with the government and had been hanged; the remainder were, comparatively speaking, 'in clover'. The legal niceties of a non-military man, a civilian of a British colony the United Kingdom was not at war with, were not of top priority.

'So, Bill, let's go over those times and places just once more,' said the DMO.

'Yes, Bert, I'd like that. Everything turns on our getting it exactly right.'

'Before that I want to talk about young Mason's remark about the Jiffs' message not making sense if it were meant for India has set me thinking.' He stopped, took out a packet of cigarettes from his pocket and offered the DMI one before lighting up himself. 'I don't know what to make of it,' he continued. 'I see there can be one of two reasons but each with the same result,' and he looked quizzically at the Brigadier.

'Yes, it's puzzled me, too. Let's hear your ideas before I give you mine.'

'Righty-ho. Either the operator is anti the INA so trying, unobtrusively, to foul up the system or, and this, I grant you, is a long shot, they're so ruddy incompetent they don't know their harp from their oboe, to put it politely,' and both men chuckled.

'Bert, both make sense. Now, let's take advantage of it. Let's presume the message has not reached any Indian in India so let's pretend it has by acknowledging it ourselves. As Rance knows the man being infiltrated can speak Gurkhali and has Gurkhas with him, let's send something like "Message received and understood. At sea Rabilal will be met by a Gurkha."

The DMO thought it over. 'Yes, I like it.' He wrote it down, put it in an envelope, which he sealed, and called for his ADC. 'Take this message and deliver it to the WEC as quickly as you can for immediate despatch without breaking the speed limit, getting knocked over by another vehicle or being hijacked so the message gets lost.'

All armies spend an inordinate amount of effort on their 'time and space' problems and this was the next poser to be tackled: how to get Rance's 'Snatch Group', as they now thought of his Bren gun training team, briefed and down to the coast at Haripur in time for the first possible attempt by the submarine on the 15th. Roads were not good and distances long. 'We must get everyone involved in position by D-2, today being D-10. Let's work on getting news to Rance tomorrow, D-9, to get ready to move by transport sent from Ranchi on D-7.' Nowhere else was convenient but Ramgarh and Ranchi were easily two hundred miles apart.

The DMI replied, 'Yes, this also has to be kept Most Secret,' he corrected himself, 'Top Secret, I mean. I'm still not used to using this new Yank "Top Secret" nonsense that came in recently. Not a word out to anyone except those who really have to know how we got the information, especially if we can turn the wretched man to work for us. That means not involving our Calcutta people. I think I'd better go myself. It'll do both George Riggs and me good to have a change of scenery.'

'Yes, that's wise. Again, can't be too careful. Just to make sure before you go I'll clear it with the C-in C.' He made a note on a pad and continued, 'Apart from the Snatch Group, you'll need some police to keep inquisitive people away. I feel somehow the fewer soldiers there are about the less notice people will take of you. There's seldom any military activity in that neck of the woods.'

'I'll make sure there's a powerful torch to signal back to the submarine. I can't speak Gurkhali but can manage quite well in Urdu. Once there George will arrange for a small fishing boat with an outboard engine. That'll mean money and a glib tongue!'

'Hey, I've just had an idea. Do you think we can get the Navy to sink the Jap submarine on its way back?' the DMO ejaculated.

'My! That's an idea and a half. Tell you what, let's get our tame admiral on board as soon as we can. Let's ruin his Sunday as well.'

The DMO used his secure line. 'Admiral Jenkins speaking.'

'Jo, it's Bert this end. Sorry to disturb your Sunday but we've just had totally secure news of a tempting target in the middle of the month. It would be useful if you could despatch it irrevocably for the good of us all.'

'Bert, blast your eyes but it sounds too good to miss. Area?'

'Bay of Bengal and the Malacca Straits.'

'Aye, aye, General. I'll call you back but it won't be before late tomorrow.'

'Jo. Good of you. I'll stand you a beer when we next meet,' and, with a smile, put the phone down.

6 September 1943, Ramgarh: '*Seong wai*,' Captain. A Chinese soldier saluted smartly and gave Jason a note.

'*Doh che*,' Thank you. Captain Rance returned the salute before looking at what was written.

The soldier saluted once more and left. Rance looked at the note. Signed by a Top Sergeant it read, 'Come to the main office to receive a telephone call at 12 noon'.

What now? Jason wondered. *Time to go back?* Their work

was done and his soldiers were getting bored. *Yes, definitely time for a move.*

Jason was near the phone before noon and a couple of minutes after 12 o'clock it rang. The Top Sergeant answered. 'Yes, sir, he's standing right beside me. Here he is,' and handed the phone over.

'Captain Rance speaking.'

'This is the DMI's ADC, Captain Riggs. Listen and don't ask questions. A 15-cwt truck will reach the main gate of your camp at around 1130 hours on the day after tomorrow, Wednesday. Roger so far?' he asked in signals jargon.

'Roger, over,' Jason replied.

'All of you will be taken to Ranchi for further briefing. Tell the Yanks only that you're on your way back. Once you reach Ranchi, report to the Guard Room and you'll be given directions. That'll be on the 11th and you'll leave again early on the 13th. Get it?'

'Yes, sir,' and the phone went dead.

Jason thanked the Top Sergeant and went to his men's accommodation. As he appeared the Havidar in charge brought the soldiers to attention and saluted. They were drinking their midday brew of tea.

'At ease, Guru-ji. Let the men continue drinking their tea while I talk to you.' The soldiers made themselves comfortable but before Jason could start, he was given a mugful. 'I was called to the office to answer a phone call at exactly midday,' he started, sipping the sweet hot brew. 'It was from GHQ Delhi, the ADC to a Brigadier sahib.' ADC was not a term the men knew and the version Jason gave them was *ath pahariya,* [the one who is] on duty for eight hours. *Now, when did I learn that?* 'I was told not to ask any questions. We are moving the day after tomorrow at 1130 by truck but we are only going as far as Ranchi where we have to report for further orders.' All the soldiers knew where that was. 'I don't think we're on our way back to Bhagsoh' – the Gurkhas' name for Dharmsala – 'if we were we'd have been given more notice.'

A flash of interest passed over the soldiers' faces at that. 'We have to tell the Americani, and the Chinese if they ask us, that we are on our way back to where we came from. Havildar guru, we'll only be at Ranchi for one full day. We must be ready to move on to whatever task we're given so that means getting our kit together and laundering our clothes now. They can be dry before we go.'

The soldiers set about 'internal economy' as the army knew it and Jason went to look for Colonel McCabe to give him the news. He also wanted to thank the two Chinese generals for their help, understanding and friendliness.

12 September 1943, Singapore: 'Ready to go? Not feeling nervous?' asked Raghavan.

'Nervous? No, I'm ready for everything,' answered Rabilal, with a brittle laugh, hands clenching each other behind his back.

'You haven't told me why you've volunteered for such a, well, dangerous task. I expect you know that two of your group want to go into battle by parachute.' He leant forward and said, 'I can't bear the idea of going in an aeroplane. It's not safe: on the ground, here you are; in the air, where you are is how I look at it.

I don't think it will be hard to persuade the Japanese to make an aeroplane ready for them.'

'I don't like the idea of flying either but my dislike of the English bubbled up, oh,' and he wrinkled his brow as he thought, 'in 1938 when ...' and he told Nedhyam about the incident of having indecent words used against him by a fellow named Jason Rance at Bhutan Estate. 'Of course I'll never be able to catch up with him but catch up with anyone of the English will do just as well. Is that good enough for you?'

'Perfectly understandable and I'm proud of you. Oh, before I forget, have you got that list of names I gave you? Just check once more. Your journey is useless without it. I was not in charge of the other infiltrations so did not send any list then.'

The Gurkha looked in his pack. He had wrapped it in waterproof cloth and put it between his towel and spare clothing. 'Yes, no worry. I can't lose it.'

The list was one that Mr Nedyam Raghavan was proud of. It was almost up to date. He had circulated various centres in India and asked for the names and addresses of all those willing to be used as contact were the occasion to arrive: amendments had dribbled in until postal arrangements abruptly ended.

'There's one enormous piece of luck, you know,' he prattled on. 'You'll be met by a Gurkha. I told you, didn't I, that we had a message back from our people in India the day after I sent mine?'

'Yes, I'm really glad of that as I'm not a Hindi or an English speaker although I know a few words of both languages.'

'Now, I'll once more run over the details of your journey which shouldn't take more than four days non-stop. The fleet submarine is' and he looked at his note book, 'I-203, a big powerful boat that carries the midget submarine,' he looked at his notes again, 'M-19, on its back.' These superfluous details grated but Rabilal tried not to show it. 'You'll go most of the way in the big boat and only transfer to the little one for the last short part of your journey.'

'I hope it will let me out as near land as possible as I can't swim.'

'I know, so I've brought you a pair of water wings for you and here they are. Puff into them to inflate them and put them over your pack before you jump into the water otherwise they won't be of any use.'

The Gurkha looked doubtful as they were handed over. 'Have a puff,' the Indian encouraged him.

This Rabilal did and his face creased into a smile of satisfaction. 'Yes, I've got the hang of it.'

'You'll be met by a boat or a raft so don't worry. There are two other items I have for you. This is the first,' and he handed over a torch, 'a special operational one that is waterproof. And the second is this,' and he handed over a waterproof bag. 'Put your pack into that before you get into the water. It doesn't matter about your getting wet. It'll keep you alert,' and he grinned wickedly. 'Major Fujiwara will take you to the docks.'

Later that day a rather nervous Rabilal Rai boarded the Imperial Japanese Navy fleet submarine I-203.

14 September 1943, Haripur, Orissa: At Ranchi Jason just had time to find a place for his men before being called away by

Brigadier Lambert's hard-working ADC. 'Rance,' the Brigadier started off. He was drinking a cup of tea and he looked at him over the rim of his cup, smiling gleefully. 'It's lucky indeed that I debriefed you so thoroughly when we met,' the older man purred, looking at him approvingly. 'You have a good memory and now is a chance to put it to good use.'

Jason looked blankly at the DMI and didn't answer.

Unexpectedly the Brigadier asked, 'Do you know what Anatole France said about chance?'

Jason's look became even blanker: he'd never heard of that character. 'Then I'll tell you: "Chance is a pseudonym God uses when He doesn't want to sign His own name." You see it's like this ...' and he explained the reason for the sudden recall. 'I can't tell you how we know about this but it is one hundred per cent certain sure.'

'I'm utterly surprised to hear about this completely unexpected development, sir.' A look almost of awe crossed the younger man's face.

'Do you think you'll recognise the fellow again after, what, five years?'

Jason pondered. Thinking back to their last meeting and now knowing enough Gurkhali to understand why Rabilal had been so angry when he'd thought he'd said 'Look out, I'm going to sneeze,' he still felt uncomfortable with his actual words ... 'Any recognition marks, moles, tattoos you recall?' the DMI broke into his thoughts.

Jason came to himself with a start. 'Why yes, sir. You've jogged my memory. In a letter my father wrote to me he said that they'd found a Pashto tattoo "Tor Gul" on the left shoulder of all the four ruffians.'

'How very strange! That'll be proof positive, then. Most satisfactory,' said the DMI happily.

Before they started on the second leg of their journey and thinking about a slippery and moving deck Jason ordered his men to put their boots in their kit bag, take out their canvas shoes and leave the kit bags in the stores for collection on their return.

The town of Haripur was some distance from the shore but there were a few shacks near a jetty used by the fishing community. George Riggs, who luckily came from an Urdu-speaking regiment, reported to the local police station and asked for a policeman to go with him to the jetty and arrange, with a fistful of rupees, the loan of the smallest fishing boat that had an outboard engine.

They met one owner who was willing to forego a night's fishing for the equivalent of the price of normal catch and the fuel that would have been used. – '*Aj kal tel bahut mahañga hai*', fuel these days is most expensive – 'and why is my boat wanted?'

'Oh, we're having an exercise at rescuing anyone who might be drowning from a sinking ship,' was the first thing that came into Captain Riggs' head.

'Then I won't take the boat out. I can't get muddled up in military work,' and he gave a nod to the mainland as if to say that it would go against him if found out.

'For another two hundred – think of it, two whole hundred – rupees, if you tell me how to start and steer, I'll take the boat out and pay for any damage that might happen. Not that it will,' he added hurriedly. 'It's not far, less than a mile I expect, and I know how to drive a car.'

So that point was settled. The jetty was also convenient for waiting for the submarine's signal.

'I have my thoughts about retrieving Rabilal. What are yours?' asked Brigadier Lambert.

'In one word, sir, "varied" but I've learnt that Gurkhas are bad sailors so after an underwater voyage and an in-the-water journey to the shore, even if he were a good swimmer which I somehow doubt, he'll be only too glad to be rescued. I see you, Captain Riggs, myself and a couple of my men to haul the target out of the water only putting out to sea.'

'Right. In broad outline we agree.'

Jason was encouraged enough to ask the Brigadier a question, 'Sir, is there any chance of our sinking the submarine on its way back?'

'I'll be frank with you. Of course we've thought of that but, there always is a "but", isn't there? If I tell you will you keep your mouth shut for ever and a day?'

'Of course, sir.'

'There's only one submarine available and that belongs to the Royal Dutch Navy, the RNLN. I even know its number, O24. Why we cannot use it to sink the Japanese submarine is because it is due to do on the northwest coast of Malaya on the 20th of this month what the INA is going to do near Haripur. We cannot, simply cannot abort that even if we could, after all the months of planning. But we couldn't even if we wanted to as it's observing radio silence.' The DMI did not add that knowledge of its whereabouts might jeopardise Magic traffic.

'Thank you, sir. Your confidence in me will be will faithfully observed,' was the slightly pompous answer.

Even the DMI didn't know that O24's radio was 'on the blink' and couldn't take or receive any messages even if she wanted to.

Jason and his men were a bit overawed by the presence of such a senior officer and the Brigadier seemed to sense it. 'Captain Rance,' he said, looking at his watch. 'It is now 1530. I won't interfere at all with how you deploy your men but tell me what you propose to do from now on.'

'First of all, sir, we'll have finished our meal before sundown and afterwards, with one man awake, rest till midnight on the jetty. I and my soldiers will be awake from midnight onwards. Your ADC will be woken up if not already awake just before 0100 hours to be ready to take the compass bearing on the submarine's signals: you, sir, can continue dozing until the flashes. After all, this is only Night One of Three. Once we have seen the sub's flashes, I will answer from the end of the jetty. Captain Riggs will take a compass bearing on them to steer by and go down to start the boat's engine. I might even see a body in the water with my binoculars if it doesn't cloud over and if it has a torch, so much the better. Then all aboard and away.'

The Brigadier nodded his assent and Jason continued, 'presuming we find him, I'd rather him not hear my voice in case he recognises it so I'll get my Havildar to holler out to him and once we reach him, get him aboard. I think we must quickly get to change into dry kit, one of my men's if he has none himself. I believe you'd like us to start being kind with him rather than severe.'

'Correct. Then presumably you won't bind him.'

'Maybe once we're on the road but at first he'll be too whacked to resist us.'

'Yes, we're on to this with the seat of our pants. Something new for us all, including the poor sod we hope to pick up. Once ashore I plan to put him in a closed vehicle, guarded by your men, but only bound if he shows any signs of trying to escape. Once we reach Ranchi he'll be yours no longer as he'll be totally mine. I'll also have him medically examined. As for you? I'll get someone on the staff there to find out.'

Jason had been awake since midnight when he saw three short, three long and three short flashes out to sea. Clouds covered the moon and there was no silhouette of the boat. 'Flashes seen,' he shouted out as he ran to the end of the pier and George Riggs took the bearing. 'Dead on nine zero degrees,' he called out as he left to go down to the boat as Jason was answering the flashes.

'Those detailed follow the sahib,' Jason called out. After they'd gone down the ladder the DMI's voice asked, from behind, 'Why haven't you gone down too?'

'I'm waiting in case the sub signals again. If she does, I'll need to answer. Please make your way down, sir.'

'If nothing is flashed in figures five come down and join us in the boat, then we'll be off.'

On board the I-203 Rabilal found life almost unbearable and he wished he'd never volunteered. He had not like being so completely enclosed ever since he had been locked in a windowless room for one whole day as a punishment when a five-year old. He had, however, learnt just enough rudimentary Japanese to understand basic orders, where to eat, sleep and such like.

He was much happier when the boat reached the surface and he could breathe fresh air again. He nearly refused to be incarcerated in the midget submarine M-19, as it looked so terribly small. Four really hard slaps on his cheeks brought him to his senses and he crawled into the tiny tube with his kit, the water wings and immense misgivings.

The new captain put one finger up. 'One hour,' and slapped his passenger's cheeks hard.

If the I-203 had been hellish, for the miserable Rabilal the M-19 was a living nightmare. Cooped up in the prone position, his pack prevented him from turning over so he became cramped. The boat was so near the surface that the waves kept it rolling, tossing and yawing, just enough to make him vomit. After an hour, which seemed to have passed as slowly as a week, the engine noise subsided and he felt a hand shake him. He couldn't stand so half crawling he followed a sailor up to the deck, gulping the fresh air into his lungs with an almost feverish glee and untold relief. Even wearing his torch round his neck since leaving Singapore he automatically touched it to make sure it was still there. *I'm dead without it.*

He started to blow up his water wings. The sailor urged speed but he couldn't blow any harder. The sailor snatched them, blew them up and hung them over Rabilal's pack. 'Ready?'

Rabilal nodded and the sailor showed which way he had to go with his outstretched arm. 'Go!'

As if an ice barb had suddenly entered his bowels all strength seemed to have left the man from Bhutan Estate so, unceremoniously, with a hard slap on his cheek, he was thrown overboard. The submarine again signalled its message and slowly moved seawards. It would never do to submerge and draw the swimmer down with it.

Immediately on seeing the second set of flashes Jason flashed back. The sailor on deck glanced behind him as he closed the hatch and went inside. He reported what he'd seen it to his captain. Rabilal saw nothing and the impact of saltwater in his eyes and mouth filled him with an innate urgency, buried so deep he didn't know he had it in him to cope. The waves see-sawed him up and down. He felt for his torch, managed to switch it on and waved it around his head. *I pray my rescuer can see it* he sobbed inside himself, dog-paddling for all he was worth with the other hand, not realising he was merely turning himself around as he did.

Jason quickly but carefully went down to the boat, got in and George Riggs revved up the already idling engine. Once away from the pier the Brigadier shouted out over the noise, 'Wave your torch about, Rance, so that the man in the water can see it. Give him something to paddle towards.'

'Yes, sir, and he'll soon hear our engine.'

All aboard strained their eyes and a little later George called out, 'Light, light, straight to our front. Still some distance off,' and accelerated.

Rabilal heard the engine. *The gods have answered my prayers*. He was tiring, lying low in the water, the weight of his pack pulling him down. George Riggs throttled back as the boat reached him. Jason told the Havildar to shout out to the man in the water.

'*Bhai, bhai,*' younger brother, younger brother. 'Continue paddling and we'll drop a rope down to you.'

A splutter was the only answer.

'Can you hear me?' the Havildar shouted in a louder voice. 'Shout, if you can.'

Nothing was heard even though the engine was idling. Then there he was, almost bumping the side. The rope was dangled but the man, completely wearied, cold and wet through, only had enough strength to cling on to it.

Jason saw what to do. Stripping down to his underpants, he climbed down the rope and reached the struggling man. 'Get on my back and hang on to my shoulders,' he shouted in Gurkhali.

But even that was too much to ask.

Jason caught hold of Rabilal round his waist, front to front to keep the pack away from his face. 'Pull us up. Pull us up,' he yelled. As they were dragged up it was all Jason could do to hold on to the man and the rope but manage he did until the two men were lifted over the railings. A soldier relieved the tired and sodden man of his pack and Rabilal's breast heaved with a blissful feeling filling his lungs. Dazed, he looked around. A startled expression came over his face as he tried to make out what he saw: *Gurkhas in uniform!* His gaze then rested on Jason. His mind reeled, boggled, swayed and the words of yesteryear came like a thunderbolt into his troubled mind and like a thunderbolt he fell onto the deck in a dead faint.

By that time the boat was making for the pier at its fastest.

The Brigadier said, 'someone take his shirt off. He's in a bad way and you, Rance, shine your torch on his left shoulder.' Shirt off, Jason flashed his torch and there it was, لنگ طور. 'That's him, sir, and he's out to the wide. Can't see him making any trouble.'

'I agree.'

'While you've got the torch on, have a look in his pack and see if there's anything that can help us.'

Jason rummaged around and found a waterproof envelope between the dry clothes and towel. Excitedly he opened it and found the list of IIL contacts. 'This will be of interest, sir,' he said, showing it to the DMI who shone the torch on it as he took a quick squint. 'Treasure trove, to be sure,' he murmured, grinning like a knowing goat. *It will come in extremely useful, of that I'm certain.*

They reached the pier and George skilfully brought the boat to a halt. He switched the engine off. The silence, broken only by gently lapping water, was almost loud. Rabilal was still in a faint. 'What can we do with him?' the DMI asked.

In a flash Jason's mind went back to that day on Bhutan Estate and the way the old shaman handled the woman. *Can I imitate him? I must try.* Almost desperately and inwardly struck by his own temerity, he blurted out, 'Sir, you trusted me earlier on. I must trust you now. You and my orderly will stay here with Rabilal and the others must go up to the pier and wait for us.' He looked around and saw an old sail. *Just what I need.* Rabilal started to stir. 'Hitman, get that cloth and dangle it between me and this Rabilal man. Brigadier, please take my torch and shine it so I can have some reflected light but please stand out of the man's sight and say nothing.'

Rather remarkably the Brigadier did as told, mightily intrigued by such an unexpected turn of events.

Hitman held the cloth as told and Jason lay down, head only an inch away from Rabilal's with the cloth between them. '*Daju, daju*', elder brother, elder brother, 'listen to me. Can you hear me? You can, can't you? I'm talking to you from Bhutan Estate. I'm that rude young Jason Rance, friend of Ah Fat.'

'Yes, *bhai*,' came a weak voice. 'I can hear you. Where am I?'

'I've come to say how sorry I was to be so rude. I now know better.'

'I can't see you. Where are you?'

Where am I? Quick! 'I'm in a lorry up the hill, waiting to welcome you. Waiting to ask if you'll work for me and some others. I'll introduce you to them. They are friends not like in Singapore where you were misled. They didn't like you. Come to me Jason Rance, *Daju* Rabilal.'

Jason heard a sob and a muttered, 'I'll come. I'll come.' A pause, 'and I'm sorry I tried to rob you in KL.'

'And I for hurting you. Do you forgive me?'

'I do, I do. The other three have vowed to kill you ...' and his voice faded away.

Just as Jason was quietly rolling away he heard Rabilal mutter 'one in many, many millions', which meant nothing to him. He took the cloth from Hitman. 'Tell Rabilal to stand up. Put him where he can't see me. Open his pack and take out his dry clothes. Tell him to put them on. If he's shy, make him stand behind the door.'

Jason moved over to the DMI and took the torch from him. There was just enough light to see the amazed expression on the DMI's face. 'Sir, you and I must leave before Hitman brings Rabilal out. I don't want him to see me before he gets into a vehicle.'

'Dear God above! What a performance!' breathed the Brigadier, half to himself and half to Jason.

On dry land again, the DMI said, 'Let's have a brew before we move off. Rabilal for one will certainly appreciate one. I know I will and I'm sure you will also.'

'And how, sir.'

'Captain Rance, come over here to one side and tell me about your extraordinary performance, which was like nothing I've ever seen before. I wish I could have understood what you said to him. I had no idea whatsoever that you were a ventriloquist. What was your message?' The Brigadier was noticeably unmilitary in his bewilderment.

Jason's reply was not what his senior officer had expected, 'Sir, I asked you to take me on trust as the Indian Army thinks such skills are "un-Sahib-like" so would be detrimental to me if it got out that I am one. I pretended we were back in Bhutan Estate in Malaya. I apologised for being rude when we first met and asked him to work for us. I said I'd meet him in a lorry on the road.'

'Extraordinary! But why did you make such an act of it?'

'He believes in shamans and shamanism. I know that he has seen shamans work in what I might call a "mystical dimension" which will wholly enter his mind as true. When he comes to properly he'll be a new man. Nothing more than that.'

'Almost unholy,' breathed the Brigadier, not realising the pun.

'He also told me that the other three had vowed to kill me, sir. It just could be an added dimension to my future, wherever that may be.'

'It might indeed,' grunted the DMI, shaking his head in wonder.

After their brew and a packet of biscuits for Rabilal everyone except Jason, the Brigadier and his ADC embussed. 'Come with me, sir, if you will, to the lorry that Rabilal's in. And may I ask you to shine the torch inside the vehicle before onto my face?'

'Certainly.'

The tailboard was open and Rabilal, feeling tons better, was sitting on one side. When Jason saw him, he feigned surprise. 'Rabilal, Rabilal. So you're really, really here. I saw you in a dream last night and here you are. Come to work for us, have you?'

Rabilal immediately recognised Jason, *those piercing blue eyes!* 'Oh, Jason sahib, yes, yes, yes. I felt you near me.' He beamed at them: *I'm here and I have proved myself to myself after all my doubts.*

'Your new boss is here. Brigadier Lambert sahib and Captain Riggs sahib of his staff. You will do everything they tell you – and be paid for it.'

Rabilal got out of the vehicle, went to the other two, joined his hands in front of him and, haltingly in English, said, 'I work. I work for you.' Then, to Jason in Gurkhali, 'I'd like to work for you even more.'

The DMI and Captain George Riggs thanked him and shook

hands. Jason heaved a deep sigh of contented relief and satisfaction at his huge gamble having turned out so happily.

'What did he say to you personally at the end?' the DMI asked.

An embarrassed Jason hesitated before saying, '"I'd like to work for you even more".'

'Would you if we gave you the chance?'

There was a long, long pause before Jason answered. 'I feel I ought to join an active battalion, sir, but I have to obey any orders I'm given.'

It was dawn when the staff car with the DMI and the ADC sitting in the back and a slightly bemused Jason in the front left Haripur. Hardly anyone in the area was any the wiser of the events of the previous night. The Brigadier looked at his watch. 'It's about a hundred miles to Cuttack. What I propose is we'll make that in one hop, get to the local military unit and borrow their cookhouse for a meal for our men and get a scratch meal for ourselves from the Officers' Mess. Once there I'll put a phone call through to announce "Fish caught".'

And after an exciting night and the swaying of the car, soon only the driver was awake.

Earlier that same day at 0500 hours Tokyo time, the Imperial Japanese Navy Communication Centre received a coded message which reported a successful conclusion of submarines I-201's and M-19's task. At 0330 hours Singapore time a similar message was received and, for the eavesdroppers in New Delhi, the message arrived at 0200 hours. Just after the DMO had reached his desk at around half past 8 his ADC took a phone call from the WEC saying that a Mauve message was waiting collection: the DMI's office had said that the DMI was out so a call to the DMO was advised. 'I'll call you back soon,' the ADC told the caller and, as he put the phone down it rang again. 'DMI here. Give me the DMO please.'

'Wait one, sir, putting you through,' and the DMO's black phone rang. *Blast it, why now?* The General picked it up. 'DMO.'

'Bert, Bill. Fish netted. On my way back' and the General stared at a silent phone. 'Hear that, Charles?'

Yes, Charles had.

'Details will be fascinating, I'm sure.'

The ADC rang the WEC and said that there was no need to deliver the message until it was called for.

15 September 1943, Singapore: Around 10 o'clock Major Fujiwara, Head of the *Fujiwara Kikan*, went to the INA office, a plain house at Number 3 Chancery Lane, about a mile from the residential area of Mount Pleasant. Saluted by the sentry at the gate he walked straight into the Operations Office. No knocking on the door for him. Sitting at the desk was Shah Nawaz, formerly a captain of 1/14 Punjab Regiment, now a Lieutenant Colonel and Operations Officer of the INA and a future Major General, who did not stand up – he was senior now and in his own army's HQ. The Japanese saluted. A lazy wave of 'hand to head' was returned. Against all Imperial Army's protocol, a chair was offered.

Offer declined.

'I've come to tell you that Rabilal Rai's submarine operation was successful …' and he broke off on seeing the bewildered look on the Indian's face.

'Ra-Rabilal's submarine operation? I'm lost. I know nothing about it. Please tell me.'

Fujiwara inwardly sighed. He knew how imperious and at times slap-dash the C-in-C, Bose-san, was – *what is the English expression I have heard? Yes, the right hand not knowing what the left hand is doing.* Keeping a straight face he said, 'First Mohan Singh-san then Bose-san wanted him to go to India and try and stop Gurkha recruiting in Darjeeling and at that other place. Only Raghavan-san can speak Malay so Bose-san made him responsible for arranging it.'

'So Rabilal is now in India?'

'Yes.'

To take the conversation away from his ignorance, Shah Nawaz changed the subject. 'Do you know that Rabilal's three friends learnt how to shoot with the Volunteers as you were moving south and are now enlisted soldiers in the INA. Tor Gul has already left for Burma but the two cousins are still here, kicking their heels.'

'Yes. Raghavan-san has all the details of Rabilal's episode,' and abruptly the Japanese officer saluted and left.

Neta-ji, why wasn't I told? Much as I admire you …

Shah Nawaz caught up with Raghavan later that day in his office near the 11-storey Cathay Building in Waterloo Road and demanded an explanation. Something seemed to worry the hairy one-time lawyer. 'I was surprised but tried not show it, not at the task as we've done it before but the Gurkha was one of a gang of four, the Tor Gul Gang who have stuck together ever since we've been here. It seems that he didn't tell them and now two of them, parachute volunteers, also want an active task. The leader, Tor Gul himself, is an NCO in the Nehru Regiment.'

'There's so much to this job you know, Nedyam-ji, starting up a new army, or rather an old army in a different guise, one is bound to get one's lines crossed. Yes, now I cast my mind back Tor Gul does ring a bell. Tell me, what language is Tor Gul and what does it mean?'

'It's Pashto for "Black Rose". I've spoken to them quite often and I've heard their story. Have you time to hear it?'

'Yes, over a cup of tea.'

That arranged, out came the story, '... and, having vowed vengeance against this Englishman Jason Rance by killing him in Kuala Lumpur, rather dramatically naming what they planned as "Operation Black Rose", "Tor Gul" in the vernacular. But he left for Britain the next day so they couldn't kill him hence instead of one particular man who they think they'll never find, anyone else, plus, plus, plus will do instead.'

'I like that. Muslim tenacity and solidarity with Gurkha guts, not that we don't have equal guts,' he added hastily.

'Find the two men for me, will you? I'd like to have a word with them.'

Raghavan grinned wolfishly. 'You'll make a fine trio!'

16 September 1943, Orissa, India: A puncture and a fuel blockage meant that the Snatch Party only reached Cuttack, where there was

a small detachment from the Bihar and Orissa Sub-Area, during the late afternoon. By then, 'enough was more than enough' and although Gurkhas go to sleep almost automatically in a moving vehicle because of having been rocked to sleep as babies, the DMI decided to spend the night there.

'An early night, Jason' – *Jason, not Rance!* – 'and an early start should get us to Ranchi by late tomorrow.'

Bed spaces were found. Rabilal refused to be parted from Jason. He refused to sleep with the soldiers and, armed with a blanket, crept into Jason's room and slept on the floor by his bed.

At dawn Hitman brought Rance a mug of tea and cocked an eye at the still-sleeping Rabilal. 'Can you get him a mug also?' His batman nodded and soon came back with a steaming mugful. 'Put it by him and wake him up.'

Hitman roused him. 'Here's a mug of tea for you.'

Rabilal looked at Jason and addressed him as *bhai*, younger brother, but before he could say anything else Hitman interpolated, 'Don't say "*bhai*" any more. You must call him "Captain sahib".'

Rabilal gasped with astonishment. 'Captain? As high as that?' and recovered his poise.

As he drank his tea he became talkative. 'Sahib, I'm so stiff I ache all over. But what a dreadful journey it was and if you hadn't rescued me … O-ho, I'd be dead.' He drained the mug, put it down and, in a gesture of confidence, said, 'Those other three I was with. We all wanted to kill you as you had called them by a swear word utterly repugnant to Muslims but after the Japanese conquered Malaya we said there was not a chance in a million that we'd meet up with you so we'd kill as many Mat Sallehs instead.' Jason understood the reference to Englishmen and also the unexplained remark of the night before. 'We even gave our plan to kill you a code name, "Operation Black Rose",' using the Hindi words *Kala Gulab*, 'because of that ugly birthmark on one side of Tor Gul's forehead ...' and he rattled on until it was time to leave. It brought back memories from 1938 that had lain dormant in Jason's mind since his father had written to him when he was at the IMA about the tattoo on the men's left shoulder.

By 7 o'clock, with chapattis and vegetables as haversack rations for the men and sandwiches for the three officers, they were on the road.

'Rabilal sticks to Jason like a leech,' George Riggs said after a while. 'Almost fanatical and there's no fanatic like a recently converted one. What will we do with him once we're in Ranchi?'

The Brigadier took his time to answer. 'George, it's all a gamble. We can't make him "public" so to speak until he has been fully debriefed and that list of contacts scrutinised. I can't yet tell how best to utilise him. I must get back to GHQ fastest. Can we leave him in Ranchi? No,' answering his own question. 'No facilities and too many busybodies so no security. And in Delhi? He only speaks his own Gurkhali and Malay. Who on earth can we use for an interpreter for a meaningful debrief, I wonder? Any ideas either of you?'

`A bolt of lightning struck Jason. *My oath. Shall I break my oath? Yes, I think I must.* 'Sir, my father whom you know about is in New Delhi. Years ago he put me under an oath about undercover work not to mention it unless I felt I had to, as well as both his Chinese and his Malay language ability are second to none and he and my mother both worked in Malaya for many years before the war. Now I feel it time I have to tell you about it. Isn't he your answer?'

'So if it's not you it's him?'

'Sir, I'm not the one to make the decision.'

They reached Ranchi with no more mishaps, thankful the long road journey was over.

PART THREE

PART THREE

1

16 September 1943, Ranchi, India: 3/1 GR had been training hard in jungle warfare tactics since July and earlier in September the CO had received secret orders that his battalion would join 80 Indian Infantry Brigade of 20 Indian Infantry Division, commanded by a one-time 1 GR officer, Major General Gracey, somewhere near Imphal. The other two battalions in the brigade were the British 1st battalion of the Devons and the 9th battalion of the 12th Frontier Force Regiment. Lieutenant Colonel Wingfield, who had commanded 3/1 GR since it was raised, re-raised in historical fact, had asked for Lieutenant Jason Rance as a reinforcement and was disappointed to learn he was not immediately available. However, the Camp Commandant, previously warned of the DMI's party's expected arrival, told him that there would be time to include Rance with the last elements of the battalion due out on the 18th.

16 September 1943, Singapore: The two cousins, Abdul Hamid Khan and Abdul Rahim Khan, now wore uniform and had been taught how to salute, not 'open-handed' as did the Indian Army but 'flat-handed' as if shading the eyes, the INA's preferred style. They were thrilled to be called to the Operations Officer. 'Do you

think that at long last we'll be given a proper job to do and get our own back? I'm fed up with waiting to learn how to be a parachutist and am looking forward to be able to do it for real. If so I can hardly stand to wait,' Abdul Hamid Kahn burbled, inaccurately but excitedly.

'You know, at one time, when that white-skinned *saitan* so hurt my kneecap I thought I'd never be able to walk or run again,' spouted Abdul Rahim Khan, 'but now I don't have any pain in it so I feel confident that I can make a safe landing without it hurting.'

'Yes, you're a fit man now, cousin. Let's go in.' They knocked on the door of the Operations Office.

'Come along in and sit down,' called out Lieutenant Colonel Shah Nawaz, feeling there'd be no indignity to his rank this once. Abruptly he asked 'Why do you want to put yourselves in danger in this way?' Before either could answer, he continued, 'oh, I know you are proud Indians ready to help us re-conquer India though you were not born there' – *must be tactful* – 'but details interest me.'

So the story came out – *just like Nedhyam Raghavan told me about that Gurkha* – '... and although there is less than any chance of ever meeting him ever again, I think meeting anyone like him will do instead' one of the cousins finished up.

'That's good enough by me. Have you any especial target in mind where you'd like to be dropped? If so I'll need to specify it so Major Fujiwara can pinpoint it when asking for air force's authority to fly you there.'

Abdul Hamid Khan wanted to get near the fighting and

Abdul Rahim Khan thought going to a hospital to encourage the wounded not to rejoin their units would be a fine thing to do.

'There's bound to be a military hospital to the rear of the fighting, probably at Dimapur, a strategic railhead and you could do a lot for us with so many people not feeling all that well,' Shah Nawaz giggled.

After a bit more chit-chat the two cousins left and Shah Nawaz started to process this new request. After all, *Bahadurs* were brave, weren't they?'

17 September 1943, Ranchi, India: Before Rance, in engineering terms, knew whether he was punched, bored or counter-sunk, he was approached by a senior major of 3/1 GR. 'Rance, thank goodness you're here. In case you didn't know, the CO has chosen you and your team to be the basis of our new Recce Platoon. Most of the battalion has left for Imphal. We are the last and we leave the day after tomorrow. I'm sorry but you'll have to drop to lieutenant.'

Jason's head was in a whirl. 'Understood, sir, but I'm honour bound to finish off the job I've found myself on.'

'Who with?'

'The DMI.'

'In that case, off you go and be quick about it.' *Big stuff for a youngster.*

Jason hurried off and found the Brigadier. 'Sir, excuse me but I simply must speak to you,' he blurted out frantically.'

'Calm down. What's the trouble?'

'Sir, it's like this ...' and he quickly explained what had

happened. 'May I make a suggestion? My Havildar, Dilbahadur Pun, is a wise old bird. He's serving on the Reserve and too old to go to war. Surely he could look after Rabilal in New Delhi?'

'There's no other way, is there? Your father and the Gurkha Havildar should be able to do what is needed. Tell the Havildar to report to my ADC.'

That done, Jason and his team reported to the officer in charge of the rear details of 3/1 GR. 'We're off in two days' time with the first batch of 9/12 FFR who are brigaded with us.'

One of the first results of having the list of the IIL contacts was to get an Indian purporting to be Rabilal Rai to contact each one in turn. 'I am Rabilal Rai who has just landed in India on a secret mission and I have a message for you from our Neta-ji to the effect that for security sake any message from now on that does not have the code words Mangal Pande in it must be taken as false.'

Mangal Pande was one of the best-known figures in India's historiography as the man who started the 'sepoy rebellion' of 1857.

20 September 1943. Singapore: Subhas Chandra Bose had been frantically busy after arriving from Japan. He'd had to show his face everywhere and to everybody. He needed to revitalise the men of the defeated Indian Army after the collapse of the first INA, become the self-imposed C-in-C for its renewal and to imprint his authority over it rather than it being under the Japanese, make an impact on the Indians he'd ordered down from 'up-country'

in his first couple of days, try to coax the recalcitrant Gurkhas and, in a way the most important. Also he felt it important, as a 'public relations' gesture, to be known or known about by as many people as possible.

Major Fujiwara was his essential link both with the Imperial Japanese Army's HQ in Tokyo and Southern Army HQ in Shonan, as he had learnt to say instead of Singapore. The first point he had taken up with him personally was the same point he had managed to get the Japanese Prime Minister to agree with, namely that his Indians were a fighting force and not a bunch of second-class men to act as labourers for the Imperial Army. That had taken considerable hammering home but was eventually agreed to, albeit reluctantly. He had been heartened when told of Rabilal Rai's escapade and delighted when confirmation of his unequivocal success and integration with various 'sleeper' agents India was transmitted.

'What else have we in that line?' he asked Lieutenant Colonel Shah Nawaz when they had a meeting on the second Monday after his arrival. Despite his apathy towards the British and his not being a Christian, the habit of the 'week-end' had not deserted him.

'I have to admit I was amazed to learn that the lad we sent by submarine had three Muslim pals linked to the IIL in Kuala Lumpur, ardently anti-British and good with rope and knife. From that description one might take them for hooligans or ruffians but to my surprise I have learnt they have been training as guerillas in the Tor Gul Gang as they call themselves since 1938. The leader is the son of Akbar Khan, the League's representative in Kuala

Lumpur, and all four came to Singapore as soon as the Japanese had taken the British surrender. The gang's boss has a birthmark on the side of his forehead like a black rose. His father, a Pashto speaker, gave him the name of Tor Gul, "Kala Gulab" to us in Urdu and "Black Rose" for English speakers. I'll have to find out from Rash Behari Bose what the Japanese words are. The other two are cousins: I have their names if you want them.'

Bose hid his impatience with his verbose subordinate and, mildly for him, asked for more particulars.

'They have been enlisted as INA jawans. Tor Gul has been posted to the Nehru Regiment and I believe he is already a lance naik, and the cousins,' here he gave their names, 'having once as children been taken up in a Kuala Lumpur Flying Club de Havilland Moth, they remembered the plane, and as youths being won over by a film showing parachutists, are keen as mustard on being dropped that way near the front and causing mayhem with those Indian soldiers not yet disposed to us.'

'They can hardly go in "blind", surely, never having been soldiers.' Bose had yet to be won over.

'Well, it's, it's …' and Shah Nawaz faltered before 'it's a long shot by cousin Abdul Hamid Khan who had a letter from a brother still in India saying that his sister's new husband, a fellow villager, had joined the 9th/12th Frontier Force Regiment. Who knows but that battalion or another of the 12th or a battalion of the 13th Frontier Force Rifles or, come to that, any Muslim battalion, could very well want another NC(E) for help in their cookhouse?'

'NC(E)? Explain yourself. That's meaningless to me.' Bose

hated having to show his ignorance and was still suspicious of such a venture.

'Oh, sorry, Sahib, NC(E) stands for Non-Combatant (Enrolled) and all Indian units have such as cooks and dry and wet sweepers.'

Bose breathed out angrily. 'Now, that's something we're sure to put a stop to,' he snapped.

Shah Nawaz nodded in agreement. *No good crossing the Boss.* 'I fully stand by that point of view. The jobs have to done by someone and the only thing in its favour is that the man gets paid for it.'

Bose made a moue of partial agreement although he doubted that the Japanese would agree to a demand for such a low-level undertaking. He gave vent to a sigh of nothing being straightforward. 'Our request will have to avoid all mention of anything menial. So how does the man operate after he's been dropped *if* the Japanese will be willing to drop him and where?'

Heavy weather, this. 'Sahib, those details will be up to you to fix. But the purpose is to try and convince those soldiers to come over to us. And what's more important than that?'

'Let's have a cup of tea and while they're making it tell me about the other cousin, Abdul Rahim Khan?'

Shah Nawaz went to the door and told the office runner what was wanted. 'And bring some biscuits.'

Serious matters were set aside as the two men sipped and munched. Business resumed with Shah Nawaz describing how the second cousin saw his task. 'He feels he can find work in a hospital not far from the fighting. Badly wounded and really sick men will be sent back to India but the not so badly wounded and lesser men will be returned to their units. During their time in a forward hospital, where I expect they're always short-handed, he'll have a wonderful chance to sow dissent.'

'Yes, I like it, in principle,' the C-in-C declared after mature consideration. 'How best to plan it?'

'I've thought of that, too. Let's tell the Japanese that Operation "Black Rose" is your brainchild. You have two men who have trained themselves in the Malayan jungles for such a job since they were at school five years ago. They "held their noses" and worked with the Volunteers, learning how to handle rifles and shoot on the range. Elementary tactics were also covered. Each man will have an ID card and pay book from one of our INA men who has joined the *Bahadur*s and after they have been dropped, they'll report as having been ill on their way out of Burma, nursed by villagers and, rather than return to India, stayed on. The damned English are credulous enough to believe their "loyal sepoys",' emphasised with heavy sarcasm, 'would do just that.'

Subhas slapped his knee and laughed. 'Great. I'll talk to Major Fujiwara and impress on him how very much I'm in favour of Operation "Black Rose" and get him equally interested. It may take some time for sanction to come through. Until it does, let the two men work in the Operations Room to get a good understanding of necessary background as well as mixing with the Indians, but not the Gurkhas I think, and learn how to salute properly and Indian Army words of command, such as "Stand at ease" and whatever else is in fashion.'

'Chief sahib, you always were full of sensible ideas,' came the sycophantic answer.

'I have another idea. When the two cousins drop, let's arrange that some leaflets are also dropped. Look here,' and taking a piece of paper out of his pocket, he showed Shah Nawaz the draught of one. 'I had this made up,' he said modestly as the Colonel looked at it. It began, 'Fearless Indian soldier, the ruthless British have sent you to fight your Asian brothers. Do you wish to remain their slaves? An army of free India is here in Burma, preparing to march on Delhi. Come join us! Death, death to the English!' and there was a picture of a Sikh clutching his rifle, looking fiercely into the distance. An elephant, the tricolour painted on its side, tosses with its trunk a startled and helpless John Bull.[7]

'Marvellous,' breathed Shah Nawaz in awe.

'I've given an order for a few thousand to be printed. I'll try and get a bag that opens in the air for them when the cousins drop and they can carry some themselves, easily hidden … by strapping them in a thin wodge on their back under their shirt.'

And the Chief's order was carried out.

Talk with Major Fujiwara the C-in-C did. Against his better judgement, the *Hikari Kikan* commander passed a request through to Imperial Japanese Army's *Chuo Kikan*. In a country as autocratic as Japan the only thing more dangerous than revealing your own ignorance is to draw attention to the stupidity of those senior to you. That was now working in reverse: because Fujiwara knew he'd never convince Bose or his officers that they

---

7 Quoted from an actual leaflet.

were asking too much it would count against him it would be far better for the INA people to learn from experience just how little their soldiers really did know or could achieve with their improvised command structure however dedicated Bose and his highly over-promoted officers might be.

15 October 1943, near Tamu, Assam, Northeast India: From Ramgarh the journey to the battlefront was slowed by poor roads, a narrow-gauge railway and river crossings needing steamers As the battalion met a range of wild, jungle-covered mountains, rising in places to twelve thousand feet, Jason thought of 'Vinegar' Joe Stillwell's words about the terrain. Indeed, he saw a confusion of high, steep sided ridges separated by deep valleys. He knew that when the Japanese invaded Burma in 1942 it was over those mountains that the retreating army and civilians had fled. The road, not built for army traffic so needing constant repair, climbed five thousand feet from Dimapur, through Bishenpur to Kohima and another thousand feet before beginning the descent into the Imphal plain, which was surrounded on all sides by mountains. Imphal, the capital of Manipur, about a hundred air miles from Dimapur but many more by road and its surrounding villages, became the crux of the Burmese war and had the Japanese captured 'the oval of flatter ground' they would have had masses of stores and the INA would have had more than a toe-hold in India. Touch and go for some nail-biting weeks, it was touched and went for the Japanese and their INA comrades-in-arms.

In the first ten days of October 3/1 GR waited for further orders and there being no enemy activity to deal with, the battalion 'found its wartime feet': Jason and his men melded into the unit. On the 15th the battalion marched off as advanced guard to 80 Brigade, bound for the village of Tamu on the India-Burma frontier. Tamu was at the head of the Kabaw Valley, itself separated from the River Chindwin to its east by a range of low hills.

The battalion moved twenty more miles east and made a 'defensive harbour' at Pyinbon Sakan and spent the rest of the year there in outpost and reserve areas in turn consolidating its jungle-warfare training until battle drills and procedures became instinctive for whatever the Japanese threw at it. This gave Lieutenant Jason Rance ample chance of training his Recce Platoon, now properly constituted, in the type of jungle he would have to operate in. His knowledge of fieldcraft, honed over the years, was the nearest thing to perfection his CO had ever seen in a young officer. *He'll do us proud if he's not too headstrong* was his opinion.

Between the 4th and 20th of November the Nehru Regiment started moving by rail up through Malaya as far north as the line went then marched all the way up through Rangoon, northwards towards a small village named Tamu not far from the Indo-Burma border, a four-month foot journey. They would only reach their operational area by late March 1944 and would be ready to fight by mid-April. Wearing only Khaki Drill shorts, there being no uniform trousers available, the men found the journey uncomfortable and cold during the winter months.

Lance Naik Tor Gul, his paler skin darkened by the sun but

his birthmark still visible, was finding the going tough. Unlike the Indian Army soldiers he was with he had no qualms about breaking an oath of loyalty to the *Sarkar* as he had, of course, never taken one.

October 1943, Malaya: It was also in this month that British personnel in Changi jail were sent up to work on the Death Railway in Siam. When he heard that stores from Singapore were to be ferried up as far as possible by rail QMJ Rahul Dura, now with some use in his fingers, remembered what he had told the Japanese when in Penang. He sought out Subedar Narbahadur Gurung. 'Subedar sahib, the Japanese are sedulously cajoling Chinese and Tamil coolies and our NC(E) Indian mess-waiters, water-carriers and sweepers to help move stores on the railway. This is our chance to escape.'

'QMJ sahib, I am of the same opinion as you. But can you trust the Japanese? Their minds work differently from ours: what is good for them is bad for us but even so what is good for us could be bad for them. It is dangerous for us because it could be a trap and because after the British and Indians have won it could well be seen as working for the enemy so fatal for us. We just can't be like those Jiffs. In all fairness, we must tell the Subedar Major before you approach Major Fujiwara.'

The QMJ agreed but the Subedar Major did not. 'I dare not let two Gurkha officers try and get away at the same time. It would do no good whatsoever for the sepoys' morale.'

The argument went to and fro and finally it was fixed that Jemadar Rahul Dura and one soldier, a short, squat but massively strong man from his own village, Naik Lalsing Dura, would have their names put forward. There was something special about Lalsing, a good-looking man who wore his frown of intensity as though it were a badge of office: the QMJ didn't know what was behind it was but it been there ever since his birth when, as was the custom, his mother had been taken to the cow shed in the last stages of her confinement where it was quieter than in the house. The men folk, including the father, knew to keep away. It was a Tuesday evening in early November in the Year of the Tiger, 1914, making him thirty, not twenty-nine, since Gurkhas count their years of age from one, not zero. The onset of winter had brought the snowline of the great white Himalayan masses down so low that even in the more sheltered valley it was cold. Yet his mother was sweating copiously, her clothes rank and dishevelled. Squatting near her were some village women, watching and waiting anxiously, especially the one nearest to her, the new midwife, also tired but still fully alert, with some hot water in a bowl. With the back of her hand she pushed a loose lock of stray hair from her face as she set to work. A shaft of light from a blood red sky shone on the two women at the very time the baby was born. 'It's a boy, it's a boy,' the onlookers chorused softly, happy for the family. But they were filled with dread because any baby born on a Tuesday of that particular month – only once every twelve years when the Tiger ruled the zodiac, especially in the evening with the sunset a blaze of red glory – was destined to be a mortal danger to both parents and also to anyone who crossed his path.

'I still don't like it all that much.' The Subedar Major shook his head slowly before continuing, 'yet I'd like to think you'd get to Bhagsu and tell everybody there what we've been going through and your helping the Japani is merely a cover plan. I am sure that the *Sarkar* will eventually win and your evidence of their cruelty, to say nothing of what the INA have been up to, will be of great importance. Despite the danger to you if you go, it is too good a chance to miss. It is better that I myself will fix a meeting with Major Fujiwara direct, so can bypass all those INA functionaries.'

The upshot was that the move was allowed – it had been expected earlier – but, as 'cover', the two Gurkhas were being sent to gather up those Gurkhas still thought to be in the Kuala Lumpur area. They were given officially stamped documents, signed by the Commander of Southern Army's Chief of Staff, authorising their movement north 'as far as the railway can take them.'

So the two Gurkhas left, with no regrets but with no clear idea either as how they would manage when they got to wherever Fate would send them. They had heard that there were some Gurkha settlements in Burma and to reach one of those was as good an aim as any.

Crossing the bridge over the Singapore River on their way to the railway station they saw heads of decapitated Chinese, mostly Triad gang members although they did not know that, stuck on poles. They presumed they were warnings as well as Japanese ideas of decorations. It sickened both men but armed with those two precious pieces of paper they felt safe not to be taken as Chinese themselves although they were dressed in plain clothes. They knew well of Chinese hatred of Japanese – 'monkey men' they knew them as – whose punishments were what they themselves had suffered, included executions on an unimaginable scale. Chinese could eat grass for all the Japanese cared. Some Chinese, it was whispered, had been driven to buying human flesh at night in hidden markets so hungry were they.

At the station they were taken to a siding where stores were lined up for loading. There was an INA Sikh havildar organising a group of recalcitrant coolies and the two Gurkhas decided not to have anything to do with him while they were still so near INA HQ. At last the loading was finished and it was a toss-up whether to try and ride in the guard's van and be under INA suspicion or go in one of the carriages. They decided on the latter and managed to squeeze into a massively overcrowded cattle truck. The many hours of almost unbearable jolting and raw, sweating humanity, fetid breath, soiled underpants and unrelenting stench, were almost unbearable – but had to be borne. The normal time a train took to reach Kuala Lumpur, halfway up the peninsula, was about twelve hours. At Gemas, south of Seremban, Japanese guards and the Sikh Havildar walked down beside the train. Ululations of protest greeted them – the wretched coolies were thirsty, hungry and wanted to get down to make themselves comfortable, but to no avail. The Havildar saw the two Gurkhas and beckoned, making gestures for them to get off the train.

'Havildar, I am not in any way under your command and am going to see the senior Japanese on the train,' Jemadar Rahul Dura sternly told him, 'It is none of your concern. Where we were is simply not good enough for us on government business' and with that the two Gurkhas made their way to the guard's van where the senior Japanese looked at the passes, saw they were genuine and let them travel in it.

Given a seat each they were greatly relieved to be able to travel in more comfort than before. The train trundled on, stopped at Kuala Lumpur, not in the main station but in a siding, where a Japanese guard allowed the coolies to get down. So stiff were they that this took much longer than had been expected and resulted in the Japanese moving into the trucks and bodily lifting, then throwing, the wretched men to the ground. Slops were given them to eat. The Tamils were more cowed than the Chinese, one of whom tried to run away. He was shot and left to die where he fell.

The Japanese officer in charge of stores to be loaded had had news of the two Gurkhas and showed them what had to be loaded into some empty goods wagons that were joined on to the train. It took the rest of the night to arrange and both of them were exhausted when the train moved off for Prai around dawn.

At Prai half a truck load of coolies were taken off and guided to a ferry to take them across to Penang harbour, the two Gurkhas went with them to find that their next task was to supervise the loading of stores stacked on the quay side into a small coastal steamer. That took a couple of days. The boat, with the Gurkhas but no coolies, left and three days later, after hugging the coast, docked – but where?

The hill men looked over the railings at a small town, much poorer than any they had seen in Malaya. The people dressed differently and many wore orange-coloured robes, Buddhist monks, which the Gurkhas recognised as they too were Buddhists. 'Where are we now?' the QMJ asked one of the crew, a Goan, a small, dry man with a scarred brow and shiny grey-black eyes.

'Martaban.'

'Where?'

'Mar-ta-ban,' came the answer, the deck hand talking as though the Gurkha was an unlettered child.

'And where's that?' Naik Lalsing Gurung asked, unperturbed by the other man's sarcasm, replying in Hindi.

'Burma.' The sailor peered at the Gurkha. 'I've seen many men like you around here, or I did before they were all put in jail.' A shifty look came into his eyes. 'I'll take you ashore if you want to go.' *And get a reward for turning you over to our new Overlords.*

'Jemadar sahib, this looks like a good place to leave these *banchoots* and make out own way from now on from what he says.'

The QMJ had been sizing the man up. 'I don't trust him. Say "no" and we'll make our own way off the boat when it's dark.'

However at dusk a warning of an air raid by British bombers made the boat move to a small island where the crew skilfully and quickly covered it with camouflage nets. Bombs were dropped nearby but the boat was not hit. A load of Japanese soldiers was ferried over the next day and the boat sailed back to Penang where the Gurkhas, much to their utter disgust, were frustratingly kept hard at work until the end of the year when they were suddenly taken over to Prai on the mainland with a load of railway stores and told they were to be taken as far as north as possible on the Siamese railway.

15 January 1944, Siam: The two Gurkhas were glad to be on the move after so much immobility. They had, by now, learnt basic Japanese yet their knowledge of geographical details was woefully sketchy. Nevertheless, it was with a spurt of adrenalin that their train started off just after dark. It was too dangerous from allied air attack for the Japanese to move their trains in the daylight. It came as a definite shock when, at the Siam-Malay border, they were greeted by heavy rifle fire and the train came to a sudden stop as though it had run into a block, which is what had happened. On an impulse born of taking every opportunity to get away from the Japanese and on the excuse of 'going to see if we can help', they slipped away from the wagon they were in and by the light of the engine they saw thick jungle to the east of the line. They dived into it and moved up a hill. From between the trees they could just make out the Japanese military escort attacking where the fire was coming from. Screams and yells filled the air before gradually dying down. 'What now, Sahib?' asked Naik Lalsing.

Before his question was answered there was a pounding of feet coming towards them and, cowering down where they were, could not get out of the way of someone who tripped head first over the Naik. A thump, a scuffle and, in what sounded like Chinese, another voice from behind curtly asked 'Nippon? Japan?' and shone a torch on the three writhing bodies, each of which was trying to extricate itself.

Bodies separated and the three men stood up. A torch was flashed on the two Gurkhas and the same question was asked. Lalsing quickly said 'Gurkha, Gurkha, no no Japan, Gurkha.'

'Ku-la-ka?' was asked hesitantly.

Ku-la-ka? 'Yes, Ku-la-ka,' and to both Gurkhas' relief the man with the torch came forward with his hand outstretched to be shaken. Then 'Gu-la-ka' was repeated and the man pointed his index finger upwards and, smiling, pointed in front of him. The two Gurkhas were, somewhat naturally, baffled.

The two escapees were Chinese and beckoned the Gurkhas to follow them: expertly they wove their way through the trees for about an hour, slowly, silently, before coming to a camp, well hidden in the jungle. A challenge came from a sentry, an answering password was given and the four men went inside the protected area. Candles were lit once they were inside a room where they saw a flag that had an emblem on it which meant nothing to the men from Nepal: it was a white inner circle and a blue outer circle on which were twelve thin white points.

A middle-aged man with spectacles came in and spoke to the two Chinese, obviously enquiring who these new strangers were. Once more was 'Ku-la-ka' heard and an order was given. Soon, to the two Gurkhas' amazement, another Gurkha came in, with manly gait and undaunted confidence. They recognised him as Rifleman Manbir Gurung who everybody had though had been squashed when Havildar Parsuram Thapa made his suicidal leap at that Japanese tank. He had been knocked unconscious and after coming round had moved off north by himself. Chinese guerillas had come across him, given him succour and allowed him to stay with them. Now, after a spontaneous reunion, there was no language problem because by now Manbir could speak Chinese. The guerillas were Nationalists who, although Siamese-domiciled, were actively working against the Japanese by doing as much harm to them as the Japanese had done to the Chinese.

An agreement was reached: 'stay here, be fed and accommodated by us and teach us tactics of ambush and tracking, weapon training and proper camp defence for six months until the end of next April and we will take all three of you by secret ways into Burma and,' showing them on a map, 'put you on the road on the Siam-Burma border. From there we suggest you move west using Mount Popa as a landmark. It is a sacred place and you can relax in a temple if you're tired until either you're fresh enough to continue or from what we hear the Indian and British army troops come as far south as there. You'll be safe then.'

Over a lifetime of working with good men and good British officers, often against people he considered his inferiors, Jemadar Rahul Dura had developed a diagnostic fluency for detecting men's loyalty, convictions and faith. Life with the Japanese and Jiffs had sharpened those perceptions. He instinctively trusted his new captors, for that was what they were. There was no alternative and the deal was accepted. Luckily Naik Lalsing Thapa was a low-level tactical expert and a cunning killer: the QMJ was no slouch either.

28 February 1944, GHQ New Delhi: The red light in the Wireless Experimental Centre flashed. 'Here we go again,' said the Duty Operator. 'Let's see how much they've got to tell us this time.'

It was a long transmission from Singapore to Tokyo, which was carefully copied. 'Call the translators. It's their turn for a spot of concentrated work.'

Lieutenant Hector Mason was on duty on his own as his fellow translator was having a day off. The message was another request from the INA: Personal from Commander-in-Chief for Operation 'Kuroi Bara' – Black Rose – a plane to drop two men by parachute, one near Tamu and the other near Dimapur for sabotage work.

Mason got up and went to look at a map hanging on his wall, glad to be able to stretch his legs. He didn't know how much fighting there was around those two places at the moment – *probably none in Dimapur*– although he thought it was quiet for a change but the Japanese were in no way exhausted and not much had gone right for the allies so far. *And now the INA Jiffs are poking their noses in.*

Mason locked his translation in his safe as there was no immediate hurry for it to be delivered to the DMI with no urgent time factor as there had been with the submarine case. He looked at his watch, *not much more time before I'm relieved.*

Another buzz made him go back to the window. 'Only a shorty this time;' said the operator, 'and here it is.'

Hector went back to his office. The transmission read, 'Request being considered. No early answer likely.'

His relief came in and Hector showed him what he had just decoded and translated and also told him about the other transmission now in the safe. 'Before I go I think I'd better give the DMI a ring on his red and tell him there's no hurry.'

Captain George Riggs would collect the message as soon as he was available.

20 March 1944, GHQ New Delhi: 'There's no peace for the wicked,' said the Duty Operator. 'Roll on Civvy Street,' as the red light in the WEC started flashing its warning of a new transmission. He had been writing a letter to his young wife, hurriedly married on Embarkation Leave, with 'time so precious, unwanted' as they waited for his train at the station, neither of them knowing quite what to say. He had put SWALK on the back of the envelope, meaning 'sealed with a loving kiss'.

Concentrating hard, for he was a conscious man, he copied the signal and called Lieutenant Mason. 'Your turn now, sir,' he said as he handed the copy through the counter and asked for a signature.

Hector Mason dutifully translated and the message. It concerned Operation 'Kuroi Bara' and that authority had been given for a Kawasaki aircraft to drop both men as requested. The plane would continue and bomb Shillong in Assam before making a circuitous return. The targets there were the State Governor's residence, a military hospital, a large reinforcement centre and a Gurkha depot. Whether the Japanese knew that a battalion of the King's African Rifles was under training there was not divulged. The two men were ordered to stand by from 25 March. Depending on weather conditions, the operation would take place as near dawn as possible the following day. One run only would be made, at an angle of 355 degrees on a line Tamu-Dimapur. Each man's all-up weight was not to be above 110 kilograms. If either man was overweight he would be left behind: there would be no second chance.

There was a textbook of Japanese aircraft in the office and Hector looked up the Kawasaki range. There he found two likely carriers, both twin-engined medium bombers, the Ki 2, code named Sally, and the Ki 48, code named Lily. The latter, Hector judged from looking at the pay load, was probably not the one being sent, *but really that's none of my business*. For interest he also looked at Tamu on the map. *Hilly and wooded. Not easy. What'll the poor fellow do if he gets stuck in a high tree, I wonder. Will friend Jason be anywhere in the area to catch either of them?* and he unconsciously gave a hollow laugh at such an absurd impossibility.

He put a call through to the DMI's office's red telephone: 'A Mauve for collection, sir, with dates on.'

Veiled speech asked when; 'in five days' was the answer.

Reading the message a bell rang 'loud and clear' when the DMI came to the operational code word, translated into 'Black Rose'. *No names. Surely the two can't be those of the two cousins that Captain Rance had given him? Doubtful: surely even the ruddy Jiffs wouldn't be so stupid as to send such untrained men, and not military men at that, on such a dangerous operation? But why not? Their way isn't ours. It was a long, long shot but that did not invalidate the target. In a way, 'better safe than sorry'.* He looked at his watch, half-past 10, put a call through to the Red Fort where the Combined Services Detention and Interrogation Centre and the Indian Secret Service were based. The former's main job, interrogation of Japanese POWs, was where Havildar Dilbahadur Pun and Rabilal Rai were comfortably ensconced. Philip Rance, now a major and still feeling slightly bogus wearing uniform, was also based there. For security reasons, only Royal Corps of Signals men were used as switchboard operators.

'CSDIC here.'

'Please contact me with Major Rance.'

'Your name, please.'

'Brigadier Lambert, the DMI.'

'Hold on please, sir. I'll call his number.'

The DMI heard the ringing tone and was just about to give up when 'Major Rance speaking,' came down the line.

'It's Brigadier Lambert calling. I'd like to have a *tête-à-tête* with you at your earliest convenience. When's that?'

'Oh, um, Brigadier, as soon as I can get transport.'

'Any available just now?'

'No.'

'Right-ho. I'll send my staff car around. Be outside the main gate in figures 20.'

Philip Rance smiled to himself: *figures 20 indeed!*

In the DMI's office the two men talked about the Mauve message's contents. 'I happen to know that 3/1 GR is about twenty miles to the east of Tamu and your son is now in that battalion. This is a million to one chance, Philip, that he is the one man who even if he can't recognise either man will know their background if, and a very big if, Dame Fortune rolls us a "double six". What we must not do,' emphasising the words, 'is to let anyone know how we got the information when we pass any message on without thoroughly disguising it.'

'Brigadier, I agree with you but, small though the chance is, it can't be wasted. I wonder how best to tackle it.'

The DMI rubbed his chin as he thought. 'Look. Why not go back and get an up-to-date description of the two cousins from

Rabilal Rai. I know that the Rance family has met them but there might just be something that he can give you to help you to help your son. Get him to describe each man and then I'll get the Chief's permission to fly you into the nearest strip near Tamu and brief CO 3/1 GR and, if possible, young Jason. Are you ready for that?'

'Indeed so. I'll enjoy it and it'll be great to meet my boy again. He seems to be doing well.'

'Aye. He's good value. I'll get the Chief to send a signal to General Gracey asking him to co-operate. Can you leave the day after tomorrow? It'll take me till then to fix up matters.'

'Sir, I can be at Palam airport any time you wish me on the 22nd.'

The DMI nodded. 'Thanks Major, I appreciate your attitude. Fingers and toes crossed for success in what I see as their Operation "Black Rose" with us using their same code word.'

20 March 1944. Singapore: Major Fujiwara Iwaichi came into Lieutenant Colonel Shah Nawaz's office and, with a bland expression on his face, saluted. 'I have an important message Nawaz-san for you. The parachute drop you asked for has been approved. HQ Southern Army here in Shonan have been slow: they so want it to be a success that once permission came through they especially dyed two 'chutes green, the better not to be seen by the enemy.' *And it's the last time you'll get anything like this. If an air raid in northwest Assam had not been planned with the same aircraft the answer would have been no.*

Shah Nawaz was greatly pleased with the idea of green parachutes: *just the right colour for the two Muslims.* 'Oh, wonderful news! That really is forethought, Chalo Delhi,' he said, getting up from his chair and proffering his hand to the Japanese. Fujiwara had learnt that the English custom of such manual contact had remained with the INA. 'Sit down and tell me everything. I'll get us a cup of tea to help our thinking.'

And so the details were given. 'How big is a Ki-2?' asked Nawaz, wishing he knew already.

Not wanting to lose face as he also didn't know, the Liaison Officer merely said, 'Big enough, otherwise permission would not have been granted. Oh yes, because the plane has to go on to Assam means that the pilot will make only one run over the target area and drop the two men as and when he has calculated their exact spot.'

'Will he be one of those who have done our previous parachute operations, do you think?'

Really these Indians can be exasperating. 'I can't tell you but I am sure the planners in Tokyo will get their most experienced crew for the task. It needs high skill for such a delicate undertaking like this.'

Shah Nawaz felt a slight rebuke so relapsed into silence as he sipped his tea.

'It so happens that I have done some parachute exits,' he didn't say 'jump' as that was the wrong bodily motion. 'Please call your two men in and hand them over to me. An exercise framework is at the air base for them to get some idea of what to do.'

'What shall we tell them to take with them?'

'Good point. There's an individual weight restriction of 110 kilograms. That means only a minimum load: a change of clothing, all government-issue if possible. Possibly not for underpants and vest. A packet of biscuits and a slab of chocolate or raisins. Oh yes, a clasp knife but no weapon. If they are overweight the plane won't be able to take off so one man will be left on the ground. I've been told that there's no second chance, now or later.'

Nawaz shut his eyes to picture what that meant. 'How can they wear a pack and a parachute?' he asked. 'Surely the one will get in the way of the other?'

'No, the pack is carried in a separate container which, in turn, is secured to the man's parachute harness.' *Really this man knows nothing outside his narrow infantry battalion work.*

The two cousins were sent for and Shah Nawaz told them that operation had been sanctioned adding, 'How lucky you've had such a time to learn the background to the troops you will be meeting.' The Japanese Major said, 'Before I take you to Kallang airfield one thing you must know. HQ Southern Army has been informed what British and Indian units are in the target area. You'd better remember them as it could be your password to acceptance. The British battalion is known as First Devons, the Indian is 9/12 Frontier Force Regiment and the Gurkha unit is 3/1 Gurkha Rifles. The Indian battalion is to the east of the Gurkhas and west of the British battalion.'

Abdul Hamid butted in with 'Just before all mail stopped I had a letter from my elder sister's husband in India telling me that he had joined the 9/12 Frontier Force Regiment and so I could state I was trying to contact him.'

'That is useful,' came Shah Nawaz's riposte. 'Do you know his name?'

Hamid took the letter out of his pocket and read it again. 'Yes, sahib, Muhammad Taki Khan.'

Shah Nawaz laughed. 'That's the same name as the famous cavalry commander of, oh, nearly two hundred years ago. He was beaten by the British. Now's your chance to get your own back. I'll get you documented as having served in 1/14 Punjab Regiment, that's my battalion. As you know me you can talk about me so appear genuine. In fact I can get you a pay book and ID card of a man of your name. All you need to do is to remember his number, village and other such relevant details. And you, Abdul Rahim?'

'I have no such contacts but I'll need to go as a medical orderly. Can you, sir, get me an ID card and a pay book to take with me?'

He could and did but it never occurred to him to ask if Abdul Rahim knew what the initials, IAMC, stood for. Neither would 'Indian Army Medical Corps' have struck any chord with its new soldier.

The Colonel then gave each of them a flat package. 'Inside these are some leaflets to distribute to Indian Army soldiers to help them make their minds up to switch sides. A couple of bundles will be dropped with each of you so the men you don't meet will get the same message.'

'We will guard them most carefully,' one of the cousins averred.

At the airfield there was a mock-up of an aeroplane's door almost at ground level, a platform from which a rope was suspended to help the man go through the motions of trying to steer the parachute and a fibre mat to practise rolling on when the ground was hit. These last two were more of a morale booster than for real use as the descent would be too dark and too quick to see where to try and steer away from or towards, while preparing one's body for landing in the dark was almost impossible. Both cousins were thrilled that, at long last, they were getting ready for what they had wanted to do for oh so many years.

One of the few men trained for parachute operations by the German Military Attaché in Tokyo when war broke out was ready for them. They were shown the training aids. 'It is quite simple,' translated the Major, 'watch the exit demonstration,' and he barked an order to his soldier. The man stood in the mock-up door with his right foot overlapping the edge, the other leg behind, one hand flat on the inside of the fuselage with the other over the stomach and back straight. 'A red light above your head will mean "get ready for exit" as you stand in the door. When a green light comes on you step out, bringing the rear foot forward and using both legs for momentum. There will be what we call a "dispatcher" who will hold you steady and tap you on the shoulder as an added signal to leave the aeroplane.'

The two Indians absorbed that while the soldier showed them how a few times. 'Now it's your turn. One by one,' and they practised it. It soon came to them easily.

'You will be dropped from about 250 metres so there will be only about twenty seconds in the air.'

One of the cousins interrupted him. 'Excuse me but we only

know feet not metres. How high is that in feet?'

Fujiwara's face didn't alter but inwardly he cursed. Luckily, having operated in Malaya for so long he soon gave them the answer. 'About 800 feet. As you reach the ground try to land like a spring with your feet and knees tightly together then roll like a wheel. Watch,' and at the end of the demonstration added 'Whatever else keep you head tucked into your chest.'

'Next on the list is the container you put your kit in. For that we give you an issue bag into which you put your haversack. You tie it round your body and secure it to your leg. In the air you pull this quick-release pin,' showing it to them, 'and let the bag swing below you.'

Relaxing at the end the Japanese Major had one most important point for them. 'You must hide everything less your personal stuff just as quickly as you can. There may not be all that time at your disposal. But where? In the bushes out of sight is one answer, drown it in a river is another, at the back of a cave is a third but supposing there're none of those? Your only option is to dig a hole and bury it, leaving as few traces as possible. It is for that reason I'm going to issue you with a small spade. Once you have got rid of your kit and thrown away the spade, get out of the immediate area and only once you are sure no one is looking for you start on your task, otherwise,' in a theatrically rasping voice, 'you'll be dead meat.'

The two cousins tried to visualise what they had been told. 'Happy now are you?' the Major asked. 'Any points you'd like to ask me?'

'What happens if we get stuck in a tree, Fujiwara-san?' asked

Hamid.

'That's something we've also thought of. The rope your container hangs from is 24 feet long. Tie one end to a branch and climb down.' Both cousins nodded appreciatively.

Major Fujiwara sincerely wanted the Indians to be their own masters in India so tried to be helpful. 'What is your plan if you're caught?' he asked.

Startled looks were the answer he thought he'd get. *Haven't thought of one, obviously.* 'I have an idea. Listen to what I suggest.' He had both men's full attention. 'You'll be dressed in British uniform, won't you?' Nods of 'yes'. 'So you are British Indian Army on a secret mission sent by parachute so that any Jiffs,' said scornfully, 'that might be lurking around will make contact with you and the British will the easier capture them.' A glow of appreciation at that cunning showed on both cousins' face. 'You will be interrogated and you'll have to say that details were rushed and anyway you were not responsible for the planning of the operation, only doing it.'

For once Major Iwaichi of the *Hikari Kikan* was not up to date: when the Indian Army men were captured they were dressed in Khaki Drill shirts and shorts. Now the uniform was shirts and long trousers coloured olive green. If their mission were real, that would be what they would be wearing: anything else would be sure to invite suspicion. None of them knew the proverb 'for want of a nail a kingdom was lost'.

Before they turned in for the night Hamid turned to Rahim and said, 'Cousin, what we have been told is that I go out first. That means we will say goodbye on the plane.'

'Well, let's hope it's not goodbye forever and that we are both successful. Chalo Delhi.'

20 March 1944, GHQ New Delhi: In the Red Fort Major Philip Rance was talking to Rabilal Rai. 'Rabilal, can you remember when you first saw me?'

'Tuan, it would be in the middle of last month, I think.'

'Are you sure?'

A tiny, tiny something nagged at the back of the Gurkha's mind but it was too shadowy to get a hold of. 'I think so.'

'Do you know the name of the man who lifted you out of the water before you could have drowned?'

'Yes. Jason Rance.'

'I am his father and it was I who spoke to you in the Police Station after you had tried to burgle that hut of mine at the back of my garden.'

A gasp of horror escaped from Rabilal's lips. 'Tuan, no, no. It couldn't have been yours.'

'But it was. Don't worry, that incident is long ago but what I want now is you to tell me anything about those two cousins in the Tor Gul Gang, not the "mawar hitam" himself. Can you describe them to me?'

'Tuan, yes. Abdul Hamid Khan and Abdul Rahim Khan are both tough and useful with knife and rope. The former has one ear larger than the other and his knee hurt when Jason sahib attacked us and the latter's Adam's apple is protrudingly triangular and his feet are turned out as he walks. Both speak good English.' *Yes, that's how I remember them.* 'They are anti-

British and pretending to be anti-Japanese joined the Volunteers to learn weapon training, range work and minor tactics.

'And Tuan, when we were in Police custody, we vowed vengeance on your son by killing him because he had insulted us and foiled our attempt to revenge ourselves against the British. Since it seemed so unlikely that we'd him ever meet again we vowed vengeance on any Mat Salleh. We even called our plan Operation "Tor Gul" after our leader's nickname and birthmark. Of course they are taller and stronger than they were. They have been enlisted as soldiers of the INA.'

And now I'm being called to help my son in what is a reverse Operation 'Black Rose', Philip thought with a grim chuckle.

The phone rang. It was the DMI. 'There's a plane with a spare seat leaving for Dimapur in ninety minutes time. You're booked on that and will spend one night there before moving off on the morrow. I am sending my car now so get ready,' and before Peter had time even to draw breath, the line went dead.

He got up, thanked the two Gurkhas and saying he had another job, he departed in a hurry.

25 March 1944. Singapore: A signal, sent the previous day from the *Choho* branch of the Imperial Japanese Army's *Chuo Kikan* to the Southern Army HQ in Singapore, which, of course, was also picked up in Delhi, caused great excitement when it reached the INA office at Number 3 Chancery Lane.

'Tell the two cousins that their aircraft is shortly arriving and they must report to Kallang airfield at 1400 hours tomorrow for familiarisation of a Ki 2 aircraft before emplaning for their secret task,' Shah Nawaz excitedly told the office runner, 'and that I want them here with their kit as soon as they can get ready.' *They would never have been enlisted in the old Indian Army but they're certainly good enough for us.*

The two men soon came and gave a salute, exclaiming 'Jai Hind' and were answered by 'Chalo Delhi'. The atmosphere was tenser than normal: the whole escapade was risky and hadn't Neta-ji said more than once that 'blood maybe freedom's price'? Shah Nawaz seemed to have forgotten that, as far as the two cousins were concerned, they were Malayan not Indian citizens.

All orders from Tokyo were taken as having come from the Emperor personally so, although privately the crew were not too happy to undertake such a mission, nothing could ever be said against it and undertaken it would be. Apart from there being hardly any room for movement even without two extra bulky parachutists to be clipped on to the static line, the accuracy of direction of flight with outside winds not being able to be measured and the subsequent onward journey to bomb Shillong meant immense concentration by the four crew, the pilot, co-pilot, navigator, who would also act both as bomb aimer and dispatcher, and the flight engineer; if enemy fighters or anti-aircraft fire imperilled the mission, it would have to be aborted. Sorry! Even so, each prayed to their personal *kami* spirit to be extra careful for them.

Major Fujiwara and Lieutenant Colonel Shah Nawaz took the two cousins to Kallang and introduced them to the crew. The dispatcher's job was to ensure that the two men's harness and parachute were in order, to open the door of the aircraft shortly before the target was reached and to let them know when the green light was on as they would be looking straight ahead so not see it. The flight time would be a little over four hours, exactly how long depending on the wind.

Having looked round the plane from the outside, the cousins climbed the ladder into the fuselage and were shown where to sit and how to 'stand in the door' in the correct position before exiting.

It was the dispatcher who asked Major Fujiwara a pertinent question. 'What will the two men wear on their heads, Fujiwara-san? Without a helmet it could be fatal when they land.'

The Japanese Major inwardly cursed. He knew that British soldiers had been captured with steel helmets but that type of headgear was unsuitable for parachute descents as the flat rim would be lifted by the wind and the chin strap be an impediment. 'The only thing to do is to give them each one of ours and to get rid of it with the other gear after landing.' He gave orders for two to be brought, the newer ones shaped like normal steel helmets but made of cork covered with cotton drill. As the two cousins were trying them on, he debated whether to go through with a mock *Genpuku*, Coming of Age, ceremony as the two men were about to become real soldiers but *no, neither are of Samurai stock*.

'Early night tonight, both of you. You'll doss down here, be awoken at 0200, given a snack and a mug of tea. Take-off is at 0300.'

25 March 1944, near Tamu, Assam, Northeast India: It was mid-afternoon and the DMI, his ADC, Major Philip Rance and the 80 Brigade IO landed on the airstrip on the last leg of their journey. CO 3/1 GR, Lieutenant Colonel 'Sammy' Wingfield, had had a separate signal to say that the area had to be searched and properly guarded by the evening before. As a cover story for Jason's presence there and the list of those to attend included Lieutenant Rance's father, the CO had been asked if the son could be responsible for clearing the area so that the two could meet. Yes, so Jason's Recce Platoon, with rations for two days, had been sent out the previous evening.

Jason was thrilled to the core to see his father. *Dad's really into something*. Salutes and handshakes all round and an embrace for father and son. 'Mother sends her love', father Rance whispered into his son's ear.

After necessary introductions the small group settled themselves in a hut that was as heavily guarded as was the surrounding area. The DMI said 'Gentlemen, smoke if you wish. Personally I don't.' None of the others did either. 'Before I start, I have to ask you please to forget everything I have said as soon as what I have briefed you about has eventuated and that this meeting never happened. Now a quick briefing …' In essence it was that at dawn on the morrow a Ki 2 aircraft was expected to fly overhead with two Jiffs, one to drop in this area and thirteen minutes later the other near Dimapur. The plane was scheduled to bomb somewhere farther on. 'We can, I think, risk trying to shoot it down but only on the way back as we simply dare not alert anyone for specific reasons and that is why we have decided to try our best to get at least one of the two, if not both, alive.

Young Rance here will, with his CO's permission, be in charge of the near search party and try to capture the Jiff and not to kill him unless escape would be inevitable. We've seldom been able to get our hands on a Jiff on such a mission as this and *if* we're lucky, the debrief will be of the greatest value.'

The meeting broke up and the DMI called Jason over to him. 'Do you know what Haddon Chambers made the main character in Act 2 of *Captain Smith* say?' he asked with a throaty chuckle.

At it again! Jason gawped, blinked and stuttered his ignorance.

'Then I'll quote it to you: "The long arm of coincidence".' In a quieter voice so only Jason could hear, 'the enemy code word for this operation is *Kuroi Bara*, Japanese for "Black Rose", so that's why you've been asked for.' Smiling he shook Jason's hand, wished him good luck and strode off to catch up with the others who had gone ahead.

After the senior officers had left Jason's CO called him over. 'What did the DMI have to say to you?'

'He quoted something about "the long arm of coincidence", sir.'

'Did he? I wonder why. That's quite a task you've been given. How will you tackle it?'

'Sir, off the top of my head, our first job is to try and pin-point where the parachutist has landed.'

'You will hear the plane and see it so there's every hope of watching the wretched man drop. And then?'

'We'll go looking for him. I don't know about clearance in other unit's areas and have you a time limit?'

The CO pursed his lips and scratched his head. 'Clearance?

You won't want more than two square miles, if that. I'll fix it. You didn't come rationed, did you?'

'Yes we did, until the day after tomorrow.'

'Good. Solves a lot of problems. Stay here the night. It'll be cold so I'll send up some blankets, one for you and one for each pair of men. And after you've had a meal and a brew, brief all your men remembering to use "veiled" speech.'

'Yes, sir, I will.'

'Time limit: say until noon unless you are hot on his tail then back here by evening if you can't find him. Best of luck and who knows Dame Fortune might throw us a Double 6.'

At Dimapur the DMI had a brainwave at least that is what he called it: there was enough time before his plane was ready to leave for New Delhi so he visited the hospital. After introducing himself to the Colonel in charge, he said, 'Just a bit of hush-hush, don't you know, but if you were to find a patient who doesn't ring true, I'll ask you to let CO 3/1 GR over in 80 Brigade as soon as you can. During that time, if the person you suspect needs medical treatment, by all means give it to him. But please, do not let him escape whatever else.'

'Brigadier, I'll do anything you tell me to do, provided it is not medically against my oath,' was the pompous reply. 'As for keeping him, bed spaces are always at a premium and if he is not ill, I will not detain him.'

And with that the DMI had to be satisfied.

Jason called his men in and told them to cook a meal in

daylight. 'We'll keep alert till then and after our meal I'll brief you.' He sat down and dwelling on what the Brigadier had told him, found his mind drifting back that time in 1938: *Coincidence? That old Nepalese shaman in Bhutan Estate, rheumy-eyed, long haired, with a wispy grey beard and who exuded an aura of authority. I was shown a board and where to put some unhusked rice on it. I had placed a ten-dollar note on the ground beside the board and was bidden to sit. The old man started off by putting his liver-spotted, grave-marked hands in the rice, feeling it, lifting some, letting it fall and gently kneading it. He'd asked me my name and my age, all the while staring hard at me, forcing eye contact. Covering the wooden board, which was not much bigger than a child's slate, with fine dust, he picked up a stick and started drawing lines on the heaped rice, seemingly at random, scrutinising the grains carefully. 'Four* mawa hatas *in four years and after that three more at ten-year intervals with different names,' had been his cryptic findings. I had sat riveted, hardly knowing what to say or believe.*

He came back to the present with a jerk. *If Rabilal was the first, are these two parachutists numbers two and three? Is this what the old men had meant when he had said 'Four in four years and after that three more at ten-year intervals?'* He felt a goose running over his grave then another thought struck him. *If what he said was true, then I won't be killed till the very end of his prophesy* and the ghost of a smile hovered round his lips.

After the meal he gathered his men around him. 'You will have wondered at all the senior officers here earlier on in the day ...'

Yes, they all had *and even the sahib's father had come. Now that was a surprise.*

'... and I will now tell you about our most important and unusual task. The Brigadier sahib says that two Jiffs are to be parachuted into this area tomorrow morning at dawn, one is due to jump out of the plane here and the other over Dimapur.' It was dark and his men's faces, strong and expectant, were shadowy in the flickering firelight but Jason could see all were intensely interested and determined to capture the renegade. 'All those senior sahibs know that it is up to us to try and nab this one, it will be to our shame if we miss him.' The men nodded: it would indeed be a personal and a regimental shame if they missed their target. *Those Desi Jiffs who are not true to their oath of salt ...*

'At dawn we'll be able to see him but he won't be able to see us. His great disadvantage is that his white parachute will be visible from a long way off. The plane will be flying almost due north' which he indicated with a thrust of his chin. 'We must be ready to go to where we see the parachute drops and try to capture the Jiff alive as he will certainly have much information to our advantage. We will shoot him dead if capturing him becomes impossible. Shortly before dawn two men will go to the nearest high ground, never have one man alone, and move towards him as they see where he lands. Havildar, detail two.' This the Platoon Havildar did. Jason continued 'One man will climb that tree there,' shown with another chin thrust, 'and take a bearing with my compass, just in case the wind catches him drifting off course. We'll have our brew before dawn. Havildar, please detail the best tree climber. Any questions?'

A sentry was posted and they turned in for the night. Rifleman Hitman Gurung felt something was wrong. But what? As he turned over to go to sleep on the hard ground, it struck him. *Djinn. I must guard my sahib tomorrow as I fear he'll be in danger.*

2

26 March 1944, Singapore: Detailed preparation and implementation from rough idea and hazy expectation came as suddenly as does milk come to the boil and precipitously brought the two cousins' yet-to-be-experienced adventure to a 'here and now' point: result, a 'white night' for both of them. Although in their own way they were brave men, those who should have known better would have seen the whole venture as irresponsible and foolhardy yet such was the strong personality and the ability of not taking 'no' as an answer of the INA leader, Bose, that the tenuous nature of such an operation was put to one side and doubts were not to be gainsaid.

Despite the magnitude of war and adventure, mingled with the romance of what was seen as a worthy escapade, by now much of the cousins' earlier enthusiasm had drained away as cold reality set in. They were neither as daredevil nor as fiery as they had shown themselves with Lieutenant Colonel Shah Nawaz and, if not quite as fragile and brittle as an oat cake, both of them would, secretly, have been happy if the operation had been cancelled at the last moment. But that was not to be. Yet 'face', that display of public potency which makes for personal prestige, is never far below the surface of an Indian, nor, come to that of a Japanese, so, with a brew of hot tea and tasty chapattis inside them, by the time for emplaning both men had regained sufficient cockiness to impress those who saw them. The Colonel asked them if they had their secret package strapped on their backs. Indeed so, how could they have been forgotten? Neither he nor Major Fujiwara checked to see if the two packages of leaflets had been put in the plane, which was a pity because they were left behind.

Both Fujiwara and Shah Nawaz went to wish the cousins good luck and after a barrage of 'Jai Hinds' and 'Chalo Delhis' they emplaned. They sat on a small bench with their 'chute by their feet and the door was closed. First one engine was fired and revved, then the second, the plane shuddering fearsomely. They had to be shown how to fix their seat belts. At the end of the runway more shuddering, then accelerating, a lurch in the stomach and a push to one side on take-off. Everything new, unexpected and slightly terrifying: so different from that short flight in a monoplane when youngsters.

Once safely airborne they undid their seat belt. The noise of the engines was too loud to talk. Looking at each other with wan smiles and they shook hands. A long and tiring day and a 'white night' they closed their eyes ... but what little sleep they had was fitful and fretful.

27 March 1944, somewhere above northeast India: The pilot of the Ki 2 once more glanced at the compass that glowed among the other dials: 355 degrees. *On course despite turbulence on the way.* His practiced eyes automatically took in other relevant data as well. The sky to the east on his right had started to lose its darkness: from the altitude he'd have to drop those two, 250 metres was the operational height, it would still be dark … and dangerous with those hills on either side. He bit his bottom lip as he started to make a slow descent, throttling back and letting out the wing flaps to reduce speed. There were no landmarks to help him: he had worked out in minute detail the speed needed to arrive at dawn which the meteorological people had told him was 0603 hours. He sent the flight engineer into the fuselage and said, 'rouse those two and get them ready. The first exit will be in,' and he looked at his watch, 'twenty-four minutes.'

The engineer did as told and the change in the noise of the engines struck him, their background threnody having so melded itself into his unconscious he'd lost the sound of it. Interior lights were switched on and the two cousins, who had spent the time dozing on and off despite the unexpected cold, were roused into some semblance of alertness. During the flight turbulence had been severe and the cousins made to fasten their seat belt. The plane had buffeted them and the sickening drops into air pockets made them think they were on their way down to crash into the earth. Had they not fastened their belt both would have hit their head on the roof. They were so frightened that they clutched onto one another, puking down their shirt front as they did; now the taste in their mouths was revolting.

The pilot throttled back to near stalling speed and the noise of the engines decreased. 'Twelve minutes,' the co-pilot told the dispatcher on the 'blower'. The dispatcher, wearing his head set, acknowledged the order, told the first cousin to stand up and put on his equipment. He then checked that the 'chute was correctly buckled and clipped onto the static line, and the container suspension rope was properly fastened. He put on his own safety belt that was attached to the side of the door. The pilot looked at his watch. *Two minutes.* He motioned to his co-pilot who switched on the red light over the door. The two cousins merely nodded goodbye. The dispatcher opened the door and a blast of cold air swirled around the inside of the plane. Abdul Hamid was beckoned to move into the doorway. Abdul Rahim, still seated, watched with mounting concern.

Standing in the door Abdul Hamid had never thought anything could be so terrifying. His heart thumped and he wet himself. *This must be what* Zamhareer, *the worst and coldest Muslim Hell, is like: pitch black and unbearably cold.* 'Face your front,' shouted the dispatcher forgetting that the hapless man didn't speak Japanese.

In the cockpit the pilot, sweating slightly with the effort, had his mind solely on the speed of the plane: the difference in stalling speed of the aircraft, below which he simply had not to fly, and the speed of the strength of the slipstream that ripped the stitching of the parachute gores, above which he simply had not to fly, was a mere four and a half knots. To maintain the speed of the aircraft in the middle of that small zone needed his total concentration. That, the dark and the unknown territory below him, to say nothing of being over enemy territory, was a nerve-stretching business. He unconsciously squirmed uneasily on his seat. The co-pilot was equally tense and had his hands on his joystick ... just in case.

'Green on,' the pilot said and the co-pilot switched off the red and green light shone above the exit door. The dispatcher rapped Abdul Hamid on the shoulder but the cousin was rooted to the spot with fear and could not move. The dispatcher sharply pushed him out – *Gomen ne*, So sorry. No samurai but a barbarian – and his body, not straight enough, caused the rigging lines to twist, delaying the opening of the parachute. It had not fully developed when he fell heavily into a tall tree, crashing through the smaller branches, bumping against the larger ones, being slapped on the face by the leaves. His bare knees were scraped by twigs but so cold had they become in the plane he hardly felt anything. He hit his head hard, colours exploding in his brain, and knocked himself out before coming to a juddering halt in the cleft of two large branches high up. He hadn't even thought about unhooking his container.

When he regained consciousness he could not remember where he was. Then it came to him in a sudden rush. *I've managed it! I've managed it! Chalo Delhi!* His head ached and he managed to take off his helmet and found a large bump. Something too heavy for movement was lying on him. He fumbled around, found it was his container and unclipped it. He was still restricted in his movements and started to panic until he realised that he had not undone the 'quick-release' knob of his 'chute. Finally he did unharness himself, felt a bit more comfortable but it was still too dark to see the ground below. He wondered where an unpleasant smell came from. Sitting in the tree waiting for the dawn, he realised that he had thought the whole operation would be easy but how wrong he was: he'd taken it so much for granted but in fact he'd known nothing. *But I'm a hero, aren't I!* he told himself, exulting.

Dawn came. He looked at this shirt, saw the puke and tried to wipe it off with water from his water bottle. He heard what could only be a troop of monkeys. That scared him for he hated the brutes. He tried to pull his parachute down towards him and was almost frightened out of his wits by the monkeys rustling about above him investigating it. As he looked up a large lump of monkey turd fell onto his face, which he wiped off, spluttering, with his sleeve. *I'll leave my parachute where it is. Doesn't matter as it's green and high up so no one will see it.* He threw his container onto the ground, gingerly climbed down the tree, tied the rope round one of the large bottom branches and slid down.

Once more on firm ground felt marvellous and instinct told him to move off in the direction of the rising sun. *If I am in the 3rd/1st GR area I'll be better off to the east towards the 9th/12th* he decided, remembering his briefing. Fully confident once more but forgetting that the rope would show someone had climbed up or down that tree he moved off east humping his container. About a quarter of an hour later he found a stream and tried to clean himself as much as he could. In a marshy patch he dug a hole with his little spade for his container, which he put inside it before covering it up as inconspicuously as he could. He still had the Japanese hat on his head so threw that away into some thick bushes and only then realised that he had forgotten his issue hat when he'd put on his helmet so it was still in the aeroplane. Curse it! Needing a rest, he sat down behind a tree and finished off his hard tack and his water before moving off, hearing the sound of artillery fire in the distance, another first for him.

His incipient beard would show another Indian soldier he met that he was not a 'local' soldier. *But who will I meet first?* he wondered hesitantly as he moved off, mentally running through everything he had been told for his cover plan.

At about twenty past four the Gurkha sentry on duty glanced at his watch. 'Wake us up at 4.30,' was the order. *Time to blow on the embers of last night's fire and start brewing the tea*, he thought, moving to where it was. That done, he went to each man and softly woke him up, the Platoon Commander, Captain Rance, last. Hitman poured some of the hot water into Jason's mess tin and took it over for him to shave with. Tea ready and, with one man armed and facing outwards, they drank it up. They still had a couple of chapattis and cold vegetables from the day before to eat later on in the day. 'Pack up now and be ready to move as soon as we hear the plane,' Jason said, looking at his watch. 'Twenty minutes before we need to move so make yourselves comfortable.'

Twenty to six. 'Off up the hill you two go, with your full gear and try to pinpoint where the parachute drops,' he told the two men detailed for that task and they vanished into the dark. The tree-climber, to whom Jason had already given his compass to take a bearing on the fall of the parachute, had already gone.

Pre-dawn noises of the world awakening had started to make themselves heard when one of the men said, *'Jahaj ayo'*, the plane has come, and suddenly it whooshed overhead. Only the tree-climber saw a tiny and darker shadow against the sky as the parachute opened – *looks smaller that I thought it would* – and it seemed to lodge in one particularly taller than usual tree. *A chhatiwan like those in the forests above my village? I should be able to recognise it* he thought as he shinned down and handed the compass back to Jason. '335 degrees, sahib. I think I'll be able to recognise the tree.'

'Packs on and off we go, lads, to look for him. Let's try and get him before he knows where he is,' and away they went as quickly as the growing light allowed.

Nineteen and a half minutes after his cousin had left the plane, Abdul Rahim stepped out into the cold air and as he was buffeted by the slipstream found his body parallel flat before gradually dropping feet first. There was a momentary tug and he glanced up and saw that the parachute had opened. *What now, what now?* he almost panicked before remembering to pull the retaining pin out from where his container was suspended from his belt. He immediately felt a tug on his right side as it dropped. So intent was he in getting the drill correct he did not notice the increased noise of the plane as it accelerated and started to climb. The pilot, one hand off the controls mopping his brow before changing his compass bearing to 273 degrees for the last one hundred and fifty miles of this unusual and never-to-be-repeated mission, never did know how near he had been to scraping the belly of his aircraft on the top of the trees on the high ground. Had he, his hair would have been white before he touched down, which he did, on time, much to the relief of everyone in Singapore, his bombing mission at Shillong having been completed on schedule. On landing he thanked his *kami* as did the other three crewmen theirs.

Rahim hit the ground, scraped and jolted his bare bad knee on a stone as he rolled over, surprised to find himself all in one piece and, except for a throb in his knee, unhurt. It had given him no trouble for ages until the rolling practice when he had landed on it and felt a slight twinge. *But now pull in the parachute*. He pulled it in. *Stuff it in its bag*. This he did. *Take out my kit from the container*. Yes. Done. *Now what?* he asked himself as he stood up. *Get rid of the stuff. But where?* Dawn was breaking and there was enough light to see a small pond a few yards away. *That'll have to do*. He sniffed the stink of stale puke *and I can rinse my mouth out*. After wetting his mouth with the pond water which had almost as foul a taste as there was before and which he would never have touched in normal circumstances, he tried to clean the front of his shirt. He stubbed his toe on a rock and that brought him up with a jerk. *The stuff won't sink by itself*. Feverishly he probed around under a large rock, put the little spade there, stuffed his 'chute in its bag, the container and the Japanese hat under it and blocked where he'd done that with some large stones. That took him quite a time but manage he did. *All clear*. He let out a great sigh of relief but being wet, started shivering. *And now? First change my clothes and dry the wet shirt and trousers when the sun comes up then find someone to tell my story to and act my part*. It only then came to him that he had actually achieved something that had only been a dream before and he laughed aloud at his success. 'Chalo Delhi,' he sang out before realising that that was a foolish thing to have done. He put his pack on, looked around and seeing a footpath roughly going north, blundered along it, mind still a-whirl, taking no sensible precautions. It never occurred to him to wear his hat, which he too had left in the plane. His knee had started to ache and he felt woozy. He saw an empty shed and decided to hide there. He felt hungry and nibbled his rations. *I'll lie low for a bit and see what goes on.*

It was not long before the WEC in Delhi had another Mauve to be translated and sent to the DMI when his office opened.

It is not at all easy to move on a compass bearing in thick jungle at any time and to guide oneself to a particular tree, especially when in an area where a Japanese patrol might have been sent to escort the parachutist to wherever he had to go, is slow work. About ninety minutes after they had set out they heard a troop of monkeys in front of them. 'Something has frightened them,' the tree-climber softly said to Jason and, not all that long afterwards, 'Sahib, I'm sure that's the tree, the *chhatiwan*.' It was about twenty paces in front of them. He saw the dangling rope. 'Sahib, look at the rope. Proof that he fell into the tree and let himself down to the ground with it.'

'You are probably right but we must make sure. Let's hope it is not a booby-trap decoy as we should be able to see a white parachute up the tree,' cautioned his Platoon Commander.

Jason made the hand signal for 'halt, all-round observation'. After ten minutes, during which time any movement would have been heard, the men carefully searched around for any other suspicious signs. They saw nothing irregular from 'normal' jungle. They had looked all along the line they'd seen him drop but neither a man nor a speck of white was to be seen. There had been no sudden draught of wind to take him in another direction although it had rained during the night.

'The *djinn* took him,' grunted Hitman Gurung. 'It makes me uneasy. He'll appear from somewhere without any of us knowing about it.'

Jason, with Hitman, went up to the tree and there was a mark in the ground but no footprints as those made in the dew had dried but in one place the undergrowth had been disturbed. Jason called his tree-climber over to him. 'Climb the tree as high as you safely can and see if there are any marks that will prove you are correct.'

At the bottom of the tree Jason heard a rending noise and seconds later a triumphant Gurkha came down dragging a torn green parachute after him. 'Sahib, I was not wrong but the *banchoot* didn't have a white parachute.'

'Now that is something none of us would ever have expected. What a clever ruse to have come up with. We'd better take it with us as evidence. HQ will most certainly be interested in it. Now we know for sure we can track him,' and track him they did as he had not been a careful walker. They came across the marshy patch and saw how it had also recently been disturbed. Jason made a couple of his men poke around and the container was found. 'Pull it out.' A man who had gone behind a bush to relieve himself found the hat. 'Great work! Brigade will want to see both items, especially the hat. We'll have to carry both items with us rather than leave them here in case someone, native or enemy, takes them away,' ordered Jason. 'While we're here we'll have a look round but it is too risky to go far as we may wander into the 9/12 FFR's area.'

Look around they did and could only confirm that the man had moved east. 'That's going towards the sound of the guns,' remarked one of the soldiers.

'Let's finish off our rations then it's back to our night stop,' Jason told his Platoon Sergeant. *What a pity we don't have our own wireless set.*

Back at their temporary base, they brewed up once more and, as they were enjoying their hot tea, the IO of 3/1 GR and his opposite number from 80 Brigade, suitably escorted, drove up in two vehicles. Looking around and seeing no prisoner, he called out 'So you didn't get the renegade! We were hoping against hope but, truth to tell, we'd rather doubted it. It was such a long shot.'

'Well, we were unlucky. One of my men saw the actual tree the Jiff landed in but by the time we got there the blighter had left. However, it was his good and our bad luck that he dropped with a green parachute not a white one which we might have seen well before we actually reached the tree so have reached it sooner. Who knows but we might have got the blighter. I sent one of my men up the tree and he found the green 'chute and tore it down as it had got stuck. We tracked him, came across some fresh digging and uncovered a container with a Japanese hat under a bush nearby. They're here if you want to take them away for investigation. We tracked him eastwards but didn't want to go too far as I was not sure where our boundary with 9/12 FFR is.' He put his hand over his mouth and stifled a yawn.

A soldier brought the stuff over for the IOs to have a look at. 'Hm, interesting and unusual. Goes to show how much the

Japs are helping the Jiffs,' opined the Brigade IO. 'They'll have to go to Brigade HQ with us as, in any case, I have been ordered to take you with me, Jason, to make a full report of whatever has happened, successful or otherwise.' He looked at his watch. 'We'll go back just as soon as we can.'

'And my platoon?'

'Take your batman as escort and I'll take the rest of them back to the battalion with me,' said the Battalion IO.

A few minutes later Jason and Hitman got in the back of the Brigade vehicle and were driven off.

Abdul Rahim Khan had been briefed that Dimapur was at a railhead and he'd find what was described as 'organised military chaos with a floating population' there so it would be comparatively easy to 'get lost in the crowd'. He had been given the pay book and ID card of a man with the same name who had been in the Indian Army Medical Corps and had learnt enough about the man's background, village, recruit training and service until he was captured to be able to answer most questions put to him and evade suspicion. It had, somehow, seemed so easy when he was being trained for his new character but now he felt lost, faint and unsteady as the air journey had upset him and his knee aching. *What to do now?* he wondered, nearly in tears, and not feeling at all sure of himself. He had sat in the shed till after the sun came up and put out his wet clothes to dry. The clothes were still damp when he decided it was time to move off. An hour or so later he came to a place that sold tea and refreshments. He smelt delicious cooking and, forgetting he'd no money, asked for a plate of rice. There was a table outside where he sat and waited for it.

A British Military Police vehicle on patrol slowly cruised by. The Corporal in the passenger seat said, 'Bert. Stop. There's something wrong with an unarmed soldier wearing KD sitting here alone so far from town at this time of day.' He peered and said, 'Let's get out and see what's what. Something's bloody fishy.'

Rahim saw the vehicle stop and wondered why the two British soldiers got out and approached him. He saw they carried pistols and wore white belts and peaked hats with red tops but not being a soldier such details meant nothing to him but somehow they spelt danger. *Run?* Too scared to move he stayed where he was. On reaching him they looked him up and down and asked him in execrable Urdu who he was and what was he doing.

Rahim's mind went blank. He dimly remembered from Malaya days that *Gora*s only spoke English so he answered in English. 'I don't understand what you're trying to ask me,' in a tone of voice that offended the two Policemen, who took it as gross impertinence.

'You'd better cut out that ladida lark and answer properly, you bleedin' 'orror,' the Corporal said. 'Show me your pay book and ID card,' holding out his hand as he did.

Rahim caused more suspicion by not having them on him as he searched around in his haversack for them. He found them and show them to the Corporal who looked at the pay book, Army Book 64, and, on a sudden whim, said, 'Wot does IAMC mean?'

Even if Rahim had known his mind remained a blank. He stared uncomprehendingly at his questioner.

'There's more than meets the ruddy eye, 'ere. The blighter

speaks English but doesn't seem to know what IAMC means. We'll have to take him in, Bert, and I'll give the APM a bell once we get back. Strewth, look, he's grazed 'is knees.' He faced the unfortunate Rahim and coarsely and unnecessarily asked, 'Didn't take enough weight on yer elbows, eh?' But first let's see what's in 'is pack.' The younger, a Lance Corporal, picked it up and emptied it on the ground. 'Corp, that's bloody odd, damp clothes. Shows he's been somewhere else, don't it?'

'Yeah. Does, don't it? Put your titfer on.'

The hapless Rahmin had no idea that 'titfer' was rhyming slang for 'hat' and stared blankly at the Corporal.

'Your 'at, you dolt, your bleeding 'at,' pointing to his own.

Rahmin suddenly realised he'd left his hat in the aircraft and shook his head. 'No hat.'

'Come on, then, hold out your paws.' Not understood. The Corporal demonstrated and as soon as Rahim obliged, he found he was handcuffed.

As they led him away to the vehicle the shopkeeper brought out his meal. Dumbfounded, he shouted after them that he needed money, but he merely wasted his breath.

So mentally 'at sea' was Rahim on being handcuffed after such an exhausting journey and unusual parachute descent that he forget his cover story, 'dropped by the Indian Army to root out Jiffs', so from the garbled interview with the APM it was obvious that something simply did not ring true. The question 'why are you wearing KD?' merely evoked an unconvincing and muttered 'uniform'.

'He's gone doolally, or in medical parlance of unsound mind, is my reading of the situation,' said the APM and told the Duty Medical Orderly to escort him to the Duty Medical Officer.

'Doc, we've a rum'un here so please have a look at him. Could be genuine but somehow I don't think so.'

A cursory inspection saw a swollen and grazed knee but nothing else untoward. The man was not emaciated in any way but mentally he just was 'not with it' to the extent a normal soldier should be. 'Don't be afraid,' the doctor said to him through an interpreter, not realising that the man was a good English speaker. 'Stay here for a while and have a full check up. There's nothing to be afraid of.'

The upshot was that Sepoy Abdul Rahim Khan was to be kept under surveillance and to have a medical check up as he was obviously in need of one. He was put in the Isolation Ward and given a meal, which he wolfed down.

When the Medical Colonel was told he had a look at the man himself, remembered what the DMI had asked him to do so got a message sent to CO 3/1 GR by way of 80 Brigade HQ to that effect. 'I'll come back this evening. Have a long rest in bed now,' he said in good Urdu.

Decidedly odd to me was his inner comment as he left for his office, easing his neck and jutting out his jaw defiantly.

The wireless operator in the Brigade IO's vehicle was contacted and a voice cackled 'Fetch Acorn'.

'Wait out.' The British operator leant forward and tapped Acorn, the IO, on the shoulder. 'Sir, you're wanted on set.'

Acorn took the microphone. 'Acorn on set.'

'Sunray on set. Go straight to Dimapur and talk to Starlight

Major then report back.'

'Wilco. Out.' The vehicle drove on. 'Jason, something's come up but I don't know what. We're to go straight to Dimapur hospital and talk to the chief Quack.'

Something or someone? Jason asked himself.

Driving faster than was really safe they reached the hospital late afternoon, reported in to the Registrar, told him who they were and what they wanted. They were obviously expected as they were immediately taken to see the Colonel, Starlight Major himself.

'I don't know what you fellows are playing at,' the Colonel said moodily. 'The man you want to see is suffering from some kind of trauma but, essentially, is not ill.' He did not mention that the medical check-up was cursory in the extreme so that the propaganda papers had not been found. An orderly was called. 'Take these two officers to the Isolation Ward where that Indian soldier was put earlier on today.'

The three of them traipsed off. Once at the ward, the Brigade IO proposed Jason should go in alone. 'From what little I've heard today I think that's best. I'll be just outside in case I'm wanted.'

In the Isolation Ward, Rahim, left by himself, knew that he had got things badly, horribly badly, wrong. *I'll have to escape. I have my knife and in the dark anything can happen in my favour* and he chuckled, morale rising at the thought. *I'll wait till it's quite dark when there's less chance of anyone coming to see me.*

He had gone back to lie on his bed when he heard footsteps and voices outside his door. When the door slowly opened he got up and went over to the window, poised for action. In Jason went and saw a man standing near the window. With the light against him, he could not see who it was so he switched on the light. The result was completely unforeseen. The man 'did a double take' as the light lit Jason up. *It can't be, can it, after all those years?* He peered harder. *Yes! Has to be him with those piercing blue eyes. Revenge for that damning insult at last.* All else was forgotten and with animal instinct for the kill, he took his knife out of his pocket and in one fell swoop plunged at Jason in grim silence, knife arm to the fore. Taken utterly by surprise Jason stood stock still while the other man jumped at him and dashed his arm down as though to thrust the blade well into Jason's stomach, shouting 'Revenge! *Jai Tor Guuuuuul*'. Jason fell over and the attacker fell on top of him. Looking through the opened door the Brigade IO saw what had happened and dashed into the room with the medical orderly and Hitman Gurung. They leapt on the 'patient' and dragged him away.

'Are you hurt?' the IO asked Jason who was rubbing his stomach.

'Not really. Just a hard thump. See what he's holding? A clasp knife. Take it from him before he opens it.'

The 'patient' slumped in dismay. *In my hurry I forgot to open the blade* he inwardly fumed.

By this time there was a crowd of interested people ghoulishly hanging around at the door and in the passage outside. 'Put the blighter in the Guard Room,' came a voice of authority from outside, 'tomorrow we'll see what it's all about. Too late in the day to start anything now.'

'Before you do,' broke in Jason, 'I need someone to help me take his shirt off.' People stared at him. 'Please, I mean it. I'll tell you why in a jiffy.'

The shirt was taken off and there, tattooed on the man's left shoulder, was لگروط. Jason broke the silence that followed such a surprising discovery by saying, solemnly and with great authority, 'His name is either Abdul Rahim Khan or Abdul Hamid Khan. I first met him in 1938 but haven't seen him since.' Remembering his strict instructions, he made no mention about the man's provenance.

'And what's this?' asked the Brigade IO, tearing off the package strapped by medical plaster off his back. He opened it, the two British officers gasping in revulsion on seeing the text and the pictures. 'Blasted spy, that's what he is. Jolly well ought to be hanged.'

When Jason was pressed how he knew so positively who the man was, his reply was 'Ask him' and, when asked, the spitting reply of shouted obscenities confirmed the truth of Jason's unexpected diagnosis. Two ward orderlies had already gagged him and were now ready to take him away to the Guard Room with strict instructions not to let him out under any circumstances, unless heavily escorted nor anyone to be allowed to talk to him.

The Medical Colonel soon turned up, spittingly angry. Turning to the Brigade IO, he almost shouted, 'Take him away then go away yourself. I don't like you here or want you here.'

'Sir, he's to go into your Guard Room and it's late,' said Acorn with unruffled clarity.

'Then tomorrow morning first thing, without fail,' the Colonel thundered as he stormed away, jutted jaw well to the fore.

Jason thought back to Rabilal's briefing. *I must really have upset those wretched hotheads. If, only if, the joker in the tree who got away is Number 2, then this nut case must be Number 3. One more to go if we can find Number 2* and he shook his head in wonder as he remembered the prophesy of five years previously. *Profoundly disturbing to have this hanging over my head. Does Rabilal's 'conversion' mean only two more?*

28 March 1944, near Tamu, Assam, Northeast India: Abdul Hamid, hoping that his luck would hold having come so far, instinctively knew that he could not stay by himself for any longer than necessary. He rather hoped that most wild animals would have been so scared by all the noise and movement that they would be lying low although he didn't really believe it. Nor, come to that, could he rely on meeting a sympathetic person. He came to a ridge and, to his amazement, the trees he saw on the precipitous hills in front of him were bare of leaves. It was only when he heard a loud crump and saw mud and dust rise from an artillery shell explosion and the distant sound of small-arms' fire that he realised he was approaching a battle area and that the leaves had been blown off. Down below him he saw a village and decided to go there: food, shelter and news were what he wanted, so down he clambered.

The houses were built on a different pattern from what he was used to, with one grander looking in the middle. Cursing himself for not having learnt any basic Burmese phrases, he went to it and called out, first in Hindi, then in English, 'Is anyone here to help me?'

An elderly crone shuffled to the door, looked at him, shook her head and turned back inside. *Now what?* He decided to wait a while as there was no point in going any farther if there was a chance of finding out what was happening in the general area.

'Is anyone here who can help me?' he called out again, using both languages.

'What do you want?' he heard in English from behind him. He wheeled around and saw a middle-aged, bespectacled man coming towards him. So intent had he been he had not heard him. 'Can I help you, you look lost? I am the village headmaster but I cannot speak Hindi, only Burmese and English. But first, what do you want so far from your unit and by yourself unarmed?'

'Oh headmaster, sir, how glad I am to have found you. I have been on the way for some time, am tired and hungry and am looking for an Indian unit, the 9th/12th Frontier Force Regiment which I believe is somewhere around here.'

The headmaster shook his head. 'Excuse me. Apart from not knowing or caring what unit is where, somehow that does not sound right. You are unarmed and wearing a different coloured uniform from the soldiers I have seen and have no hat. Also soldiers do not move around by themselves, armed or unarmed. If you tell me the truth I'll see if I can help you: if not I'll consider you a danger and won't.'

Different coloured uniform, did he say? Think this one out: act naturally. 'Sir, I can tell you all but I need to sit down. Can you provide me with a glass of water, please?'

The headmaster looked him up and down. *Strong, could be*

dangerous. But why unarmed? Something's surely wrong but it's not my business to put it right. 'Come with me,' and he took him to his own house where he called to his wife to get some refreshments ready.

Abdul Hamid, grateful for the kindness, came out with his story, 'I was in Malaya with 1st/14th Punjab Regiment in Captain Shah Nawaz's company ...' and on went the rigmarole about escaping before the battalion was captured, how he had been ill, how he had lost his rifle, how he was determined to get back but, one thing and other ... 'and here I am. I have a relation in 9/12 FFR but I don't know where it is.' With a realistic sob, out came 'I have to admit that I'm lost.' *Convincing enough? I hope so. Might also explain the colour of my uniform.*

'Your story could well be true,' admitted the headmaster, 'but I am not convinced. I have my doubts: for one thing your clothing is too new to have lasted all that time. But we civilians keep out of the way as much as we possibly can. It's not our war. What I do know is that quite often an Indian patrol comes to where I teach and I can tell them about you. Until then I'm afraid you can't stay in my house as were the Japanese to come and inspect, both of us would be dead straight away unless we were tortured first.'

'That is kind of you. Where will I stay?'

'In my cattle shed. I can feed you but not much. If there are no troops in the area you can repay me by weeding my vegetable patch.'

Luckily on the morrow a patrol did visit the school and the headmaster, who knew no Hindi, spoke in easy English to the Naik patrol commander. 'Indian sepoy hiding. Wants 9/12

Frontier Force.'

The Naik understood English better than he spoke it so, pointing first to himself before waving randomly around him and nodding his head, let the Burmese headmaster know he wanted to speak to the man. The headmaster led the patrol to the cattle shed and, as they approached, called out loudly in English, 'I have some friends who want to meet you,' before turning on his heels and leaving them.

The Naik ordered his men to take all-round positions before calling out, 'I am Naik Hakim Beg of 9/12 Frontier Force Regiment. Who are you?'

Abdul Hamid Khan gave his name, number and battalion while pulling his pay book and ID card out of his pocket as he emerged from the shed. He raised his right hand and gave the Arabic greeting, 'As-salamu-alaykum.' The return was only 'Salam'. 'I can't tell you how glad I am to see proper Indian soldiers again,' he gushed. 'Are you from 9/12 because my brother-in-law is in that battalion?'

That caused a spark of interest. 'Yes, we are. His name?'

Indians refer to relatives and siblings by the relationship between them, seldom by name, and although Hamid's sister would not know what her husband's name was, Hamid did. 'He is Muhammad Taki Khan, the same as the famous cavalry commander of, oh, nearly two hundred years ago.'

'Yes, I know of him. I think he works in the B Company cookhouse but we are A Company men. We'll take you back. But what are you doing here in the first place, dressed in KD?' By now Abdul Hamid Khan knew not to ask what KD meant. 'Where's your weapon? If we are to take you to the battalion we must be sure to be doing right otherwise the Adjutant sahib will be angry.'

So out came the story again and the Naik then asked, 'So I suppose you'll want to go back to your village.'

'Oh no. I can't give up now I've come so far, can I?'

'They're always short-handed in the cookhouse and another pair of hands will be useful. However, it's not up to me. I will have to take you to the Adjutant sahib. If he accepts you you may be allowed to stay.'

'Good, I'd feel safe there after all my difficulties.'

'Got any kit?'

'A pack.'

'Go and get it and we'll be off. It's quite a way to go.'

Hamid just had time to thank the headmaster as they moved out of the village. *I'll have to think up a good story about my uniform being KD and not looking old …*

28 March 1944, near Tamu, Assam, Northeast India: As soon as Jason had regained his battalion he learnt that a Japanese push, rumoured to be 'supported' by INA troops, was expected. Immediate battle preparations were made, ammunition, bullets and grenades issued, medical packs checked and refurbished and, where possible, battle drills rehearsed. Jason found himself with his Recce Platoon moving back along the road he had recently travelled for about eight miles to a bridge over a small river, named Lokchao on the map. After crossing the bridge he took his men up a hill, named Top Point by the battalion, and moved north to act as a Standing Patrol. The terrain was ridged hills with steep slopes but many trees had been denuded of leaves by violent artillery fire from both sides. From being used to thick jungle he felt almost naked. His platoon had a wireless now and he sent a message to Battalion HQ giving the position of a strong Japanese group he saw to his front, using what cover there was, moving south west, seemingly heading towards the bridge. With the Japanese accurately pin-pointed, battalion mortars and supporting mountain guns, mixing smoke and high explosive, set fire to the undergrowth and flushed them into more open ground. Jason left where he was and although outnumbered felt he could ambush them.

A change in the wind blew the smoke in his direction so he was unaware of a Japanese who came through it until he was almost on top of him. So intent had the Japanese been in killing an officer that he did not see Rifleman Hitman, who, quick as a flash, tripped him as he passed and cut his head off as he fell. Jason's platoon charged the enemy who, unusually and unexpectedly, retreated fast. The dead man was a Japanese second-lieutenant and documents he was carrying showed that he was commanding a special engineer unit intent on blowing up the bridge and a major attack in roughly the same area planned shortly.

30 March 1944, near Tamu, Assam, Northeast India: The Adjutant of 9/12 Frontier Force Regiment, Captain Ranjit Singh, an outstanding Indian officer from a noble family, received a report daily from the Subedar Major. Battalion HQ was in a house that the Pioneer Platoon had managed to improve somewhat in the remains of a village and at midday on 30 March the Subedar

Major marched in, stood to attention emulating *rigor mortis* before coming up with a cracking salute. 'Sahib, I have my report to make. Have I your permission to do so?'

'SM sahib, please do,' replied the Adjutant courteously.

'Hazur, my first point is a patrol has brought in a man who claims he is an escapee from 1/14 Punjab Regiment which as you will know was taken prisoner in 1942. He is still wearing KD uniform. He was found in the house of a Burmese headmaster,' he looked at his notes and gave the name of the place. 'He was brought back by an A Company patrol and, when asked by the NCO in charge if he wanted to be sent back to India, replied that he had a brother-in-law in our battalion and would be happy to stay on with us.'

'Sahib, have you the brother-in-law's name? I will need that before I go and report to the Commanding sahib.'

'Hazur, that I have. He is, or rather was as he was killed in the last Japanese attack, Sepoy Muhammad Taki Khan.'

'Yes, SM sahib, I well remember him, the only man in the battalion with that illustrious and historic name.' The Adjutant ran the top of his right index finger under his ferocious moustache and moved a pencil on the table as he thought out his next move. 'Has he been seen by the RMO?'

'Hazur, yes. I felt it prudent that I had such a report for you. The Doctor sahib says that although the man seems to be in a daze, bodily there's nothing wrong with him. But he doesn't have the bearing of a soldier nor does he look like one because his feet turn out rather more that a *rangrut* normally has when enlisted.'

The Adjutant knew that his SM was a 'stickler' for a perfect stance in his sepoys. 'Yes, that is a point but SM sahib he need not have been a peacetime soldier. There was such an increase after war started that we rather had to take any man who wanted to be a sepoy. What is your recommendation, SM sahib, before you tell the Commanding sahib about it?'

'I will suggest that we keep him for a month and then make a report on him for Brigade. We can always use more help in the cookhouses. Even if he can't cook there are lots of fatigues he can be used on until the month is up.' The SM actually thought that a month was probably too long.

'A report will have to be made now, SM sahib,' countered the Adjutant. 'His people at home will want to learn that he is still alive as I doubt if the Japani have ever sent news of any POW. Higher Formation must be told about him. Let me go and see the Commanding sahib. I'll give him the outline then you go and make your normal report.'

The Adjutant came out of the CO's office and nodded to the SM. In the SM went to report to the English sahib for whom he had the greatest respect. His recommendation was accepted and a report went on up the line: an answer was not expected back at least until the month had ended.

When Sepoy Abdul Hamid Khan was told his future he was delighted. *Now I can really start on my work* he told himself.

29 April 1944, a few miles southeast of Tamu: For the past week there had been severe battles between 80 Brigade and the Japanese. Atrociously difficult country often resulted in hand-to-hand fighting with front lines only being a matter of a few yards apart.

Many brave acts took place under these almost unprecedented conditions and there were horrendous casualties on both sides, with more Japanese casualties than 14th Army's.

It had been rumoured that a Jiff battalion was in the area, behind the Japanese, but contact with them was only made once by 3/1 GR's Recce Platoon, Captain Jason Rance leading an attack. The Jiffs quickly melted away, leaving many of their dead and wounded as they did. Ill-fated souls, they were bereft of much equipment as re-supply was their 'Achilles heel'. Rance chased them as far as he felt prudent before returning. He had a wounded man who needed urgent attention and he saw some Indian soldiers crouching behind some rocks to his front. He called out to them in simple Urdu, 'we're 3/1 Gurkhas, are you 9/12 FFR?'

A havildar stood up, grimy but smiling, with his rifle to his side. 'Yes, Sahib, we are. What do you want?'

'I have a wounded man with me and your Regimental Aid Post is much nearer than mine. May I have your permission to come into your area and take him there, please?'

This one speaks so kindly and sincerely. Of course I must help him. 'Sahib, I'll give you a guide.'

Jason left the platoon with his Havildar and a 9/12 FFR Naik took him and the wounded man, helped by a man on either side of him to hold him up, away to the RAP. Once there Jason handed him over to the Medical Officer and said, 'I'd better see the Adjutant while you look at him. I'll call back afterwards to see what's what.'

The Naik said, 'Captain sahib, come with me. I'll take you to the Adjutant sahib's office.' A sentry at the opening of a tarpaulin-covered hut asked him what he wanted. 'I am Captain Rance of 3/1 GR I want to see the Adjutant sahib and tell him that a wounded man of mine is being looked at by the RMO sahib.'

A burst came from inside. 'Jason? You come to see me without making a cuckoo noise? How dare you?' and, grinning broadly, hand outstretched in greeting, there was Captain Ranjit Singh. They shook hands, both delighted to see each other once more, so far from peaceful Dehra Dun. 'What can I do for you?' he asked.

Jason told him what had happened and about his wounded man.

'That's no problem and no trouble. Let the Quack have a good look and, if necessary, we'll keep him until it's safe to send him back to you.'

'That's kind of you and a relief to me. Thank you.'

'Think nothing of it! Like a mug of hot tea before you return?'

'Couldn't think of anything I'd like better,' answered Jason, delighted with the idea.

'Runner,' called the Adjutant.

'Hazur,' the runner answered, coming in and saluting. The Adjutant said, 'Go to the cookhouse, order up two mugs of hot, hot tea with lots of condensed milk and tell that new man we've got to bring it.'

The runner saluted and went off. 'I'll tell you why I've asked for the tea to be brought over by a particular man, Jason. From what I remember of you in the IMA you are a pretty good judge of men and there's a new man I have my doubts about. While I talk to him I'd like you to stand back and form an opinion about him? Okay with you?'

'Of course it is,' Jason replied, not linking the request with anyone in particular. While waiting for their brew, the two of them swapped yarns about where they'd been since IMA days. The runner popped his head in and said that the man from the cookhouse had brought the tea. 'Send him in,' called the Adjutant and Jason only noticed the man as he was putting two mugs on the table. He looked him up and down then ... *click. A large Adam's apple and feet turned out. No. Can it really be that man? The man whose parachute we found? Yes!* The man, placing the two mugs of tea on the table, 'felt a presence'. *Danger?* He turned to leave and saw those piercingly blue eyes. Gasping in disbelief, *it can't be but it really is. Revenge, here and now!* Recognition of the man sitting in front of him as the one who had so insulted him, hurt him so badly, prevented his plan from working out so many years ago all came back in a blinding flash, putting everything else completely out of his mind. Before anyone could react, in one fell swoop he took one mug of scalding tea off the table and threw it straight at Jason's face, shouting '*Jai Tor Guuuuuul*'. There was just enough time for an alert Jason to duck, closing his eyes, and the hot liquid spread all over his hat. The runner, watching, was on to him in a flash, but was not prepared for the angry man's strength. He was thrown off and Abdul Hamid Khan dashed out of the office. The Adjutant quickly followed and ran after him. Jason overtook him and brought the escaping man down with a splendid rugger tackle. Soldiers of the 9/12 FFR Defence Platoon came, picked him up and frog-marched him back to where the Adjutant was.

'Jason, why did he do that to you?' asked the Adjutant, as the outraged man struggled to get free.

'Ranjit, take off his shirt and look at his left shoulder and then I'll tell you if what I see proves what I think.'

The shirt was taken off and there, tattooed on the man's left shoulder, was لگورط.

As Hamid Khan writhed he turned over and revealed the incriminating package on his back. That, like the one his cousin was carrying, was ripped off and the offending material produced more gasps of surprised horror. 'Give that to me and take him to the Guard Room where he is to be kept under the tightest security.'

The CO, alerted and alarmed by the noise of chase and capture, called out from his own office.'What the hell's going on Ranjit? Come in and tell me.'

Back in the makeshift office the three of them sat down and the CO asked Jason, with a fresh mug of tea, to tell them what he know. So Jason told them about what had happened in Malaya, 'where I used to live, sir, in 1938. His name is Abdul Hamid Khan. I first met him in 1938 but haven't seen him since.' *Time for a white lie.* 'By knowing me then I can only presume that he has nursed a grievance against Europeans ever since. My guess is as good as yours here, he somehow managed to join the Jiffs even though he was never an Indian Army soldier. That can come out in his debriefing, sir. As for the leaflets, they show that planning was done at the highest level.'

'If what you have told me is true, as I am sure it is, it means that he is, therefore, a Malayan and not an Indian citizen so not a turn-coat from the Indian Army and therefore cannot be tried for revoking his military oath,' was the CO's comment

The SM, who had joined them, said, 'I always thought he was a badmash. Now I know.'

'I forgot to mention one fact,' Jason added. 'He's high-school educated and can speak and understand fluent English. Best to be careful what you say in his hearing.'

The CO, uncurling his legs from under the table, sagely noted 'we're here to fight the Japs first and the Jiffs second. I'll send the man back to Brigade under escort as soon as practicable but first we'll have to send a signal as his presence has already been reported and with what you've told us, Rance, another and fuller report.' Jason got up, saluted and asked permission to leave. 'Yes, off you go and how lucky you came to see us,' the Adjutant said. 'If your soldier had not been wounded ...' and his voice trailed away.' Meanwhile I'll get a message sent telling your battalion you are with us and are now on your way back.'

Alone in the Guard Room and heavily guarded the thought of having got so far was almost as if the gift of credence had been withheld by the whim of some divine comedian came into the prisoner's mind in his bleak despair – *but that is blatant heresy. It was God's will* and he knelt in prayer to try and calm his writhing and bitter soul although he didn't know in which direction Mecca was.

That evening, when Jason got into his trench to go to sleep his thoughts turned to what had happened earlier on in the day. *So Number 2 has been accounted for* and again he shook his head in wonder as he remembered the prophesy of five years previously ... *Not only a* mawar hitam *but three more like it. That means*

the one left can only be Tor Gul himself. Luckily I can recognise
him. But as I'm to face three more at ten-year it means I won't die
by what Number 4 tries to do with me – but, of course, I may be
wounded, perish the thought. I hope it'll be less lethal that a mug
of hot tea … and sleep overtook him.

It was soon after that that 3/1 GR were sent first on six months' rest and then taking in much needed reinforcements before retraining. Before the battalion's return to Burma the Japanese Imperial Army had suffered the most disastrous defeat in its history up to then. Five of its divisions had been broken up with crippling losses in men and material, leaving over fifty thousand counted bodies behind with maybe up to twenty-five thousand more uncounted. Only six hundred prisoners had been taken, proof of the fanatical nature of their resistance. But, although the tide had turned against them, they were far from finished.

May 1944, south-central Burma: The man whose name had been shouted as a battle cry of revenge was also finding life far from how he had imagined it. The Nehru Brigade, in which Tor Gul was serving in the 2nd Battalion, had been the last to leave Singapore. In the battalion was a whole number of southern Indians, Tamils mainly, recruited from the Singapore docks' labour force and workers from rubber estates up-country had joined the INA without any idea at all of what they had let themselves in for. Simple folk, they had been easily hoodwinked both by the IIL and also by the C-in-C when he lectured the whole of the *Azad Hind Fauj*, using clever propaganda at which he was an expert.

Propaganda is that branch of the art of lying which consists in very nearly deceiving your friends without quite deceiving your enemies by inducing people to leap to conclusions without adequate examination of the evidence: it had worked its magic on them, a perfect example of what happens when the plausible meet the gullible. He had, of course, spoken in Hindi to start with but, for the non-Hindi speaking southerners, he had used an interpreter. After a heady farewell from Singapore, they had only got as far north as Kuala Lumpur when they mutinied against their NCOs who tried to instil discipline into them as though they were normal Indian Army recruits. Not only that, the NCOs, northerners who only spoke in the *lingua franca* of the Indian Army, Urdu, and no English, were up against an impenetrable linguist barrier of speaking in a language that was not understood as the southern Indians knew no Urdu and spoke English as a second language. About three hundred of them refused to go on any farther. They were all dismissed by the battalion commander but, after considerable toing and froing, Subhas Chandra Bose insisted they be reinstated. Keeping them or sacking them was, in a way, a choice of the grotesque. It didn't make much difference as most of them ran away. In any case much time had been wasted over the un-thought-out consequences of enlisting them willy-nilly and more time was taken up in the INA's only being able to move by night because of British aerial domination.

By the time the Japanese were driven back from the Imphal battle, the Nehru battalions were still far to the south. Lance Naik Tor Gul, with his ugly Black Rose of a birthmark, managed to keep up with the soldiers but found life much harder than ever he had imagined. Often tired, hungry and 'feeling out of it' by not having any regimental experience, from time to time his thoughts turned to the other three of his gang, wondering how they were faring: it was just as well for his peace of mind that he had no idea. He had heard that Rabilal Rai had volunteered for a submarine journey – *plucky one, that*– and he had also known about how keen both cousins had been on making a parachute descent. *A spunky couple, always inclined to be flamboyant. Should have made a good job of it if Allah has been willing …*

May 1944, GHQ, New Delhi: … which had not been the case. News of Cousin Hamid's capture, as had that of Cousin Rahim, had 'gone up the line' to GHQ and although neither cousin was of much relevance, both the DMI and the DMO, especially the former, were interested enough to have a chat about it. 'Bert, that makes three out of the four that young Rance was talking about. Not all that bad to have found three needles in three disparate haystacks or three niggers in three different woodpiles. In themselves they are minor indeed but both show the power with the Japanese that the Jiff commander seems to have. From that point of view an in-depth debriefing might give us another insight of what goes on than we already have. But it is quite uncanny that both those parachutists were captured where Rance just "happened to be". Jinx, voodoo or whatever, it's impossible that the last of the gang will fall into his hands.'

'I agree with you, Bill,' said the DMO, straightening his already straight line of pencils. 'What I'd like is as much of the INA's comings and goings as possible. Like you it could be that the two men were more involved with their planning people than the other Jiffs we've captured.'

'Yes, that's more your line of country than it is of mine. We've got to get them here first. The reports I've had show that Rance has handled their capture most carefully, that's to say, he has recognised them by their tattoo and by being in Malaya with them pre-war but that's as far as he's gone. We can't keep their capture a secret but the fact we knew in advance of their plan, our "Magic", is safe because only a very limited few know about their parachuting escapade.'

'So how do you propose to play it?'

He unconsciously scratched his nose while he pondered: 'I'll brief the Military Police to keep them separate and not to let either know that the other has been captured. I'll leave it to them to bring them here, BORs only, no IORs in this case and put them in the Red Fort. This has to be kept, to put it really crudely, 'duck-arse water tight'. Once there I propose, and this is off the top of my head, to get that Gurkha, Rabilal Rai, to pretend that he's still unfriendly to us and secretly record conversations he has with them. Only that way will we be able to find any flaws in what either says or, indeed, what they would have cooked up together had they met up previously.'

'You don't think you're in danger of knocking the nail out of sight?' There was an undercurrent of irritation in the question. 'We've already had a lot of stuff from the Jiffs who have surrendered.'

The DMI fluttered an airy hand and his lips twitched into a small ironic smile. 'Yes I agree. We've heard a lot about the poor conditions in their operational doings but nothing from the angle that these two Malayan Jiffs could give us and who knows but we may find a nugget.' The DMO nodded but did not press the point. 'In any case it will have to go to the very, very top, to the Viceroy himself.'

Major Philip Rance had once more been called to the DMI's office and, to his surprise, was told that 'Your son had once more thrown a Double 6. Listen while I'll tell you what I want to happen.' Jason's father was particularly interested to learn that yet a third of the so-called Tor Gul Gang had been captured and that his son had been the catalyst for the capture in the 9/12 FFR's lines. 'That, sir, is indeed extra-ordinary and one minuscule chance in how many myriads.'

'I agree. What I believe is that, unlike the Jiff soldiers, these two may well have been quite near to the planning people in HQ. What I'm about to order is that only BOR policemen will handle them, keep conversation to a bare minimum, not let either know that the other has been captured and then hand them over to you in the Red Fort and then use your Rabilal as a stool-pigeon. What I am particularly looking for is any details about the Jiff HQ, personalities, methods et cetera. How, off the top of your head, will you play it?'

'As you suggest I'll get Rabilal Rai to pretend that he is still pro-INA and talk to them, one at a time, in Malay, which I too will fully understand. The talks will be recorded. Somehow I don't think I'll be able to turn them as we have done the Gurkha as their visceral hatred of my son and us British is too engrained for us even to try.'

'Hear, hear,' broke in the Brigadier.

'I won't necessarily let them know when I talk to them but they can be legally charged with a number of crimes, such as attempted murder, to say nothing of falsely emulating Indian Army soldiers, carrying fake documents and anti-British propaganda, trying to undermine morale, acting as enemy versus the Viceroy and/or the Governor of Singapore and/or of Malaya and dressed in military uniform when civilians as starters.' He paused to draw breath. 'There may be more,' he added with a glint of a smile, 'if those are not enough to make them swing for what they've done.'

'Thank you, Major. We are thinking along the same lines, I'm glad to say. But of course we need confirmation from the very top for that to happen.' He made a note of something on a memo pad. 'What are the odds of son Jason finding the fourth?'

Father Rance laughed. 'Even if I were a betting man, I'd say all the stars in the Milky Way to one against!'

3

Late May, 1944, 1 GRRC: The officers and men of 3/1 GR
were delighted to be given six months' away from the fighting
for a good spell of home leave for the soldiers, local leave for
the officers before re-manning the battalion to make up grievous
losses. At Dharmsala the Gurkhas were paid an advance before
going home. Jason had gone with them and after seeing his Recce
Platoon men off went to see the Adjutant. 'Welcome back. And
where will Jason Rance do his poodle-faking during this time or
do you want me to try and get you on some kind of weapons'
course?'

'If there's a sniper's course going and it's not too long, I'd
like that. But first I'd like a warrant for me to go to Delhi and
spend time with my parents. I haven't really had a chance to see
anything of them since I left Malaya in 1938.'

'Lucky for you they're near. What's their job? I'm told that
British officers out from England aren't allowed to have their
families with them. But wait one,' and he called the Chief Clerk.
'Subedar sahib, please look at the courses schedule and see if there
is a sniper's course we can send Captain Rance on during his leave
period.'

Jason didn't bother to answer the question and the Adjutant didn't press the point.

The Chief Clerk came back. 'Sahib, there's a four-week course in Saugor', pronouncing it as Sagar, 'running from mid-June to mid-July.'

'How about that, then? It'll be hot and wet.'

'No matter. Please put my name down for that. By then I should have got the twigs out of my ears and be ready for something to do.'

'Once I get confirmation I'll send a signal to the GHQ Camp Commandant. He'll get you to and from Saugor and give you a rail warrant for wheresoever Destiny will send you – and I wish it were I not you,' he added gloomily.

Mid-June, 1944, Red Fort, Delhi: *It must be about six years since that incident when Jason foiled those stupid lads in their attempt to break into my office that I had in one of the sheds at the bottom of my garden. Until Rabilal Rai so unexpectedly came on the scene I'd dismissed them from my mind,* father Rance thought when he was told that two prisoners, known as Item A and Item B for security's sake, had been put into separate cells somewhere within that spacious yet, in places, claustrophobic warren of red-coloured buildings. *Nor is it a question of 'chickens coming home to roost'* but an apt proverb did not come to him.

He sent for Rabilal Rai. His 'warder', Havildar Dilbahadur Pun, had been sent on home leave but Rabilal was now trusted enough to be by himself. He regarded Major Rance with almost as much awe as he did his son. 'Rabilal, I have a surprise for you,'

Philip Rance greeted him, as usual in Malay, their only common language, once the Gurkha was seated. 'What would you say if there were two new prisoners in the isolation cells by the names of Abdul Hamid Khan and Abdul Rahim Khan?'

'Tuan, if anyone other than you had told me I would not have believed it. How …?'

'All in good time but I will tell you that my son was present when each was caught. He is coming on leave quite soon and I'm sure he will want to meet you again.' He noticed a look of pleasure spread over Rabilal's face. 'What I want from you is something difficult but by now you have my complete trust so here it is: you will interview each one as though you, too, are a prisoner. You will not let on that the other is also in the Red Fort. You will be recorded and only after I have listened to their evidence will I become known to them. Can you manage that?'

'If you say so, Tuan, I'll have to. But after that I will also ask for something.'

'Can you ask me now?'

'May I?'

'Of course. I wouldn't have said so otherwise.'

Unexpectedly the Gurkha broke into silent tears, which he wiped away with his sleeve. 'Tuan, I've had enough of life here. When you son goes back to fight, as I'm sure he will, may I go as his servant, please, and look after him as he looked after me when he saved my life?' *So he has learnt about that part of his rescue!*

'I can't promise but I'll keep it in mind and ask my son. Now let's get down to details …'

Abdul Hamid Khan's mind was in a whirl. The journey from when he had so unexpectedly been confronted with his life-long enemy was engraved on his mind. It had become magnified and distorted beyond reality and he still could not believe in his inglorious capture. But that had become dimmed with the seemingly unending railway journey, always handcuffed to a British military policeman who only spoke to him when he gave him orders. He had not seen much during his journey but the amount of military might, vehicles, artillery, armour and men he had seen had made a deep impression. *Compared with what we had it is overwhelming. We can't, surely, win against that lot?* He was taken out of the train where he could not see the name of the station and driven in a windowless vehicle, obviously through heavy traffic by the stops and starts and horn blowing, to ... where the vehicle had stopped and the escort sitting in the front of the vehicle interrogated. Then off again and a few minutes later the doors were opened and he was taken to a cell. His handcuffs were taken off. His gaoler left him. He looked around and saw a bed riveted to the ground, a basic lavatory and wash basin. Light at the upper part of one wall showed a small, barred window and an electric bulb dimly shone. He had no idea at all where he was. He lay on the bed and tried to doze, thankful that the jerking, jolting, juddering journey that had taken so long was now at an end.

He heard footsteps outside his cell that sounded hollow in the hush. The door opened and he was totally thrown on seeing Rabilal – *Rabilal of all people* – come in with a mug of tea and some parathas. 'Hello, Hamid. I've brought you something to eat,' he began in Malay but was almost knocked over by Abdul's delighted embrace. 'Rabilal, is it really you?' ecstasy in his tired voice.

'Yes, they got me as they seem to have got you. I'm allowed to work in the kitchen and I overheard your name so I managed to bring this for you. I can't stay long but I'll be back with some excuse or other fairly soon,' and with that he left then went and did the same with Rahim with the same result, total surprise and unmitigated delight.

The wiring system had been checked but even so after each first visit it was rechecked and found effective, so, over the next few days, Rabilal visited both cells and spoke at length with both men. His 'excuse' was that he was off duty and had bribed the gaoler not to look in. He was accepted at face value: after all, bribes always oiled the works, didn't they?

The two cousins became more talkative and eagerly answered the Gurkha's questions. All of what had happened poured out of each in a controlled, cathartic cascade: about how they had joined the INA, how they had acquired the ID cards of real soldiers, how many people worked where, what Neta-ji was doing, office routine, how were relations with the Japanese and much more including details of their parachute adventure and how they had found that arch fiend from KL days until Philip Rance felt he had enough to write a long report for the DMI to forward to the C-in-C and the Viceroy: all particulars had to be 'just so'.

'According to English law a witness who can be cross-examined would be needed to stitch up an unanswerable case against them, surely?' the DMI commented to Philip Rance after calling him in. 'That one person has to be your son.

Where is he now?'

'He's just started a month's sniper's course in Saugor and won't be available until mid-July, sir.'

The DMI looked at a wall calendar. 'We mustn't go outside the law, even on this one, much as I'd like to. I do know that The India Army Act of 1922, as amended, requires death for a soldier caught like these two were but what we need to know now is if what the Manual of Military Law, Part II, says about what it calls camp followers, namely civilians attached to the army, applies to these two. So what we must do now is prepare a case for whichever way the Law needs it to. That will take time. It will fit in nicely if I can get the "Legal Eagles" to have their case ready by the time your son finishes his course. I'll keep you informed and there's no need to tell your son anything till he comes back.'

'Understood, sir,' and with a passable salute, Philip Rance went back to his office in the Red Fort.

25 June 1944, Somewhere in South Siam: By now the two escaping Gurkhas could speak simple Chinese and had rendered sterling service to their protectors, not only in laying successful ambushes and false trails so confusing follow ups but also in such matters as weapons training, camp sentries and even siting latrines downwind from any camp. They had also led the guerillas on some daring raids, Naik Lalsing having made some audacious and spectacular kills with his bare hands, once against a Japanese captain armed with a sword. They had had to move their base a number of times for although, contrary to expectations, the Japanese were not expert jungle fighters, being far too noisy, local

Siamese were scared enough of them not to inform them when asked if they knew where the Chinese were.

After their meal that evening the QMJ said to the senior Chinese anti-Japanese fighter, 'Friend, by my reckoning our six months' help to you finishes today so it is time we moved on north. Lalsing also wants to move with us. Do you agree?'

The senior man took a draught of *samsu*, 'triple-distilled' rice wine, coughed, deftly spat, cleared his throat, wiped his lips and, after a long pause, said yes, he did. After talking rapidly and at length with his comrades, he said, 'Movement overland in the south is unwise and as the man to lead you, Lee Soong, has an uncle who owns a fishing boat at Songkhla on the east coast he will take you there and arrange to sail up the coast by boat to any village to the southwest of and about a hundred distance-apart-by-direct-route miles from Bangkok. The skipper of the vessel will know where best to land you. Once off the boat go by bus or train up as far as the Golden Triangle where there are our people who hate the Japanese.'

The Gurkhas looked blankly at one another at the mention of 'Golden Triangle', not understanding what was meant. The senior man saw his mistake and corrected himself: 'Up in the north, near the borders of Laos, Siam and Burma, is an area of poppies that gives a good harvest of opium. Some of our forces give the Nippons opium as a way for a free pass. Lee Soon can fix it for you with them. You will travel as Siamese peasants. We can fix up your clothes for you.' He looked quizzically at Lalsing as though weighing up some important point. 'You're a short man. If you can kill a large male honey bear, skin it and wear it. The other two can lead you as though taking you to a circus. In any case, if the Nippons stop you, you could always dance for them and,' chortling at his own joke, 'you won't need to be taught how to!

'I will write them a letter asking them to help you and I believe they will be able to give you enough opium balls to bribe the Japanese soldiers with to give you safe passage. Then you move west, making for the Mount Popa area. After that it'll be up to you.'

Roars of earthy and robust laughter greeted such an absurd idea. That evening they held a council of war to decide how best to help the three Gurkhas, for Rifleman Manbir Gurung also wanted to try and get back. The more innocent the group seemed the more likely it would be that their passage would not be prohibited and, wearing local fig, they planned to move up the coast, finding out from each village they sold their wares to what might lie ahead of them.

The Gurkhas never knew how payment would be made but it was, in fact, in rubies and opium, both to become 'available' at the far end of their journey.

Next morning, brimming with good humour and thanks resounding in their ears, the small group set off for the next stage of as unpredictable journey as any they had previously taken.

Mid-August 1944, GHQ and Red Fort, Delhi: After Jason's sniper course, for which he received the highest grading and a request from the Weapon Training School authorities that he be kept on as an instructor, he returned to finish his leave. He was happy enough in Delhi: there was a surprising amount of social life and a pleasing mixture of single and married but unattached women to let him go so far but no further, but under the surface he pined to go back to his unit. One day he was called to the DMI's office. He was told to go in by the Personal Assistant so in he went with a cracking salute.

'Sit down,' was the peremptory order. 'I am sure you can remember my quoting to you about "the long arm of coincidence"?' Before Jason could answer 'I have another for you, a translation, "Though the mills of God grind slowly, yet they grind exceeding small". It is, in fact, an old, old quotation. Do you know it? I'll give you a clue: it was translated from the German by Longfellow.' The Brigadier rather fancied himself as knowing just a little bit more than others did.

'I haven't heard it since I was at school, sir,' Jason answered, wondering what on earth the Brigadier was on about.

'Okay, I'll stop trying to be clever and come to the point. It's about those two men who tried to kill you, one in the hospital in Dimapur and the other with 9/12 FFR. The case against them must be water-tight and I want you to write out a report of exactly what happened, with background in 1938 and your unexpected meetings with both men. The report, with one I'll prepare about what the two men themselves have to say, will go to the C-in-C and Viceroy for further action. It must be "chapter and verse" in every respect. Today is Thursday. Bring it in manuscript to me, personally, by midday Monday. I will have the necessary amount of copies made and call you in to sign them.'

'Sir, that'll be no problem. All the facts you need are fully embedded in my memory.'

'Good. Until the Viceroy gives his verdict, you'll have to hang around here.'

'So I am to stay here till then?'

'Yes, that's right. Once your leave is finished we may give you the odd job but there's no going back to your battalion or the Centre for a while.'

'Understood. Is there anything else, sir?'

There wasn't, so he left the office with another cracking salute. Shortly afterwards the Military Secretary's Branch, which looks after promotions and some postings, sent advice to 1 GRRC at Dharmsala that the-by-now Captain Rance had been temporarily posted to Camp HQ in GHQ as a supernumerary.

The Viceroy's decision was announced towards the end of August. The two accused, who had yet to know about the other's existence, were brought together to hear their future. They exchanged agitated glances but were not allowed to speak to each other. It was all over in a morning. The charges were read out and the verdict was announced by the President of the Court, the Judge Advocate General, who put a black cap on his wig. 'Guilty!' He then pronounced the sentence: "You will be taken from here …" he paused. The cousins looked up, a happy expression on each face, perversely presuming they were being allowed to go free. This was dashed into one of deepest dejection as the full import of the next part of the sentence was uttered, '… to a place of lawful execution and there you will be hanged by the neck until you are dead. And may the Lord have mercy on your souls.'

Jason was somehow troubled by those damning words: he

would have felt more troubled had he somehow known he would hear them again in another eight years.

Late August 1944, Central Burma: The Mahindra Dal, having shown a greater ability to operate in a major war than had the other units of the Nepalese Contingent, had crossed the Chindwin with the 14th Army and entered central Burma. The CO, Lieutenant Colonel Ksatra Bikram Rana, had the guts to disregard the order against going into Burma and a crisis arose once it was known about it because it went against what the Maharaja had specifically insisted on. The battalion was ordered back into India and the CO sent for by General Krishna, the Maharaja's representative in Delhi, to explain why the Maharaja's implicit order had been wilfully disobeyed. Leaving his battalion where it was he managed to get onto an aeroplane that stopped at Kandy in Ceylon where he had an unexpected meeting with the Supreme Allied Commander, Admiral Lord Louis Mountbatten. The result was that the Admiral personally wrote to the Maharaja praising 'The Mahindra Dal' as being of such a high standard it would ruin its morale if it was recalled. Armed with the letter the CO continued on his journey to Delhi and delivered it. While waiting in the Nepalese embassy for a reply he was interviewed by both the DMO and DMI where he asked if there was any chance of his battalion being given some sniper rifles – Lee Enfields No 4 Mk I (T) with No 32 Mk II telescopes – and an instructor to help out. *This is a good chance to show willing. Captain Rance will be the ideal man to send to them.* The case was put up to the C-in-C who agreed to it and that Captain Rance would deliver them when they were ready. Another posting order was initiated by the Military Secretary's branch for that to happen.

The Maharaja was so pleased with what had been written, especially by a close relation of the King-Emperor, that his original stricture was not to be applied to the Mahindra Dal. It was also announced from Kathmandu that the 'The', as written in the Supreme Commander's letter, was to be uniquely included in its official name.

General Krishna made a phone call to the C-in-C's office, as protocol allowed, to tell him that the battalion would remain in Burma. 'Lieutenant Colonel Ksatra Bikram Rana has told me about his request for sniper rifles. Have you any answer please before he leaves Delhi?'

'Yes, General sahib. It has been authorised and I have detailed a Captain Rance from 1 GR to be attached to the Mahindra Dal if you approve for as long as the CO wishes him to be there. He will be the instructor for how to use the weapons as he has just passed out top from a sniper's course.'

'Thank you, General sahib. That is good news and will strengthen our two countries' relationship.'

'Indeed so. Please tell the CO to report to the DMO, Major General Arnold, tomorrow afternoon at two o'clock by which time I will have arranged for Captain Rance to be there so the two officers can meet up.'

And meet up they did and both liked what they saw. Four weapons were deemed enough and they would be taken personally by Captain Rance as soon as they were ready. Jason told his parents that he had a new job and it was then that father Rance mentioned that Rabilal Rai had asked if he could go with him. 'I'd like that but I can't very well take him as a civilian, can I?'

No, he couldn't so it seemed that Rabilal would be unlucky. Father Rance then had an idea: 'I'll talk to the one man I think can help us, Brigadier Lambert,' and rather daringly he thought, put a phone call through to the ADC asking for an interview, 'just a short one, please.'

A time was arranged. 'What can I do for you? I'm rather busy,' was the gruff riposte.

'Sir, I apologise for taking up your time so I'll keep it short. My son, as you already know, is to be attached to the Mahindra Dal. The man Rabilal Rai wants to go with him. My son is happy to take him but he's a civilian yet I feel that, with his background, he might well recognise any other Jiff infiltrator from Singapore and so would be an unusual asset to the Nepalese battalion.'

The DMI thought that one over. 'No harm in that, I suppose, but why come to me?'

Trying to show no exasperation, Philip Rance said, 'Sir, quite honestly, you are the only senior officer I feel will listen to me. How can we get Rabilal Rai enlisted so he can be officially my son's, er, batman?'

'I wouldn't normally do anything but the Gurkha worships your son so I'll talk to the Military Secretary's Branch and they'll come up with some clever scheme, I expect. It'll take a day or three but leave it with me. By the time the box of sniper's rifles is ready for your son to take with him, I'll have an answer.'

And the answer was that Rabilal Rai found himself a soldier in 1 Gurkha Rifles. He was overjoyed and promised Jason that he would not let him down. 'Wouldn't it be strange if I came across that Tor Gul man?' he laughed. 'However much I might curse him, if it hadn't been for him you and I would never have met up in India, would we?'

Both laughed and Jason took his 'batman' to the Camp Commander's Quartermaster to be kitted out.

Late November 1944, Siamese-Burmese border: The first six weeks of their journey by fishing boat was without any untoward incident. Once Jemadar Rahul Dura became used to the boat's movement he was glad of the enforced rest. The other two Gurkhas, the naik and the rifleman, found the inactivity boring but moved around in the villages where their wares were sold. They eventually left their boat at a place they never learnt the name of and after many thanks, managed to get a bus at Nakhon Pathom as far as the main north-south road at Phitsanulok. It was then a question of going to Chiang Rai in another bus.

Loo Soong kept them cooped up in a small hut at the edge of the town for a day or so while he tried to find out what the situation was. As he said, there was no point in going head first into a dangerous situation if it could be avoided. 'I have found out that the journey to the area of the Golden Triangle, the route we mentioned before we set out, is unsuitable for your purposes. I will therefore take you west to the border then I'll make my own way on by myself.'

In the guise of locals they moved across country until they reached the border. These last five months had not been easy for the three Gurkhas and their small escort, without whom they would have never got as far as they had. It was seldom that they had a sustaining meal and the mental 'wear and tear', ever since the disaster of 1942, was taking its toll. The naik and rifleman, being younger, had managed reasonably well but the QMJ, being so much older, had found the going hard, yet he simply would not give up and the other two Gurkhas and their Chinese escort respected him for it so helped him unobtrusively as and when they could.

Loo Soong gave them enough balls of opium before they parted company – *where had he kept them all this time or had he somehow got them on the way in exchange ... for what?* the Gurkhas wondered – for a couple of months' barter. 'This next part of your journey will be dangerous,' the Chinese let them know. 'You will be on your own and the area in full of Japanese troops. I have heard that the British and Indian soldiers have won great victories but that the Japanese are fighting back strongly. There are also Indians moving up from the south. Aim for south of Inle Lake, which is almost due west from here, then move towards Mount Popa, which can easily be seen from far off. I haven't been there myself but from what I've heard about the place it is an extinct volcano in the middle of Burma's "dry belt" which never dries up and is full of lush jungle. Nats who some people say are rogues live there. If you can find one you can talk to, he will give you news about any fighting in the area and where to avoid. I advise you to keep a ball of opium for him.'

They made their farewells with reluctance: seldom had the Gurkhas met more reliable allies.

January 1945, Mount Popa area: If the Japanese, along with some units of the INA, could hold Mount Popa, which dominates the surrounding countryside so was a natural observation post, it would not, in itself, secure the Irrawaddy but it would be a distraction that might hold the 14th Army advance up sufficiently to let the Japanese manoeuvre their south-going troops more effectively to prevent their enemy from getting to Rangoon before the monsoon started. Its defence was all-important.

The Japanese were still fighting with undiminished fury and they, too, were suffering from a lack of supplies, their Higher Command not having envisaged such a fighting retreat without any 'Churchill rations' to keep them operationally impervious as had been the case to start with. Their forces comprised two armies, the 15th on the left facing their adversaries and the 28th on the right. However, after sustaining more casualties than there were reinforcements to make up numbers, there was a gap between them and it was the Nehru Brigade that was detailed to fill it. As the INA had always claimed parity with the Japanese as a fighting army, the defence of parts of Mount Popa was also given it. So far almost untouched by battle or the wasting effect of rain-sodden hills, it was expected to be the best formation the INA had.

At Popa's higher levels it was wonderfully cooler than elsewhere and jungle fruits were an almost unheard of luxury. Colonel Shah Nawaz, glad to be in the field after his office job, was commanding the battalion of the Nehru Brigade that was covering the most likely 14th Army's axis of approach, based on the village of Legyi, where there was a Buddhist temple, known for its kindness to travellers, a mere military 'stone's throw' to the north of the main Mount Popa feature. The INA CO had as his batman-cum-body-guard Lance Naik Tor Gul who had shown that he had it in him to withstand the difficulties that were thrown at him without murmur, mutter or mumble more than was the case with most other Indians who had been recruited from Malaya. Those who had mutinied and had needed punishment had been forgiven by their unarmed C-in-C but were a burden to any CO who wanted a unit that knew how to fight and could be relied on so to do.

By now conditions in the INA were worse than many of its soldiers had ever imagined or had been trained for. Everything a campaigning soldier needs were either in short supply or non-existent. Desertions back to the Indian Army proper were increasingly taking place and battalion commanders had started to execute men they had found trying to in front of others as a warning not to.

Part of the Nehru Brigade had had one success that raised morale considerably: when the South Lancashire Regiment tried a river crossing over the Irrawaddy at Nyaung many of their boat engines, which were only to be started when they had pushed off, failed and as the boats drifted the men of one of the Nehru battalions inflicted casualties on the British troops and sank some boats, killing two company commanders and the engineer officer responsible for the boats. Aircraft were called in and the boats returned to their own shore. Later, another crossing also failed but, to the surprise of all the attackers, a small boat bearing a white flag put off from the opposite bank. In it were two Jiffs who, on coming ashore, said that the Japanese had marched out of the attacker's target, Pagan, leaving the INA to garrison the town. The aim of the INA, now that there were no longer any Japanese to bully them, was to surrender, and that is what they did.[8]

What fighting there was between the INA and the attacking army mostly took place at Kyaukpadaung, farther south, above which from not far away the heights of Mount Popa frowned. It was in that general area that the by-now-under-strength units of the Nehru Brigade were located.

Quite why Colonel Shah Nawaz had Lance Naik Tor Gul, with that 'black-rose' birthmark on one side of his forehead, as a batman-cum-runner when there were 'real', more sophisticated men than he to choose from was as much a show of unanimity with Malayan-born Indians as anything else. But the lad was a devout Muslim, which the Colonel also was, and that was a strong bond.

One evening, after their meal, the Colonel was visited by his friend, Colonel Gurbaksh Singh Dhillon. Tor Gul, ever faithful, sat in the background. By now he was fully trusted, which pleased him greatly.

'Sardar-ji, we have come a long, long way from where we started back in India. We have vowed to re-conquer the country from the British but …' and his voice trailed off. 'Tor Gul, if there is any, go and make us each a mug of tea,' he started up again, then 'but the odds against us are frightening. Apart from the British

---

8 In his *Defeat into Victory*, the author, Field Marshal Slim, noted that 'This incident was, I think, the chief contribution the Indian National Army made to either side in the Burma War.'

troops we killed when they were crossing the river, and their boats failed them – more like an exercise with live ammunition than real war – and that troop of dismounted State Force Gwalior Lancers led by Jemadar Gajendra Singh surrendering to our *Bahadurs,* along with those few hundred sepoys the Japanese had captured in the Arakan and let come over to us, we haven't had any success at all ... doesn't add up to very much, does it, after the extraordinary efforts and privations we have all suffered so far and are still suffering?' *It's a wonder we've managed to do what we have,* he thought dejectedly at the human price paid. *If what we've coped with had been on the other side bow many bravery awards would we have won*? and immediately cursed himself for such give-away thoughts.

'No, it doesn't, militarily for all the effort put into our operations, I agree with you but the spirit shown by the rank and file has been, in the main, of an extremely high standard, in fact far higher than would have been expected of them when they were enlisted.' Shah Nawaz nodded his agreement but did not interrupt. 'Personally I cannot see military success coming our way, except maybe, in an odd skirmish. But if the spirit shown to date can, after the war is over, also be shown when we govern India by ourselves, it can only do good for us.'

'I agree. The Britishers, individually I've come across a lot of jolly good chaps and I have always admired the way they look after their soldiers. They often care for them better than some of us do. But, and it's a big, big but, they can't rule India for ever and I for one have committed myself so far I dare not ... do anything other than what I am doing.'

His friend took that to mean that there was no idea of his surrendering. Tor Gul returned with the tea. 'I am sorry, Hazur, to be so slow but while looking for some sugar I heard a rumour that some Nepalese Contingent troops were not far away and I thought you'd be interested.'

'Nepalese troops?' both men chorused. Dhillon continued, 'They don't have all that good reputation, do they, compared with our Indian Army Gurkhas. Do you think we could induce some of them to join us?'

'Now that's a thought worth considering,' echoed his friend and they sipped in silence, thinking out possibilities.

Before Colonel Dhillon left Lance Naik Tor Gul came to collect the empty mugs. 'Tor Gul, I know why are you so keen to see India free although you've never been there because you told me when I was planning. But tell me what your thoughts are now.'

Tor Gul stroked his luxuriant moustache as he carefully considered the question. He found it difficult to express the thought that 'not so easily can mankind escape from the rigours of his pilgrimages' but he made a stab at it, haltingly to start with 'Hazur, it began as a personal vendetta as a result of a misconceived raid on a house in Kuala Lumpur when I was no more than a kid. I even named it Operation "Tor Gul", which is Pashto for "Black Rose",' unconsciously touching the ugly birthmark on the side of his forehead. 'That would be,' and he counted on his fingers, 'seven years ago. My father also taught me about the doings of the IIL which has lodged in the back of my memory, merely as a goad to good performance rather than my ultimate goal to kill as many Britishers as possible. So far I have yet to kill anybody,' and with a painful laugh, 'except myself on our long, arduous and often hungry marches and have learnt what inspired hope can do against great odds.'

'That's a fair enough answer. You have done well, very well considering you never had the recruit training that normal Indian Army soldiers have. What if you were to catch up with … by the way who is the person who made your anti-Britisher quest into your personal vendetta?'

'His name is Jason Rance and he is about my age. He is a Chinese linguist and also speaks good Malaya but never bothered to learn Hindi or Urdu.' *Should he have, in colonial Malaya?* the colonel wondered. 'He left home for England the day after we raided his father's office. I expect I'd recognise him again but the chances of ever meeting up with him are' and he sought for a simile. 'Even if I were a betting man, I'd say all the stars in the Milky Way to one against! – but it's still Operation "Black Rose".'

The two colonels laughed. 'Right, if there is any real news about the Nepalese Contingent unit coming, your job will be to disguise yourself as a monk and go to the temple at Legyi to observe and report even though there is no way a British officer will be found serving in a Nepalese army unit.'

Late February 1945, near Mount Popa: Captain Jason Rance and Rifleman Rabilal Rai, resplendent in his jungle green uniform and armed with a pistol, had taken the sniper rifles to the Mahindra Dal. They had been welcomed by the CO, who warmly thanked them for helping out, and as soon as there was a lull in activities Jason and the Second-in-Command arranged a short training course. The Nepalese soldiers were intrigued by the Englishman, never having set eyes on any such as him before leaving Kathmandu, nor having spoken to one ever. They were unaware that any foreigner could speak Nepali and Jason's fluency both pleased and puzzled them. But what really made him a favourite was when one particularly dumb soldier simply could not get used to shutting one eye Jason had taken hold of the rifle and, as though it was the rifle itself speaking, told the soldier that 'you are no use to me if you can't shut your left eye.' That was pure magic, the men never having heard a ventriloquist before: it cemented relations and so convinced the erring soldier that he just had to close his left eye that he did, and he became the champion marksman.

'Colonel sahib, I think your men are as well trained as I can make them. It is time for me to return to my battalion,' Jason announced one morning.

'So soon, Captain sahib? If you go, where will you go to? What I know of your military postings it could take months before you could get to an active unit again. You'll go to, where is your centre, Dharmsala, isn't it?' Jason nodded that it was. 'And then they'll keep you there as a Weapon Training Officer to teach the recruits how to use sniper rifles!' and he laughed at such an idea. 'I've just had orders that we are to go to the Mount Popa area where I believe the Nehru battalions of the Jiffs are. Our axis of advance is towards the village of Legyi, a short distance to its north, which may well have Jiff standing patrols in it. And after that? There might be some good sport sniping up at the top of Mount Popa, if we get that high, as there is plenty of *shikar* I hear and *shikar* with two legs is more valuable, certainly around here, than *shikar* with four,' and he laughed delightedly at his own joke.

On hearing the words 'Jiffs' and 'Nehru' Jason's mind went back to the information the two cousins had given Rabilal about Tor Gul. *'Providence finds the python's food' is a Gurkhali proverb I've learnt: am I somehow being led into getting a 'full house' with Number 4?* He felt dizzy at such a thought. 'Colonel sahib. Your words fill me with encouragement. Please send a signal to your higher formation asking that I be kept with you for as long as it takes to see if my training is successful on operations.'

The signal was sent and Jason was allowed to stay until the end of April.

The Gurkha group of three, wearing Buddhist monks' vestments, had slowly moved to the south of Inle Lake and could easily see Mount Popa to their west. The QMJ was tiring badly and the other two, much younger, were also finding the going difficult, not so much because of the terrain but food was in short supply. They had managed to use some of their opium balls in exchange for enough rice to last them a week and as they rounded the lake some delicious fish, fresh and sustaining. One evening, as they sought sanctuary in a Buddhist temple, they came across four Jiffs who were cooking their evening meal. Pretending to ignore them as they prepared their own food they were able to hear the drift of their conversation. It seemed that they were on patrol from Mount Popa. 'This won't be the last time we'll come so far south if the Indian Army has anything to do with it as they are so much stronger than we are,' a Havildar was saying. 'They're coming down south and we must meet them to the north of Mount Popa. If the Britishers have any sense they'll keep away from the village of Legyi as the Buddhist temple is famous there and the monks deplore anyone with weapons. But then will they bother about the natives here if they never bothered about us?'

'I was a pre-war soldier,' said one of the patrol, 'and the sahibs were always decent with us. It was their defeat in Malaya that made our leaders lose faith in them.'

'Certainly our recruit training was cut short. But not as bad as the Gurkhas who had trained for the desert in Africa but were sent to Malaya instead.'

There was silence until a sepoy asked, 'and what about us? What we've been doing is far harder than I ever thought when I volunteered for the army. I've just about had enough,' and turning his head away from the others silent tears poured down his cheeks.

The Gurkhas saw the Havildar waggle in head in agreement. 'So have I,' he said and looking conspiratorially at the other three. 'How about you? Tell me truthfully as we are alone and this is important.'

Two of them agreed but the youngest had an objection. 'If the sahibs hear about it, won't they shoot us as they shoot deserters?'

'I don't want to be shot after all we've been through. Can you ensure we can get away safely?' asked one man.

The Havildar suddenly looked pleased. 'Got it! I overheard a rumour that a Nepalese Contingent battalion was moving south and the village of Legyi is on their axis of advance. We've a standing patrol there. You may not have heard but because we are so short of ammunition our men are going on recce patrols as Burmese monks. I believe one or two of them have even managed to overhear Britisher soldiers talking. It's a pity they didn't understand English. On our return I'll volunteer to take you out on a recce patrol forward beyond the village and we'll surrender to the Nepalese. We have no quarrel with any of them. They are good men.'

The three others clapped their hands with joy and the Gurkhas looked meaningfully at one another, fingers to their lips.

After the Jiffs had finished their meal they settled down for the night. They felt safe enough not to bother about having a sentry. The QMJ whispered to the others, 'Do we take advantage of what we heard? Do you think we can convince the Havildar to take us as far as Legyi temple where we can rest up until the advancing troops reach us? What do you think?' and he first asked Naik Lalsing then Rifleman Manbahadur. It was decided it was worthwhile and that Naik Lalsing be the spokesman. 'They won't have gone to sleep yet, go and talk to the Havildar.'

'Havildar-ji, are you awake?'

The man must have been dozing off as half leaped to his feet with an agonised, 'Who are you? Who are you?'

'My name is Naik Lalsing Dura and my unit is 2/2 GR. I was never taken prisoner and I have been working with the Chinese guerillas in south Siam until I could find a way of escaping back to India. There are two others with me and we are in disguise as Buddhist lamas ...'

The Havildar broke in, 'How can I trust you? How do I know you are telling the truth?' He was obviously worried.

''I don't know how well you know us Gurkhas but if you do even a bit you will know we have a reputation for telling the truth. Other than that you'll have to trust us. We never joined the INA so we are not spies. About six months ago I managed to persuade some Chinese guerillas I was working with that I and two others, one the 2/1 GR QMJ who's finding the going really tough and the other a rifleman, to let us go. It's taken us seven months to get as far as here and we heard what you were talking about.'

That convinced the Havildar who said, 'So why have you come to talk to me?'

'Well, we think that if we all go in a group it will be safer for us. You will be seen as helping three monks ...'

Again he was interrupted. 'Monks, yes, you said you were dressed like as a Buddhist lama. What do you think about us four also being dressed similarly and we all go as one bunch?'

'It might look strange to have seven monks all traipsing along together but,' he paused, 'isn't it Buddhist Lent soon?'

The Havildar laughed. 'I'm a Muslim so I can't tell you but it sounds a sensible reason for so many to be together at one time. And anyway I'm sure hardly any of the INA or the Indian Army have much of an idea about it. But seven monks all together might make people ask questions.'

'Come and talk to the Jemadar sahib. He may have an idea. While you get ready I'll go and brief him.'

It was decided that although there were enough opium balls to get enough cloth for four men the Jiffs did not have the features of most Burmese. As they knew the way to Legyi it was proposed that the four Indians would walk with the Gurkhas as far as the village. The QMJ offered to write a note to the Nepalese battalion stating who he was and that the four men had helped them so would they please look after them.

The Gurkhas had lost all sense of time but the Havildar remembered the date. 'I think I'll try and collect some rations and, say, we part from the outskirts of Legyi on ... the 15th of March. How does that sound to you?'

'For us any day will do provided we get there as speedily as safety allows,' was the shrewd answer.

Mid-March 1945, near Mount Popa: Reports coming in to the Mahindra Dal told the CO that the Japanese and the Jiffs were on Mount Popa but were operating separately, the Japanese on two of the highest pieces of ground and the Jiffs along the base of the mountain. The CO sent for Jason. 'Captain sahib, I have a job for you and your snipers. We are in quite open country, look,' and he pointed out on a one-inch map the salient features. 'If you take a pair of binoculars you may well see a target to snipe at on Popa's lower slopes. If there's a two-storey house with a flat roof in Legyi village – and I'm hoping here – rather than your going nearer the base of the feature looking for a tall tree, use the house. Whatever else, stay clear of any temple there will probably be there. The last thing we need is your being chased away by angry monks, not that you couldn't outstrip them, but it's the rifles I'm worried about,' and once more he laughed delightedly at his own joke.

'I like it, Colonel sahib. It is something after my own heart.

Can you give me a possible date?'

'Plan for the 15th and come and see me before you go. We won't be far behind you.'

Before he went to sleep that night Jason's mind latched onto something he had learnt at school: the Ides of March were on the 15th and in 44 BC was when Julius Caesar was murdered. *What does that portend* as he worked out the length of time *one thousand and eighty years later?*

Earlier that same morning, the 13th of March, Colonel Shah Nawaz called Lance Naik Tor Gul over to him. 'You already know about my sending out jawans dressed as monks on recce patrols.' Tor Gul nodded. Of course he knew: who didn't? 'I am concerned at being taken by surprise of an advance, either by the Nepalese battalion we have heard about or a unit of the Indian Army. You and two men will dress as monks. The two will recce northwards towards the fighting and you will stay in the temple precincts in Legyi. Your combined reports could well be of great use to me in deciding how to defend our positions here. I want you there just after dawn tomorrow and the next day, the 15th. Both days take some haversack rations and come back at dusk. It may be boring for you but the size of your moustache is not to be found locally and your gift from the Almighty, your Tor Gul, is not suitable for you to go on active patrolling. So, what shall I say, "Covering your head in meditation" could be your pose if a suspicious target comes along. Do you have a weapon?'

'Yes, Colonel sahib, I do, two in fact. One is a thin rope round my body I can strangle a person with and the other is my extra sharp clasp knife. Both need a religious baptism and Allah will forgive me, I am sure, for using the precincts of a Buddhist temple for such to happen,' and they both laughed.

15 March 1945, near Mount Popa: The Gurkha trio, accompanied by the four Jiffs, crossed a small rise where they rested. They had heard the sound of artillery since the day before and now it was much louder, away to their northwest. Mount Popa had been in view for some time back and from where they were now, they could see the shrines on the lower slopes. 'Jemadar sahib,' called out the Havildar, 'do you see that village in the middle distance?'

The QMJ's eyesight was failing but he was too proud to let anyone know. His own two men guessed it by the way he felt around for something that was right in front of him. 'Yes,' was his answer.

'That's Legyi and we can see the temple on the far side of it. What I propose is that together we go as far as the first track that leads off to the west where I and my three men will leave you. I won't ask you your plans as a precaution.'

Naik Lalsing Dura objected. 'No, Havildar. Tell the people you surrender to about us so they can be on the look out to help us,' and he nodded at the QMJ who had shut his eyes.

A few minutes later they moved off.

Before moving off at first light Captain Rance briefed his fighting patrol, which had one of the battalion's four snipers. 'My aim is for the sniper to kill any Jiffs visible on the lower slopes of

Mount Popa and in the village of Legyi. We can only decide on the best place for him once we're near the village. I hope we find an unoccupied house that has a good view of both places from an upper room. The rest of the patrol will be in defensive positions. It is a pity there are no houses with flat roofs. If we see a tree that is better than a house and is suitable to climb up, the sniper will find a place in it. Before we move I'll inspect you.'

Once ready, they moved forward from where the battalion had spent the night, on the roadside a couple of miles back. On the near side of the village was a school, now empty, which was a two-storey building but with a sloping roof. Jason and his sniper went inside and found it suitable. From one window there was a good view of the side of the higher ground and a track leading down and from the other was the village temple. They could hear its bells mellifluously tinkling in the light wind so near were they to it. 'We'll take turn and turn about with the binoculars to give the other's eyes a rest.'

It was shortly before midday when three weary Gurkhas reached Negyi. 'Let's go to the temple for a rest and ask the monks if they know anything about the fighting. We might even find a Jiff with some knowledge. We can ask for water and, maybe, rice for a meal.'

Except for the background rumbling of artillery and the crump of bombs, all was peaceful in the temple compound. There, at one end of the open space, they saw a monk sitting down with his head covered. 'I'll go over and ask him,' volunteered Manbir. The others sat on the balcony under the temple roof and watched him.

Manbir went up to the monk and spoke to him in Burmese. 'San, yea. Be ma?' There was no answer to 'Where is rice and water?'

Tor Gul simply hadn't thought about being spoken to by another monk so had no answer.

Manbir remembered the Tibetan monks who periodically came to his village and asked his mother for food. They would put their right hands to their mouth and say 'Say-ma ochheñ.' He tried it but again there was no reaction. *Strange! Maybe he's deaf and dumb. He won't know Hindi but I'll try.* Try he did and the monk answered him, devastatingly. 'I don't know and leave me alone,' abruptly turning his head; the covering slipped and was quickly pulled back over it. Manbir was surprised at the luxuriant moustache and saw the birthmark, in which a vein throbbed like a black worm, on the side of his forehead but gave no sign that he had. He went back to the others and told them that they'd have to ask the head monk and the other man somehow didn't seem like a monk. 'Got such a moustache I've only ever seen on a north Indian and he has a birthmark like a, a, black rose on the side of his forehead.'

'Do you think he's a Jiff in disguise?' asked the QMJ.

'Why not? I hadn't thought of it?'

'I'll go and talk to him. I think I know who he is.'

By now Rance was getting bored as nothing had presented itself as a target. From the school window he could easily see the temple and its grounds. He watched the entry into the precincts of three monks and did a double take as he saw the one at the back had hard eyes, a determined jutting chin with furrows that resembled the marks of a leopard's claws on a tree trunk – *no I can't believe it, Rahul Dura of all people?* He watched the leading monk of the three who had just entered – *is he a Gurkha too? Are all three Gurkhas?* – go up to the monk who had been there all the time, sitting on the balcony with his head covered – *I'd like to know what they're talking about.* Suddenly an obvious altercation arose. Jason saw the old monk pull the head covering off the other's head and was just near enough to hear him shout out in Hindi 'you are no monk. You are the Jiff who was so rude to me when we were in Singapore. Why are you skulking here?'

The QMJ's bile was volcanic in its intensity and, with a temerity justified only by spiritual prompting, slapped him hard in the face. 'You traitor, you traitor,' he screamed. The monk put his hand into his clothes and brought out a large clasp knife which he opened but before he could plunge it into the QMJ, shrieking obscenities as he did, the two Gurkha monks ran to separate them and just managed to pin the 'enemy monk' on the ground ... and Jason, without further thought, ran downstairs clutching his rifle and dashed towards the temple precinct, not hearing Rabilal Rai shouting ''Sahib, don't go, don't go' before closely following him.

As Jason reached the temple he saw another monk dash in and stab the QMJ in the back from behind. The two Gurkhas loosed their hold and Tor Gul jumped to his feet then heard, rather than saw, someone enter and, on looking around, saw ... *can it be?* ... *yes it is* and his dark and perpetual resolve saw unexpected and imminent victory. He threw himself at Jason in one almost unstoppable bound, clasp knife to the fore, ready to plunge it into his enemy.

It was Rabilal Rai who saved Jason. Regardless of any religious sanctity associated with the temple, he shot Tor Gul in the side of the head from close range and the clasp knife merely slashed Jason's sleeve. It was Lalsing who, with his kukri, decapitated the man who had stabbed the QMJ, thereby again reinforcing the prophesy of his character made at his birth.

For a second or two no one moved then the two Gurkhas who, recognising Jason as a Gurkha officer, immediately and incongruously saluted him, still in their monk's garb. Jason took his First Field Dressing out of his pocket. 'Bind the wounded man with this and we'll take him to safety but quickly, quickly.' By now the rest of Jason's section had arrived and another First Field Dressing was applied as the others took an all-round defensive position.

Jason looked at the shattered head of the corpse, still unaware of who he was. Some almost feral instinct made him rip off the left shoulder of the dead man's shirt – and there it was, تورگل: Tor Gul, the Black Rose himself at long, long last albeit so unexpectedly.

The young British officer shuddered and went to a bench to sit down while his men made a rude litter to take the wounded man back to the Mahindra Dal. They carefully lifted the QMJ onto it and slowly moved off, his men carrying their burden as gently as they could.

'Sahib, how lucky I was you were there to save me,' croaked the QMJ but, before Jason could answer he had fainted.

On their way back they saw the Jiff Havildar and his three men in front of them. It was the worst of luck for them that one of the two patrolling Jiff 'monks', a Malayan-born man, had witnessed what had happened in the temple as he skirted it on his return. He recognised Rabilal Rai and wanting revenge followed Jason and his slowly moving ambush party. Unnoticed he moved ahead and waited. As the small group passed him, he softly called to Rabilal in Malay. It was only when they arrived at the battalion that they realised Rabilal was not with them. Jason wondered where he could have got to.

Lieutenant Colonel Ksatra Bikram Rana was happy with what the recce patrol had done and while they were away a company of the Nehru Battalion had managed to surrender to him.[9]

The four Jiffs who had accompanied the three Gurkhas surrendered at the same time. Sadly the QMJ succumbed to his wounds that night. Jason was mortified when Rabilal failed to appear and feared the worst.

There was enough spare clothing for the two other Gurkhas, Lalsing Dura and Manbir Gurung, to be re-kitted before being sent back up the line, overjoyed at being safe once more and no longer needing to worry about hunger, capture and exposure. They were sent back on the morrow, rejoicing in their reprieve from hunger, fear and exposure.

Two days later the battalion moved off towards Legyi, Jason still most unhappy about Rabilal. They found his body, killed by strangulation, and there was just enough time to bury him. Jason

9 In his memoirs the by then retired Major General Sir Ksatra Bikram Rana, KCVO, CIE wrote that a British officer of 1 Gurkha Rifles was with his battalion when the Jiffs surrendered. The name he used was wrong and he said that his nickname was 'The Fox'.

felt it was his attention to the wounded QMJ that had distracted him from keeping track of his by-now friend and was heartily remorseful.

On hearing the news of Tor Gul's death Jason's father marvelled how the 'one' had bettered the Milky Way! On saying farewell to the DMI on before being posted back to England, the latter observed that, in its own small way, Operation 'Black Rose' had been a 'minuscule but somewhat different challenge' for both parties. Your son reacted properly in all four cases but, sadly, such is the policy for decorations, he has done nothing above the average to merit official praise.'

Jason himself was posted back to the Regimental Centre and he took the other two Gurkhas with him, both thankful for liberation but sad for the QMJ and Rabilal. *One cannot understand the ploy of the gods.* On the way through Delhi he bade farewell to his parents and had an interview with the DMI and the DMO, both of whom congratulated him.

Back in the foothills of the Himalayas the war for Jason ended 'not with a bang but a whimper'. He asked to be considered for a regular commission with Gurkhas, was granted one and after partition in 1947, sadly saying farewell to his 1st Gurkha first love, was posted to the 1st/12th Gurkha Rifles, a regiment of eastern Gurkhas, reaching Rangoon at the end of that year and going to Malaya in early 1948. *A new life, still with Gurkhas ...*

Strangely it would never strike him as strange that he would be the personal target three more times in ten year gaps, even though the shaman in Bhutan Estate had warned him – he had got used to it. It somehow never occurred to him that he might not win out all four times.

By the same author

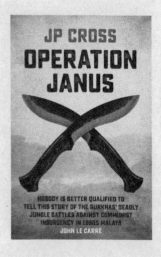